# FIONA FROST

## MURDER AT THE FOSTER MANOR

### CASE FILE 206

## DR. BON BLOSSMAN

Zakkem Publishing Dallas, Texas USA www.zakkempublishing.com

First Paperback Edition: March 2012

The characters and events portrayed in this novel are fictitious. Any similarity to real persons, alive or dead, is coincidental and not intended by the author.

Blossman, Bon, 1970—

Fiona Frost: Murder at Foster Manor / by Dr. Bon Blossman

Summary: Fiona and her team are put to test when she's thrown on her first murder case in an old mansion that is rumored to be haunted. Fiona finds herself drawn deep inside of a dark world that causes her to question her desire to be the world's preeminent forensic investigator.

ISBN: 0985036303
ISBN-13: 978-0-9850363-0-0

*[1. Crime- Fiction. 2. Mystery – Fiction. 3. High Schools – Fiction. 4. Murder – Fiction. 5. Forensic Science – Fiction.]*

I dedicate the Fiona Frost series to my nieces: Lauren, Madison and Ella. May you enjoy my mysteries in your upcoming years and may I instill in at least one of you, an undying love for science. I love you!

# CONTENTS

*Science is the only impartial justice*

# ACKNOWLEDGMENTS

Thank you to each member of my wonderful family for your perpetual support in my endeavors. J- you are my soul mate, Whitney and Zakkem – you are my everything.

Thank you to the original Dr. Blossman, my father, in the early days for teaching me how to write and giving me the motivation to succeed. You are my mentor and my idol. Thank you to my mother for her endless support.

Thank you to Vivian Nugent for reading *Take Heed to your Nightmares* many, many years ago and encouraging me to proceed with my writing career. Brandi and Susan, thank you for always believing in me and being the first to read my stories. S/O to STK, P'Dub, Frank and L'Dub for always being there for me.

I appreciate one of my very dear friends, Sylvia Ruck Branam, for being the first to read this novel and for giving me the most helpful feedback that I could ask for – you are an essential part of my life and I appreciate you!

Thank you to Maddie Poe for her beautiful face, her brilliance and for agreeing to be the official spokesperson for the Fiona Frost series. May we work together for a lifetime!

Thank you to my wonderful friends and family for being genuine and allowing me to love. Thank you to my enemies for giving me the experiences necessary to make me whole.

# I BLAST

"Hey Lauren!" I sang into the phone, as I pulled out my homework spiral from my red leather backpack.

*"Fiona! Guess what!"* The raspy feminine voice belonging to Lauren Hope teased.

I hated guessing games, but figured I would play along for the sake of Lauren's enjoyment.

"Are you sick? Are you going to miss school tomorrow?" I hedged cautiously.

*"No! I just got off the phone with Duncan Doyle. You know him?"*

"Isn't that Carden Doyle's older brother? The rodeo guy?"

*"Yes, exactly! He's at Hartford University!"* Lauren exploded.

My eyes rolled uncontrollably. Lauren Hope was the friend who would find a new crush every week. This was nothing new. When Lauren discovered a new boy, she'd make the rounds calling everybody in our circle.

"Lauren, you're seventeen years old, don't you think he's a little too old? Go for his younger brother Carden. They look identical, and Carden's only a year younger than we are. And, Carden just applied to become a member of our club!"

*"I thought your grant only covered five members? Is somebody dropping out? It's not Wolfe Nero, is it?"* Lauren's voice turned from excitement to panic.

"No, silly. He'll be a replacement member for next year. We're graduating in May, remember? We have to find our replacements and train them by next summer."

I sighed. I thumbed through my spiral and pulled out my favorite mechanical pencil from my drawer.

*"Did you get the grant renewal? Will your program continue next year?"*

"I haven't found out yet, I should hear in about three to four weeks. Leave Duncan Doyle alone, Lauren. It's always bad news when high school girls go for college boys."

*"Fiona Axalia Frost! I am not trying to date Duncan Doyle! He's studying Paranormal Science. Their group from Hartford is going on an overnight trip to Foster Manor."*

My demeanor hardened. Paranormal science was a sore subject with me.

"Not interested, Lauren! It's not science. Our club is focused on tangible data, not playing ghost catcher in an old farm house with a bunch of frat boys!"

Lauren and I had spoken about this issue to no avail. She had a growing interest in paranormal science and had tried to include paranormal research techniques in our investigations. I found it to be a fictional waste of time. I wanted to be a serious forensic scientist one day - an expert that would be taken seriously in the courtroom.

*"Have an open mind, Fiona. I was calling to see if you'd be interested in tagging along. Willow can't make it because she has to go to her grandmother's seventieth birthday party, and it would be nice to have another girl with me. We're headed out there right now. The owner of Foster Manor contacted Hartford University yesterday. He wants his mansion certified as a haunted house so he can charge people to stay there or something like that."*

Deciding to relax and give up on my homework until I got off the phone, I threw myself among the furry pillows scattered on the pastel pink comforter of my mahogany sleigh bed. While all of my friends ran from the pink of their early years, I embraced it – it was still my favorite color.

"Oh, Lauren. What shall I do with you? I'm not going, and please don't try to recruit anybody else from the club. Keep it real, Lauren. Have fun! And keep your boy crazy eyes off Duncan!"

*"Duncan isn't even the hot one, his friend is,"* Lauren squealed and continued, *"Don't say that I didn't ask. When I come back with cool stories, don't have one ounce of regret for not going!"*

"It's a promise!" I stifled my laughter. "See ya tomorrow at school!"

After completing my homework and catching up with the television shows on my DVR, I quickly drifted to sleep. As soon as the sun hit my face the following morning, I jumped out of bed and headed to the shower. After tossing on my clothes, I stood at the oval mirror of my mahogany dresser for a final check before leaving for school. My makeup was minimal, as my ivory skin was like a sketchpad, every color and every line showed up magnified.

My hair had grown impossibly long, even for someone at five foot nine. My mother talked me out of cutting it short every time I went to the stylist. I wasn't a brunette, and I wasn't a blonde - I was dead in the middle. I wanted to add highlights or dye it pitch black, but my mother was always there to say *no*. She warned that I'd lose the shine if I messed with my natural color. I vowed to one day cut it short and dye it black.

I did have a crazy blue clip-in hair extension that I wore on occasion. I wore it when I had the urge to be wild, but my mother didn't approve of it. I kept it hidden in my drawer because she said if she found it, it would disappear forever. That was the extent of my rebellion with my parents – putting a removable blue streak in my hair behind their backs. I suppose we all have our vices. With only minutes before I had to leave, I struggled through five different hairstyles before giving up and wearing my hair bone straight.

I grabbed my black marble-rimmed glasses from the nightstand and gave them a quick polish. I preferred the fashion aspects of glasses to contacts; they enhanced my fawn-colored eyes and made me appear more credible. I never knew when I'd get a call from Detective Chase about a new case and would have to go to the Godley Grove police station.

I grabbed my backpack and headed toward the kitchen of my Tuscan decorated home. As my feet hit the weathered wood floor, the pungent smell of bacon overwhelmed my senses, as I laid eyes upon my portly house nanny, Janice Parker. Undergoing her morning routine of preparing breakfast, her glistening silver hair was coiffed into a meticulous low bun with not one hair out of place. Minus the red velvet dress, she reminded me of Mrs. Santa Claus in many ways.

"Hello my dearest Fiona!" Janice sang, facing the steel gas stove as she flipped an egg in the frying pan.

I had always thought Janice was gifted with telepathy or the power of sight in the back of her head. She always knew where I was and when I had done something wrong. Nothing got by Janice.

The petite Emma Frost was at the sculpted round wood table reading the morning paper. A twenty year older yet smaller version of me in every way, she was a chemist at Hartford University. Her gleaming tawny locks fell on either side of her face like curtains, meeting into a point at her chin. She gazed at me adoringly, her eyes the exact shade of taupe as mine. An avid dollhouse collector, I admired her for the unique hobby, but always found it to be quite bizarre for a woman of her age.

I decided to skip breakfast. I knew I'd have to be quick with my getaway or my mom and Janice would band together and force me to have a seat to eat eggs at the table.

Janice didn't think you could start a day right without eating eggs. Lauren's phone call had thrown me slightly off schedule, and I was far too anxious to get to school for my meeting with my biology teacher.

"Hello Janice, g'bye Janice. No breakfast for me! G'bye mom! Have a great day!" I said quickly, snatching my car keys from the thick wooden countertop.

"Hey, Fiona! Are you holding a club meeting today after school? When should I expect you home?" Emma Frost inquired eagerly. She was an incessant worrier, but I figured most mothers probably were.

"The club meeting isn't until tomorrow afternoon." I said, deciding to sneak a cracker and cheese kit from the refrigerator. I walked over to Emma and kissed her on the forehead. "We're planning the guest speakers for our lecture series for the next two months. I scored a guy from Princeton to lecture about maggot life cycles in mammal carcasses. Is Haley up yet? I have to go now."

Haley. I cringed at even having to say the name. She was the bane of my existence in the household. My cousin from New Jersey always chose the wrong type of friends and had gotten into serious trouble. My parents were always up for a challenge so they brought her to stay with us in Godley Grove the previous summer. My aunt and uncle's back up plan was a very strict boarding school in New Zealand. I didn't see a problem with that alternative, but my bleeding heart mother did. Haley was to stay with us indefinitely.

Haley and I were polar opposites. She was different from my over-achieving family in nearly every way. Her platinum curls and bright blue eyes stood out among my family's straight taupe locks and russet eyes. Haley also had a flaming disregard for rules and academics and scoured the dredges of society to find friends. She was a freshman at Godley Grove High School, and I was now a senior. I had a flawless reputation, and I had begged my parents to force her to go by a different last name when she registered at my school. They didn't go along with my request. My mother cherished family, no matter who they were.

"Fascinating stuff, Fiona! Gotta love maggots!" Emma chuckled. "And of course, Haley isn't ready yet," my mother sighed. "I'll run her over to school, don't worry. You do what you have to do."

"Wait! Fiona! Hold up!" Haley screamed from her room down the hallway.

I strolled toward her cluttered room and shouted, "Haley, I have to go. You almost make me late every day and today, I have an important meeting."

"I don't care, Fiona. Just wait! *Everything* to you is important. Somebody is waiting for me to hang before school so I wanna get there early!"

"It better not be Josh Coleman. I've heard rumors. He's a senior, Haley!"

Emma perked her head up from the newspaper and burned her eyes into mine.

"Excuse me, she better not be spending time with senior boys!" Emma added sternly.

I shrugged as I raised my eyebrows in derision.

"Shut up, Fiona!" Haley shrieked. "I can't stand you, seriously. I can't stand *any* of you!" Haley hollered before slamming her bedroom door shut. "Forget it, I'll just walk!" Haley mumbled from behind her door.

Emma let out a huge sigh and shook her head slowly as she turned the page of her newspaper. Ordered footsteps sounded from the hallway. I spun around to catch sight of the tall, stately silhouette coming my way. It was the district attorney, Lewis Frost. He was an intimidating man, a stern authority figure in the city of Godley Grove. To me, he was just *Dad*.

"Good morning, ladies. I see Haley is in a pleasant mood this morning." Lewis sounded, his cavernous voice gruff.

"Yea, for her, that's pleasant," I laughed. My mother scowled at me in disapproval.

Lewis straightened his tie before swiping his perfectly structured bronze hair to the right of his forehead. Behind the hardhearted exterior was a very handsome man. His woody aromatic fragrance invaded my senses. I loved the scent of my father's cologne. It gave me a subconscious sense of security.

"Love you, daddy! I'm off to school!" I said playfully, whisking away towards the front door.

Luminal, my overanxious Scottish terrier, barked to get my attention. I stopped in my tracks, brushing my hand through his curly black fur, bending over to give him a kiss on his nose. He licked me on the cheek in response. Luminal didn't like me to leave the house without saying goodbye.

"Bye, Luminal. Have a good day today, and be nice to Janice!"

I scooted out to the front driveway into my black Volkswagen Beetle, ignited the engine, and headed off to school. I loved my car like it was a faithful friend, and the quick ride to school was always a good time to clear my head of lingering thoughts before the long day.

I anticipated the learning aspect of school, but the social dynamics often challenged me. I often experienced conflicting emotions. On one side, I was anxious to learn and interact with my teachers, and on the other, I was nervous about the snide comments in the hallways from my foes. At school, I was the envy of every science nerd because I had my own forensic science training laboratory in the science wing of the school. This had garnered me a few enemies, but my parents warned me of the price of success. I always remembered Emma's voice echoing in my head—*you will always have people who'd rather hate you than admire your accomplishments.* It was my mission in life to win them over.

I turned the corner and an aged steel gray Cadillac Deville driven by none other than Ms. Spinks, the police station receptionist, honked at me. She waved and smiled, and I countered her friendly gesture as our cars passed. Ms. Spinks was a long time friend of the family and had always welcomed me to the police station. I had accepted her offer many years ago, and the police station became my second home. Other kids would be at the park or community swimming pool while I was at the station, observing the 9-1-1 operators, assisting the jailors, and helping clean the police cars. It wasn't long before I established a relationship with the crime lab, and my interest in science and crime scene investigation blossomed.

My junior year of high school, I collaborated with my mother on behalf of the Hartford University Science Department to write a grant for a quarter of a million dollar forensic science training lab to be built inside of my high school. I got it off the ground and founded the Godley Grove High School Forensic Science Training Program. It was the first of its kind in the nation, and I got a lot of attention with the national media for a while. I was disappointed that I didn't do it sooner and could only enjoy running it for my senior year, but it was an achievement that I'd take with me for the rest of my life.

However, the training grant only covered five student members. The police station, being an integrated part of the program, couldn't handle training more students at a time. There was an overwhelming amount of students who wanted to be part of our program once the word got out – even students who were not previously interested in science. I simply couldn't accommodate them, and for this reason, I acquired even more rivals at school beyond the science nerds.

Anticipation permeated through my body as I pulled the VW into a familiar parking spot in front of school. The sign in the spot read *Student of the Month*. Here was another reason for my fellow students to despise me since I won the title nearly every month for my accomplishments. Sometimes at the first of the month, I would pretend that I didn't know I had won the title, and I'd park in a regular parking spot. It kept the dirty looks at a minimum on those days.

I glanced over my shoulder and saw Madison Christie, my best friend, running toward my car from the soccer fields. Her cheekbones were a prominent feature on her flawless, rounded face, and she wore her shimmering black hair most of the way down her back. Her dad was a blonde Caucasian, and her mother was a beautiful Japanese woman. Madison was gorgeous in an effortless sort of way, but her Japanese heritage certainly wasn't apparent. Confusion often arose when new friends and teachers met her parents as she looked nothing like either of them.

Madison's father was a retired military colonel and dentist and her mother, who barely spoke English, owned an American cuisine restaurant named *Chouko*. Nobody could convince her mother that naming an American food restaurant with a Japanese name was confusing to her customers. What could I say? Our mothers were equally quirky. Other than my dog Luminal brawling with Maddie's cat named Codis, our families coexisted flawlessly.

It was a good thing that everybody got along so well because Madison was my next-door neighbor since we were three years old. We shared many of the same interests, and I had appointed her as the second in charge of my forensic program. She was the vice president of the club and assistant director of the lab. She was brilliant when it came to science, but her interests and experience in technology certainly helped out on many previous investigations. Madison was barely panting when she finally approached my car.

"Fiona! How is my awesome BFF doing this morning?" Madison sang. "Why are you here so early?"

"Hey Maddie! How are you? I'm here to meet with Mr. Zuptus."

"Oh, okay. I'm headed to the showers. Did you hear about Lauren? She thinks she's going to be the next ghost whisperer or something. She's—

I interrupted, glaring at her with baleful eyes, "I heard. She called last night, and I instructed her not to invite any members of the club on that silly trip! We are strictly science! No time for paranormal nonsense! I can't believe Hartford University started a paranormal program, anyway! It's shameful!"

I felt a chill of irritation tingle down my spine as my blood began to boil. I knew that she would do it. Lauren was trying to recruit the club members to go along with her harebrained paranormal investigation. I realized I would need to have a serious conversation with her later. It was one thing for Lauren to invite her best friend Willow or even me since I was the leader of the club, but to ask my best friend and fellow club member to go along with her paranormal craziness was crossing the line.

"Fiona, there are plenty of people that believe in that sort of stuff. Maybe you should have an open mind?" Madison pleaded playfully, laughing as she tugged on her ponytail holder to release her straight, black locks onto her back.

I shook my head in disgust and smiled at her. We strolled into the brightly lit foyer of the school and parted ways once we reached the colorful hallways. Madison rushed off to the girl's locker room, and I set off for my meeting with my Biology teacher, Mr. Zuptus. He had asked me to help edit a chapter for a new biology textbook, and I was very honored.

I made my way to the blue-carpeted science wing of the school and toward my locker that was immediately next door to my science laboratory. Other than some athletes, teachers and office workers, the school was barren, the hallways silent.

As I drew near the lab, I detected a faint yet noxious odor, growing stronger with each step. I could tell it was a volatile organic chemical, but I couldn't pinpoint which one. I was aware that volatile organic chemicals were dangerous to human health so I held back a panic as I searched for the source. I examined the hallway carpet and didn't see a spill. At an instant, I realized the origin of the smell could have been located inside my lab. I started to lose my nerve as I realized that it could have been xylene or ether and both were highly flammable. Either chemical could be dangerous so I screamed in horror, tossing my backpack in the hallway. I couldn't afford for my lab to do something so careless for my four-year grant renewal was pending. This was just the kind of thing the government would take into consideration—that high schoolers simply weren't mature enough to run a lab, even if supervised by the science department of the school and the local university.

I rushed to the lab door, fumbling with my keys, anxiously glancing both directions down the hallway. I calmed myself as I realized that I didn't want the hallway surveillance cameras to witness me in a fluster. I jammed the key into the lock, twisted the handle, and scooted inside. My eyes searched the room in a frenzy as I inhaled the lab air with fervor. I was shocked yet relieved at the same time to find the air was clear, and the peculiar aroma had disappeared from my senses. As I dashed to each corner of the lab, I perceived a muffled trace of staining reagents, but this was the norm for my lab, and everything appeared to be in perfect order.

There were other science labs in the science wing, including Mr. Zuptus's, much further down the hallway. I exited the lab and darted down the hallway. The smell faded the further I went. I was perplexed.

Jogging back toward my lab, I looked down at my red leather backpack on the floor next to my locker, and then glanced at the hall clock. I noticed that it was nearly time for my meeting. Figuring I could get Mr. Zuptus to help me find the mysterious origin of the odor, I sprinted toward the lab to lock the door.

I jammed the key in the lock, and as I twisted the key, a huge explosion bounded from within the wall next to my lab. The blast was intense, and the earsplitting eruption pierced my eardrums as I instinctively raised my arms to protect my face. The violent force propelled me backwards, lifting me off my feet, as the heat seared my exposed palms. I forced my eyes tightly shut and curled into a fetal position in the air before I plummeted to the ground. My hands felt as though they were producing flames.

I was hurled inside of a nightmare; the ones where horrible things happen in slow motion, and you struggle to fight back without an ounce of strength. I was helpless against the blast and entirely at its mercy. The sting of my scalded hands was nearly unbearable. As I connected with the ground, my skull collided with the floor, and my world went silent.

# 2 MR. FOSTER

"Fiona! Fiona! You all right? Can you hear me?" Mr. Zuptus traced his long, bony fingers along the frame of my face, stopping abruptly to lightly pat my cheeks.

I felt his hands. I heard his shaky voice, but it sounded as though it came from a distance. The smoke stifled me as I fought to catch a breath. The hallway was sweltering, my pores spewed sweat. My body felt heavy against the ground as I drew back into consciousness. I had a feeling that more time had passed than I knew. I couldn't recall how long I was lying in the hallway since the blast.

"Fiona, we've gotta go, can't wait for the paramedics. The smoke's too much," Mr. Zuptus shouted over the chaos as he carefully scooted his arms underneath my dead-weighted body.

I opened my eyes slowly. I could barely see Mr. Zuptus's bright green eyes through the smoke clouding my vision. It burned and reflexively, my eyes slammed shut. I felt helpless, unable to assist, as I sensed my body being lifted into the air. I couldn't find my voice. I wanted to tell him to let me walk, but my deadened limbs felt boneless, like jelly, and my lungs were tightened like a corset, only allowing shallow breaths. The journey in Mr. Zuptus's arms was turbulent as he dashed through the thick black smoke. He struggled as he coughed and cleared his throat along the way.

The air cleared slightly as we reached the foyer of the school. We reached the front doors, and as he swung the heavy glass door open, the clean, cool air hit my face. I sensed the sunlight through my eyelids. I gasped, allowing the clean air to flood into my windpipe, but the residual smoke in my lungs forced a violent coughing fit. I blinked away the smoky particles as the light infused my retina. My eyes burned relentlessly so I pressed my eyelids gently with the back of my hands as my palms screamed for relief from the searing, stinging pain radiating from the burns.

"Wh-what happened?" I mumbled, fighting to recall the events clearly.

I was dazed and disoriented as Mr. Zuptus clumsily propped me on a concrete bench in front of the school. He knelt beside me, leaning close to examine my hands. He took his time as he carefully inspected me for other injuries, gently stopping on a golf ball-sized bump protruding from the back of my head. A couple of minutes passed, and he relaxed his stance. I nearly chuckled at the sight of him as the smoke had randomly smudged his face around his carefully manicured goatee. His '70s style fashion was enough to cause a grin, much less some added smudges on his face.

My brain pounded rhythmically inside of my battered skull as I ran my fingers along the back of my head, searching for blood. My hunt was futile as I found only sweat, and this served to calm me. The palms of my hands continued to throb with arbitrary sparks of sharp pain. I warily inspected them and winced, as I discerned my bright red skin sprinkled with tiny blisters. There was absolutely no position I could place them in to get relief from the pain. Mr. Zuptus reanimated and looked into my eyes.

"It appears as there was an explosion from one of the lockers in the hallway. You're lucky you weren't closer as you might've not gotten away with just a bump on your head and sore hands."

I remembered something along those lines. I recalled the explosion from the wall next to my lab as I locked the door. The next thing I remembered was waking up in the hallway filled with smoke with Mr. Zuptus standing over me.

"An explosion? In the locker? Whose locker was it? What could they have had in there to explode?" I inquired with angst.

Pondering the smell in the hallway when I arrived to school, I had known it was a volatile organic chemical. Obviously dangerous. How could I not have found the origin? I searched my thoughts with grim disdain.

"No idea, Fiona. We'll have to wait and see. Just overheard Principal Dinges say that the police are almost here, and the Silver Springs bomb squad are on the way."

"Bomb squad?"

The city of Silver Springs was next to Godley Grove and had a much larger police station. Godley Grove had a working relationship with them, and the crime lab would routinely send specified evidence via a courier to Silver Springs such as questioned documents and bomb or arson evidence.

Sirens rang in the distance, drawing closer by the second. I surveyed the students' puzzled looks as they arrived to school and warily marched through the courtyard to the front walkway. I couldn't imagine what they were thinking had happened inside of the school. I strained to see through the large glass façade of the school. Smoke curled its way into the foyer. I knew we wouldn't be allowed to go into the building for a long while. My hands persistently burned and my head ached, and time was ticking too slowly.

"Wow, somebody is going to get into big trouble for this one! A bomb? That's extreme," a familiar voice sounded from behind. "Fiona!"

"Madison!"

It was Madison Christie hurrying by my side. Her eyes flickered with horror. Her lengthy locks, wet from an interrupted shower, drained onto her olive-skinned shoulders, soaking the back of her shirt.

"I just heard you were injured in the explosion! Are you okay?" Madison shrieked as she inspected me for injuries.

"Yea, I think so," I stuttered, inspecting my hands.

The stinging sensation in my hands had weaseled its way back into the forefront of my mind. I held out my hands and rotated them for Maddie, who gasped, cringing dramatically at the sight.

"This hurts like heck, and the bump on the back of my head is pretty sore. But I'll be fine."

"Oh my gosh! What happened? I heard a really loud noise all the way in the showers, and then the coaches yelled at us to get dressed and get out into the parking lot!"

Madison took in a deep breath, her face turning ashen and mouth twisting into a line of apprehension.

"No idea. I smelled something in the hallway, like xylene or something like that. I thought it might have been our lab so I checked inside and didn't smell anything weird in there. I went down the hallway toward the other science labs, didn't find anything, and then I was locking the door of our lab, and the wall exploded. It was one of the lockers next to mine. The blast knocked me backwards and to the floor. I passed out, but I'm not sure how long I was there."

"Oh my gosh, Fiona!" Madison hissed through her clenched teeth. Her face was bleak, forehead creased with worry.

"I lost consciousness when my head hit the floor, and that's all I remember until I was brought out here. There definitely isn't any padding underneath that carpet in the hallway! Don't know how long I was out, but I was lucky Mr. Zuptus rescued me. *Thank God* he did because I could have inhaled a bunch of smoke and maybe *died!*"

Madison cupped her mouth as her eyes widened.

"Oh my. Let's not think of that, Fiona. You're my best friend, and I think I would *die* if anything happened to you! Come here!"

Madison leaned over and gently hugged me, and her wet strands clung to my face as she leaned back, inspecting me for more wounds.

"Darn! I left my backpack in the hallway!" I screamed and rose from the bench to face the school.

"Don't worry about it, the police will get it for you! Just wait out here," Madison assured, tapping me on the back. "By the way, Fiona. You've got soot all over your face," Madison giggled and wiped my cheeks.

"Figured that I did," I laughed, wiping my forehead with the back of my hand.

My phone startled me as it rang from inside my jeans pocket.

"Well, at least I still have my phone. Mom probably heard about the explosion already. News spreads like wildfire in this city," I said abruptly, pulling out my phone from my pocket. I glanced at the picture across the screen to check who it was before I answered, "Detective Chase?"

Detective Chase was not only the city's medical examiner but also directed the Godley Grove Crime Lab. My federal grant outlined a working and training relationship between my lab and the police department. Detective Chase was the primary contact and had an obligation to include my team on all cases. However, our group was only allowed to *shadow*, to watch investigations from a distance. We were not allowed to contribute to the primary chain of evidence. However, on occasion, we had helped the crime lab solve cases by communicating leads from our own analysis of the data.

There was always a nagging imaginary line that couldn't be crossed when the police worked with my team. The defense attorneys knew about the training program, and they watched carefully for any breach of our team being in too far on a case. After a few scares in the courtroom, Detective Chase had to establish the policy of *100% no touch* at crime scenes, and we weren't allowed to physically be in the police lab during the analysis of primary evidence. It was annoying, but we all knew that one day we'd be on the other side of things.

My palm ached as I held my phone so I adjusted and grabbed it with the tips of my fingers, bowing out my hand. It looked strange, but eased the pain. I listened intently as Madison's irises froze on my face. A call from Detective Chase meant that we would have a new case to help solve. He was a very friendly man but never called just to socialize. Madison impatiently leaned in to hear his voice.

*"Fiona! I heard about the explosion at the high school. I understand it happened early in the morning before school started so nobody was hurt. Is that true?"*

"Yes sir, that's correct," I lied.

Madison relaxed her stance.

*"Well, the reason why I called is there has been a murder in Godley Grove. Are you up for assisting?"*

I felt a spasm of anxious bliss in the hollow of my stomach.

"Of course, I'm in! Tell me when and where, and I'm there! I can't believe that there's been a murder in Godley Grove!"

Madison Christie's dark eyes widened as she stared at me, bewildered. As soon as I spoke the words *murder in Godley Grove*, you'd have thought I kidnapped her cat and won the state lottery at the same time. She displayed a rainbow of emotions as she jumped around in front of me. There hadn't been a murder in Godley Grove in over a year—not since we established the official relationship with the police department. This was huge. We would graduate from document forgeries, burglarized garages, and stolen antique broaches to *murder*. Maddie leaned back in to hear Detective Chase.

Detective Chase continued, *"It happened at the Foster Manor. Either late last night or early morning. The CSI team is on the way now. I am pulling up to the location as we speak. You told me that you wanted to shadow the next homicide. This is your chance."*

At that moment, I was taken over by a bleak feeling. My heart detached and floated in the middle of my empty chest. I struggled to swallow the lump in my throat as I remembered that Lauren Hope had asked me to go to Foster Manor with her and the Hartford University boys. She had been there. As if we shared the same brain, Madison had the same epiphany and threw herself into a panic, her face melted into a full grimace as she drew her eyebrows together in untainted terror.

"Who. Was. Murdered?" I reluctantly inquired, tilting my head to the side to ease the scorch of the impending bad news.

"Oh my gosh. No! Lauren!" Madison shrieked, waving her hands frantically in the air in front of her face.

Time ticked slower than normal as I waited for Detective Chase to respond. My eyes bulged from their sockets, and the blood escaped my face, leaving it insipid as I pressed two fingers against my temple. I wasn't equipped for this. I didn't know if I could handle the news if Detective Chase spoke my friend's name. A huge sense of regret overcame me.

*"He was an elderly man named Gilroy Foster."*

I gasped for air, grabbed Madison by her sculpted shoulders, and gave her a gentle squeeze. Shaking my head, I patted her on the back until she calmed down. My heart scampered to find its original pace.

*"He was the owner and heir of the estate. Meet us out there, if you can get out of school. If you can't make it, there will unfortunately be another opportunity to observe us investigating a murder scene. We will share our data analysis of this case with your team - either way. Even with this case, your team can investigate the scene after we've cleared it as long as the homeowner agrees. You never know what you'll find that we miss. You've been such a great help on the last cases you've worked on, Fiona. I'd love to see what your team can do with a murder case."*

"Thank you, Detective Chase. I appreciate the opportunity," I stated flatly, sliding my phone back into my pocket.

"Well? What happened? Lauren's okay, right?" Madison rasped impatiently.

I shook my head *yes*. The megaphone static and sirens took over the sound waves in the air. Principal Dinges, megaphone in hand, took his place on the top stair in front of the school. The megaphone siren blasted obnoxiously, signaling the students to gather in front of him. Holding the megaphone far enough away from his gigantic nose, he quickly dismissed the student body that was anxiously lurking about. Like ants in a flushed out mound, the students scattered, seeming exhilarated with the unexpected vacation day.

"Let's get out of here," I urged, tugging at Madison's arm as I clumsily leapt off the concrete bench.

"Fiona!" a familiar authoritative voice called out from across the courtyard. "Young lady, you're not going anywhere. The paramedics need to check you out before you do anything!" Mr. Zuptus shouted as he escorted me back to the bench amidst the commotion of the mass exodus.

"Madison, go ahead. Can you please arrange a club meeting in an hour? Let's all meet at my house," I ordered, my voice a tad sour as I sulked back to the bench.

Mr. Zuptus waved a bony finger in front of Madison's face.

"Make it later this afternoon, Miss Christie," he added sternly. "Your pal has to go to the hospital to get these burns and bumps checked out. The school is responsible for her since it happened on our property so there's no way out of it unless Fiona's parents refuse treatment. Moreover, I happen to know that her father wants her checked out thoroughly," Mr. Zuptus turned to me and continued, "I just got off the phone with your father, Fiona."

I let out an arduous sigh, and Madison's face wilted.

"Please make it for 5 PM, Madison. No matter *what*, I'll be home by then," I whispered, winking at her in a private field of vision.

Madison nodded with a sheepish grin, and then jogged amidst the other students toward her electric blue Mini Cooper.

"Now, let's get you checked out. Don't move," Mr. Zuptus exclaimed, sprinting toward a paramedic.

As Mr. Zuptus moved into my periphery, a pudgy detective with black receding hair marched toward me, followed by a much thinner yet taller, large-nosed Principal Dinges.

"Are you Miss Fiona Frost?" The dark-suited man snarled, notebook in one hand and the other strapped across his vast belly.

Confused, I answered cautiously, "Yes, sir."

"Fiona was the one caught by the blast. The paramedics are taking her to the hospital. I've spoken to her father," Mr. Zuptus reported anxiously as he hurried beside me, a paramedic trailing a few steps behind him.

"Excuse us, Mr. Zuptus. We need a very quick word with Fiona. She doesn't appear to be in imminent medical danger so give us one minute," Principal Dinges added, his wire-frame glasses appearing awkwardly tiny as they rode on top of his huge snout.

Principal Dinges slid his hand onto Mr. Zuptus's scrawny chest, gently pushing him on his way. Mr. Zuptus paused for a moment, flicking his soot-stained scraggly russet hair out of his eyes and swiping his goatee with his thumb and index finger. He recoiled back to the paramedic to give a thorough account of his knowledge of my injuries while keeping a watchful eye on me as I spoke to the squatty detective and Principal Dinges.

"Miss Frost, my name is Officer Uby Ponch. I am with the Silver Springs Bomb Squad," he said with an authoritative timbre, exposing his coffee-stained teeth. "Is this yours?" Uby Ponch said as he held out my red leather backpack.

"Yes, sir. Thank you."

Uby Ponch handed me the backpack as he looked at Principal Dinges and nodded. An awkward grin spread across his rounded face.

"I have investigated the crime scene and have been told that you own locker #230 in the science wing of this school, is that correct?" Uby said firmly while keeping his eyes on his notepad, his balding scalp soaking up the sunrays from the cloudless sky.

"Yes, sir. That is my locker," I mumbled as I furrowed my brows, exposing my confusion.

"Were you immediately present at the site of the blast this morning?"

"Yes, sir," I said, folding my arms across my chest, being careful to keep my scorched palms in the open air.

"Miss Frost, was there anybody else in the hallway when the bomb detonated?"

Confusion shortly vanished, irritation took its place.

"No, sir."

"Well, Miss Frost. After your hospital visit, we're escorting you to the Godley Grove Police Station for a full line of questioning. We need to get to the bottom of how a homemade explosive device ended up in your locker and detonated in your presence," Officer Ponch sparked. He cleared his throat, drew closer to me, and as if he flipped a switch to morph into his malevolent altered ego, he continued with an antipathic tone, "This has done a ton of damage to the structure of the school. You realize this stunt endangered the lives of many innocent people here this morning? This is a federal offense. You really need to do some soul searching as to why you would have done such a thing!" Officer Ponch stared coldly into my reddened eyes as his soured breath permeated across my face.

In a split second, my frustration melted into a fiery rage. Too confounded to speak, my brain unhinged, launching an offensive assault on my body as I searched for the true intent of his words. How could this officer conclude that someone of my status could have or would have exploded a bomb in the school? In my own locker? The entire concept was beyond my comprehension. Principal Dinges, fully aware of who I was, who my father was, was openly nervous as he inhaled deeply and tensed his posture. He countered Officer Ponch's accusations with a string of damage control.

"Fiona, no need to explain yourself now. Of course, you didn't do this, but they just need to do their job. Mr. Ponch will wait for you at the hospital and will give you a ride to the station after you're released. Your health and safety are our primary concern. I'm *sure* you had a more than valid reason for being the only one in the hallway when your locker exploded. We all know you're one of this school's finest and didn't mean any harm even if you did do it," Principal Dinges spluttered before swiftly jetting across the courtyard to scold a pack of boys that were attempting to enter the smoky building.

My heart felt like it was swelling inside of my chest, as if it were about to burst. I couldn't stop the geyser of tears streaming down my face as Officer Ponch followed Mr. Dinges across the courtyard. I wasn't one to show my emotions, but I had never in my life been accused of something so heinous that I didn't do. Mr. Zuptus charged toward me as soon as I was alone.

"You all right, Fiona?" Mr. Zuptus fumed as he knelt down beside me, wiping the tears from my cheeks.

Two paramedics followed, and one immediately jammed my finger into a plastic jacket, and the second swiped a probe across my forehead.

"They think I did this! They think I put a bomb in my own locker and exploded it!"

"What? Nonsense! I will straighten them out! Was the bomb even in *your* locker?"

"Yes. I knew it was on the wall of lockers next to the lab, but I didn't know it was *my* locker." My tears surged as a paramedic gently nudged my head straight, examining the injuries to my skull.

"Fiona, don't worry about this. We all know you obviously, without a doubt, didn't do this!"

"But Mr. Dinges believes that I could have! That officer believes I *did!*"

Mr. Zuptus shook his head as a grimace of disgust spread across his sunken features.

"They don't know you like I do. Don't worry. Go to the hospital and worry about your health. I will straighten them out here," Mr. Zuptus assured, walking alongside the paramedics as they guided me into the back of the ambulance.

I reluctantly took my place on the gurney for my first ride in the back of an ambulance. I was still shaken from the blast and didn't like the feeling of having no control. I dropped my head in defeat as the door swung shut. After about a minute, the driver pulled away. I valiantly fought another onslaught of tears, as I watched the school disappear through the back window.

# 3 TRANSIENT

I was about to receive my release papers after five mind-numbing hours of being at the hospital. I didn't think my psyche could last another minute as I found myself looking forward to the prodding and poking of the examinations and tests if only to cure the boredom. After wasting away the day, the verdict was a mild concussion and superficial second-degree burns on my hands. I knew I used my hands a lot, but never would I realize that every simple task would discharge a painful shockwave. It was more than annoying to send text messages with the bulky bandages and the painful throbbing. I'd have to heal quickly as this was going to get old quick.

Emma Frost had pulled herself away from the university to wait by my side, analyzing every move of the physicians and questioning every test. Through pain-ridden texting, I coordinated the 5 PM club meeting at my home with the help of Madison Christie. I was more than fortunate that

Madison and I had formulated our own version of shorthand text messaging as it minimized my keystrokes.

I calculated the time carefully and upon my release, I was to walk through the front door of my home in time for the meeting after picking up my VW from the parking lot of the high school. I minimized the pain in my palms to my mother so she would allow me to drive my car. I knew I could take a little pain, and my safety wasn't at risk.

Then there was the burr in my side that I might have to deal with upon my release. The one reason why I would have been late to the meeting is if I were detoured to the station for the pointless interrogation with Officer Ponch. I hadn't seen nor heard from Officer Ponch all day, so I kept a secret hope that he had forgotten about me, or at least changed his mind about making me the main suspect in the locker bomb case. Upon receipt of my walking papers, I figured I should warn my mother that Officer Ponch might be waiting on me.

I hadn't mentioned it to my mother all day because I knew she was far too worrisome to deal with the news of a possible felony charge. She would have expected it from my resident cousin Haley, but would have been horror-struck had it been against me. There was no way that I could have dealt with Emma's incessant panic attacks while waiting in the hospital all day with her.

Knowing the answer to the question, I asked anyway, "Mom, did anybody tell you that I would have to go to the police station to talk to them about the bomb in my locker? They think that I might have had something to do with it."

Emma shot a look of angst at me as she furrowed her brows, raising her tiny body from her seat. Her taupe angled hair swung like a sparkly pendulum underneath her chin.

"No, Fiona, not a word. Why are you just now telling me this? We've been together for hours, and now you mention this? The bomb was in *your* locker of all places? Did your father know about this? Who put it there? Why?"

Emma couldn't seem to get her words out fast enough as her pale, porcelain face blazed into a bright crimson red.

"No, dad only spoke to Mr. Zuptus about me going to the hospital. I doubt anybody has contacted him about the accusations that were made against me by the detective from Silver Springs," I answered, my voice was not as steady as I wanted it to be.

I waged war against my bottom lip as it attempted to quiver.

"What!" Emma shouted, grabbing her cell phone and stomping her foot.

"Yes, the bomb was in my locker. I have no idea who did it or why, but the bomb guy from Silver Springs blamed it all on me because it was in my locker."

A mask of fury plagued my mother's face as she thumbed furiously on the screen of her cell phone.

"Absurd. I'm calling your father immediately. I can't believe that you didn't mention this until now, Fiona!" Emma grumbled, peering warily down the hallway to look for Officer Ponch.

Cautiously, I joined in on the guarded corridor search while strolling to the parking lot with my mother. Officer Ponch was nowhere in sight. A feeling of warmth emanated inside of me as I realized that Mr. Zuptus had kept his word.

"Mom, don't bug Dad. Let's discuss it later, after my club meeting. Office Ponch is not here, I'm probably all right. He must have realized it was an ignorant waste of time," I pressed.

Emma begrudgingly ended the call before my father answered as we stumbled upon the black Lincoln Town Car, license plate *Frost 1*. I was embarrassed that my parents owned three identical Lincoln Town Cars. I was even more embarrassed that all three were the same color and had numbered vanity plates. My dad drove number two and my nanny, Janice Parker, drove the third. My parents were obsessed with uniformity.

On my sixteenth birthday, I begged them not to surprise me with Lincoln Town Car number four. The morning of my birthday, I swung open my bedroom drapes and laid eyes upon a shiny VW with a gigantic red plastic bow on top. However, my father mandated the car was black to match the rest of the *Frost Fleet*, as he so named it. Of course, I had a vanity plate, and it read *Fiona*. I figured I wouldn't whine that I didn't get the hot pink sports coupe that I always wanted. I was grateful to have a set of wheels in the end, and I loved the car, it was mine.

We set out on our ride to the school to pick up my VW. I checked the clock on my phone, and we were two minutes ahead of schedule in order for me to make my meeting at home. I twisted the volume knob of the radio as a muffled ring tone resonated from inside my mother's purse. My father had obviously noted the previous attempt of a call made by Emma and was returning her call.

"Oops, Fiona. I'm going to have to get this so your father doesn't panic," Emma apologized, sliding her hand across her phone's screen to answer the call. "But don't ever do this, never ever use the phone and drive, Fiona, it's not safe."

I muted the radio and shook my head.

"Uh, I'm the one that started the campaign at my school against using phones and driving, Mom!"

Emma punched the phone on speaker and passed it to me. I held it with my fingertips up in the air toward her so she could converse with my dad. Even this made me feel hypocritical, and the bending of my hands pressed the bandages against my scalded palms, igniting painful pulses down my forearms to the crease of my elbow. I took in small breaths, hoping the conversation would go quickly.

Dad went on that he had received a call from Principal Dinges about the accusations against me regarding the locker bomb. Principal Dinges divulged that the school's surveillance cameras detected an individual with a ski mask breaking into my locker and placing a bomb inside of it only minutes before my arrival in the hallway. My story of the chemical smell was backed up by my actions on camera. Principal Dinges told my father that they would keep the case open and promised to issue a formal apology to me during the next morning's announcements at school in case any rumors had spread about the accusations made by

Officer Ponch. Dad had demanded that Dinges also include a formal apology in the *Godley Grove Times,* the local newspaper. He had obliged without resistance.

I felt a renewed sense of relief after bottling up my emotions surrounding the nonsensical pending criminal investigation against me. I was always on the right side of the law, as law enforcement was to be my career. I could never be a suspect. With a criminal record, my future career would have been severely tainted.

My mother parked next to the black VW, and I rushed to the car, buckled my seatbelt, and ignited the engine. The adrenaline masked the pain in my bandaged hands as I gripped the steering wheel. Within minutes, I was home and dashed through the front door. Janice sang a chipper *hello* from the kitchen as I marched to my pink palace bedroom with my dog Luminal trailing my steps and licking the back of my legs. Checking my phone, I had two minutes to spare.

I lunged for my computer to check my email before the meeting. I knew that I had a message from Detective Chase, but it was typically a password protected pdf file, too large to open on my cell phone. Upon clicking the icon, his email was waiting on top of the list. I skimmed over it briefly and saw it was the details about the Foster Manor murder case. Detective Chase ended the email with a formal apology to me on behalf of the Godley Grove Police Department about the unfounded accusations made by Officer Ponch of Silver Springs. He had heard the news as well.

From my room, I could hear Janice opening the front door and greeting the club members as they arrived. Her friendly voice would force a smile upon your face—no matter who you were and what mood was striking you. Everybody loved Janice, and I knew she would make my club members feel at home, as they waited for me to get ready. An unwieldy smile cracked across my face as I detected the deep booming voice belonging to the only boy in the club, Wolfe Nero. He was yet another person that would compel me to smile.

Printing the email from Detective Chase, I pushed through the pain in my hands to type the words *Foster Manor* into my search engine. I quickly scanned the results, printing a few pages that seemed informative. Grabbing the papers off my printer, I rushed into the dining room where the four other club members had taken their seats, each with a pile of delectable snacks in front of them. Janice was taking their beverage orders as she made her way around the table, complimenting each guest on his or her various attributes.

"Thank you so much, Janice," I said politely as I took my place at the head of the table, lifting a warm chocolate chip cookie off my plate.

Once everybody had inspected my injuries and had finished chatting about the morning's excitement, I called the meeting to order. With pads and pens at the ready, the club members gazed at me, anxiously waiting to hear the details of the urgent meeting. Lauren Hope, the appointed secretary, put her fingers on her keyboard to take the minutes of the meeting. Her dark curly locks were so massive; she typically wore a bandana or an armed forces inspired cap to contain them. She was wearing a beige military hat in contrast with her plain black tee shirt and jeans. Lauren was hardly seen without a masticated straw hanging from her full lips. The white straw jetting out of her mouth was mangled into a flattened, jagged piece of plastic. Janice extended a new bright blue straw on top of a napkin to Lauren. Lauren gave a shy grin and exchanged the worn out straw for the new one, thanking Janice.

"I have called this meeting of the Godley Grove High School Forensic Science Club today to discuss the Foster Manor Murder, Case File 206, with the Godley Grove Police Department," I announced as Lauren's tanned fingertips went to work on her laptop, fingernails clicking against the keys.

The members eagerly nodded in acknowledgement, grabbing their pens and straightening the notepads in front of them.

"The victim's name is Gilroy Foster. He is the heir of the Foster estate. For those of you who do not know, the Foster Manor is immediately southeast of town, past the Southfork Hills. There are legends about the Foster family that you may have heard of in the past. Many locals believe the estate is haunted. You all know my stance that paranormal activity is a pseudo-science built on presumptions and cult beliefs. Again, that's my take on it and from this point forward, I will stick to this case in an unbiased, scientific manner."

"Got it, Fiona," Lauren spluttered, widening her deep brown eyes to imply innocence.

I arched an eyebrow at Lauren and continued, "Gilroy Foster contacted Hartford University's newly created paranormal program. He requested the investigators to certify that there was paranormal activity present in the home," I halted briefly and looked in Lauren's direction, "Well, I think it is best to hear the rest of the story from Lauren since she was there last night."

Lauren gave a thumbs up and slid the computer toward Madison. Madison threw her long black tresses into a ponytail and pulled the laptop into position in front of her. She nodded for Lauren to begin.

Lauren stood from her chair and cleared her throat. "I received a call from Duncan Doyle yesterday. He's a junior at Hartford University. He switched his major from forensics to paranormal as soon as the new Paranormal Science Department was created. I don't blame him," Lauren paused to catch a glimpse of my reaction before she went on, "I met him recently when I attended the first paranormal science lecture at Hartford. I've told you guys before about my interest in the paranormal, right?"

My neurons sparked with irritation at her words as I shot a guarded look into her eyes to indicate a warning not to start a promotional speech about paranormal science. This was *my* program, not a recruiting arena for a pseudoscience. It was hard enough being a teen trying to live in an adult's world, and I knew that I would lose credibility if anybody heard about us investigating *ghosts*. The skeptics of my program from my school and from the internal affairs of the police department were looking for any reason to call me a failure. I thought angrily to myself that if Lauren wanted a ghost-catching club, she should apply for a grant herself and start her own foolish program. I couldn't allow her to tarnish my program that I had worked so hard to obtain. Lauren took a breather to widen her eyes, suggesting culpability, realizing that she had pushed me to the brink of my tolerance.

She continued slyly, "We exchanged information because I wish to work with the paranormal science department when I get to Hartford. Outside of this club completely," she paused awkwardly, I gave the go ahead, "Sure enough, he called! He was very excited about the opportunity to spend the night in the legendary Foster Manor in order to collect evidence of paranormal activity—

Madison abruptly stopped typing and cleared her throat to get Lauren's attention.

"I don't understand why Mr. Foster would care. Why in the world would he want to have his home investigated?"

Madison poised her fingers on the keyboard once again, awaiting Lauren's answer.

Lauren resumed accordingly, "Mr. Foster wanted to have his home certified by a paranormal investigator that it was haunted so he could charge guests from around the world to stay there—like a hotel or a bed and breakfast. He had done research and found that haunted locations pull in tons of cash. Especially ones that are certified by someone credible, such as a prestigious university like Hartford. His plan made perfect sense."

"Oh, got it," Madison said, seeming mollified.

I explained, "Duncan Doyle is Carden Doyle's older brother, by the way. Carden's a junior at our school who is actually going to be a new member of our program for next year, maybe even running things," a light bulb suddenly clicked on above my head, "Maddie! We forgot to invite him to the meeting today."

A couple of sarcastic moans sounded from within the group.

"Ugh. My bad," Madison added bluntly, shooting me an apologetic look. Her demeanor quickly iced into winter as she turned to face the rest of the group, "Give me a break! My best friend was nearly blown up by a locker bomb! It hasn't exactly been a normal day!"

Dead silence arose in the room until Janice appeared with the milkshakes and smoothies ordered upon the guests' arrival. Janice hummed a melodic tune, and the room warmed up as the group accepted their sweet treats.

"I know Carden Doyle. He's cool. He's into rodeos and stuff," Wolfe Nero's voice rumbled from the rear of the dining room. He yanked on his striped knit beanie, pulling it close to his eyes, his dark hair flipping up over the rim to outline his striking features.

The ever-so-charming Wolfe Nero towered over everybody at six foot three so he always took the back position in the group. His flawless tanned skin paled in comparison to his stunning gray eyes that appeared as liquid metal. He was a drummer in the marching band and skateboarded around town daily. His body was peppered with interesting scars from his numerous collisions with the pavement. Wolfe was our resident profiler in the club and had an uncanny gift to see inside of the criminal's mind.

On another note, teachers dreaded seeing Wolfe's name on their roster, as he was a notorious class clown, a wretched prankster. I had a hunch that every girl in the club, if not the school, had a secret crush on him. I might have allowed his eyes to make my heart flutter once or twice, but I'd never tell anybody if I did have a little crush. I could never mix business with puppy love.

Lauren continued, "Yesterday, after school, I met up with Duncan Doyle and his friend Ralph Booner. Duncan's not bad looking, by the way, but Ralph is the cuter one. He's a forensics major and freshman at Hartford."

"Lauren, stay on topic, please," I pleaded, infusing irritation in my tone.

"Yes, ma'am. We packed up all of the expensive equipment, drove out to the estate, and set it all up. Wow, they have some major financial backing as they have massive gear!" Lauren paused for a moment as she waited for my reprimand. I stared coldly into her eyes. She continued, "The Foster Manor is creepy, for sure. *Haunted*, I'm not convinced. Duncan and Ralph showed me how to collect electromagnetic field and EVP data. It was pretty rad."

"Lauren, what's EVP?" Madison inquired ardently, fingers waiting on the keys of the laptop. If there were anything technological that she didn't know, she would become an expert at it in record time.

"Electronic voice phenomenon. It records inaudible speech while removing the white noise from the room. Pretty wild stuff," Lauren said excitedly.

"Let's get to the murder," I said firmly.

"The recording devices were going, and they started collecting data, but then Duncan and Mr. Foster got into an argument. I don't think Mr. Foster was very happy with Duncan's progress. I think Mr. Foster thought that Casper the Ghost himself was going to pop out of the walls and say *hello* because we were there," Lauren paused, the group collectively giggled.

"When did the murder take place? Right after the fight?" I asked as my eyes sparkled at the thought of an easily solved case.

"Things calmed down between Duncan and the old man, and it seemed like a lot of time passed. It was really late, nearly sunrise. We had a snack, were chillin', watching the monitors, and that's when it happened. Mr. Foster went into the kitchen, there was a loud crash, and he was dead. On the floor, *dead!*"

My mind processed her words at a furious pace. Gilroy Foster was an old man. He walked into his kitchen and had a heart attack. Case closed. What was the big deal? Could nobody see how obvious this was but me? It was natural causes. Old people die!

"Lauren, he was elderly. Why is it a murder? Did anybody even have the slightest motive to kill this man?" I pondered rapidly, my bandaged hands in an outward gesture of confusion.

Lauren gazed at me for a few seconds as she collected her thoughts for her response.

"Fiona, they believe he might have been poisoned. His symptoms were not completely in line with a normal heart attack, although heart attacks are quite variable. Before he died, he said that he had never felt that way before and that something wasn't right. He said he was about to throw up and ran to the restroom. He definitely seemed delirious and complained his head hurt. He told us he saw blue halos around lights and that it had never happened to him. He even mentioned casually that he thought someone had poisoned him. This was about ten minutes before he went to the kitchen to die."

Willow Walker's sea green eyes brightened at the sound of a medical conversation. The stunning Willow, nicknamed Doc, aspired to be a physician since her toddler days. Everybody in town had already conceded this tiny blonde beauty to be a medical doctor by honorary standing given that her father, and every female member of her family, was a medical doctor. This also reigned true for the history of her family as well. It was clear that she would have no problem following the legacy of her ambitions.

Willow couldn't resist. She added, "Heart attacks, or myocardial infarctions, come about with various symptoms and outcomes. It would nearly be impossible to determine a heart attack's underlying cause upon sight. Poison can cause heart attacks but so can natural causes among many other things such as stress and other underlying diseases. There would need to be further tests done to determine the etiology. I can see how they could potentially consider it a murder by poison given his previous symptoms of delirium, nausea, halos around light and a headache. However, I cannot believe they'd officially deem it a murder without any *evidence* of it being so, especially with an elderly victim."

Lauren gazed glumly at me before she added, "Duncan Doyle seemed to think that Mr. Foster was seeing paranormal activity with the blue halos. He firmly believes that spirits might have killed Mr. Foster by frightening him into a heart attack. He said that it had happened before in the 1800s somewhere."

"That's gone far enough, Lauren. Spirits committing murder? Really?" I argued, disturbed the conversation had taken such a turn.

"I'm reporting facts, Fiona. Duncan and Ralph officially stated to the police that the spirits are the ones that must have frightened Mr. Foster to death or if he was poisoned, the spirits somehow administered the poison into his system. Didn't Detective Chase include that in his report to you?"

I scanned the papers in front of me.

"Actually, that's not part of it. Once we get Detective Chase's autopsy report, we will know for sure if this is indeed a murder or a death via natural causes. Willow, I understand that a heart attack can be caused by many things, but you're right, they don't typically call it murder on an elderly victim," I explained. "But there's more. That's not the only reason they are calling it a murder."

"She's right, there's more," Lauren continued, the words sounded stiff.

"Let's hear it," Willow added curtly. "I knew they couldn't just go on that and consider it a murder."

"He had two wide marks across the front of his neck, as if somebody compressed his throat. The paramedics on scene said it didn't appear as a full blown strangulation, more as if somebody took out an insurance policy that this man wasn't going to make it," Lauren described, gesturing the width and position of the marks across the victim's neck with her thumbs. "They said the autopsy would be able to determine that for sure as sometimes, strangulation is only seen internally."

"Couldn't the marks on his neck have happened as he fell to the floor? Maybe he hit his neck on a countertop or something? You shouldn't make assumptions, Lauren," Madison said abruptly.

"I'm just stating what the paramedic said at the scene. He said it appeared as a *finger touch pad contusion* and explained it can be caused by an assailant's grasp on the victim's neck. As I said, it's not official; the guy at the scene that I spoke to wasn't the coroner. Detective Chase will make the final determination of the cause of death. I'm sure when we hear back from the autopsy, it will all make sense," Lauren explained with a tone of annoyance.

Willow sat upright in her chair, squaring her shoulders to the group as she held her hand in the air.

"If you fell and hit your neck on a countertop, it wouldn't look like two opposing thumb impressions; it would be more of a straight, thin line. It sounds like someone must have compressed his larynx or maybe even constricted his carotid arteries. See, the thumb will generate more pressure than the other fingers, and it would make sense that the wounds to the victim's throat would have two separate contusions."

"Willow, what's a contusion?" Wolfe inquired in a flat voice.

"The surface venules and capillaries damaged by trauma. A bruise."

"Can't they just take the fingerprints from the victim's neck? If the murderer had their hands on his throat, well, duh!" Madison asked snappishly.

"They can, and I'm sure will try, but it's rare to be able to recover latent prints from the victim's skin. Plus, the murderer likely wore gloves," I told them. "Anything else you want to share, Lauren?"

"That's about it, guys." Lauren reported.

"What did Detective Chase say, Fiona?" Madison pressed, sliding the laptop back toward Lauren.

Since I hadn't had time to read the email from Detective Chase in its entirety, I instructed everybody to enjoy their snacks from Janice as I took a moment to scan the email more carefully. That is when I noticed something peculiar in the report. At an instant, I knew we couldn't resolve this matter during the meeting. I needed time away from the club before we spoke about this issue. I had to end the meeting immediately.

"You know what? There's no resolve in this email. Our time would be best served if we wait to meet tomorrow about this. Maybe by then, Detective Chase will have more information. He says in this email he's not sleeping tonight."

"Agreed!" Madison shouted, closing her spiral notepad. "Fiona's had a rough day, and we can't solve anything here until we have *real* data from a *real* science lab. We don't even have confirmation that this is a *murder* case and not just an elderly man's destiny."

Lauren hesitated for a short second and then snarled at Madison in an obvious response of her insinuation that paranormal data wasn't real. She gathered her things quickly and jetted toward the front door, blue straw hanging from the side of her mouth.

"Doc, you coming?" Lauren swirled around to face her best friend, Willow Walker.

Willow nodded silently to Lauren, waving to the group as she trailed Lauren through the front door.

"See ya, Fiona. Bye Madison," Wolfe said serenely, hastening toward the front door.

The butterflies in my stomach performed a ritualistic dance as I watched Wolfe leave. I tried not to look disappointed as I waved goodbye. Madison was very perceptive and had called me out on occasion by the way I acted differently around Wolfe. I had to be careful.

Madison waited until everybody had left, staying behind to speak to me privately. "Do you have a lead on the locker bomber?"

"No idea. The investigation is at a dead end. There were no fingerprints, no apparent motive, the surveillance camera footage simply served to prove it wasn't I. If I had to guess, I'd say Josh Coleman."

"Josh Coleman? The school bully?" Madison retorted, her face wrinkled with perplexity.

"Well, he's the only one that I can imagine that would be crazy enough to bomb a locker. And he certainly doesn't care for me, Maddie."

"Fiona! He doesn't like *anybody*! He'd have no reason to target you, of all people!"

"Maybe I wasn't the target? Maybe it was random?" I pointed out, grabbing the papers off the dining room table.

"What about Adro Monk? You know she is insanely jealous of your lab and your success," Madison sparked enthusiastically as she gathered her dark locks and tossed them onto her back.

"I don't peg Adro Monk as a psychotic, Maddie. Jealous, yes. Psycho? No."

"Good point, we can only hope that it was crazy Josh, and it was random. So, what does the email from Detective Chase *really* say, Fiona? I know you. You must not have had all the facts, and that's why you ended the meeting."

I couldn't help but allow a huge grin to raid my face. Madison knew me like no other.

"You're so right, Maddie. I need to do a little recon on a man named Kosmo Wilder. It seems as though Lauren left him out of her story for some reason so I didn't want to bring it up around her since she said that she had nothing else to report to us. He's the number one suspect in Detective Chase's email. She *had* to know he was there! Why would she not mention him?"

Madison's deep brown eyes gazed deeply into mine as she pondered her thoughts, searching for the answer to my question.

"Donno," she scoffed.

# 4 PARANORMAL

After performing an extensive internet investigation about the Foster House and Kosmo Wilder while corresponding with Detective Chase about his autopsy report, I finally drifted off to a deep sleep. Detective Chase had promised to send a full report via email by the time I awoke.

It seemed like only minutes of a dreamless sleep before the sunrays shined through the window and hit my face. After seconds, I jumped out of bed. I quickly prepared for the meeting and skipped breakfast once again to rush to school an hour early. I always welcomed the early hours of the morning during an investigation. The analysis of crime scene data was what drove me internally, nearly transforming me into an obsessive lunatic. Once I started working on a case, I had to remind myself constantly to eat, drink and sleep. I refused to stop working until the case was solved. I was preparing myself for a future life of being an incessant workaholic, and I was all right with that, it had worked for both of my parents.

Sprinting to my lab, I glowered at my charred locker as I passed. The entire row of lockers surrounding it was damaged as well as the wall and the carpet below. It made me cringe with anxiety, but I had a meeting so I quickly lost thought of it and amended my mood into exuberance. I arranged the reading materials that I had prepared, having an organized packet for each club member. I scattered pens and notebooks in front of five seats around the laboratory bench. The club members trickled in and started reading the documents in front of them. As Lauren finished reading, she overtly nurtured an anxiety attack, her face turned tense and rigid. She inhaled a deep breath and released it slowly before making eye contact with me.

"Fiona—

"Lauren, no matter what you say at this moment will not discount the fact that you didn't mention the number one suspect to us yesterday," I interrupted, the words came out sharper than I'd meant them.

I was now the nervous one, and my body trembled. I wasn't experienced with confrontation.

Wolfe dropped his massive hands on the desk and bellowed, "Lauren, seems as though you're covering for someone, huh?"

Lauren took a moment to gaze at me from the corner of her eye before she snapped her head toward Wolfe to deliver a tense stare.

"No, Wolfe. Obviously not," Lauren snapped. "Fiona, you'll never believe this, but I simply forgot about him. He was a homeless man. His car broke down, and he just showed up there!"

I was mortified at her defense. This would not do. Lauren was training to be a forensic investigator and forgetting to mention the main suspect in a case was unforgivable. How often would a homeless man randomly show up at a residence with a broken down car on the night of a murder? I would think something so obvious would be worth a mention - at a minimum. I was baffled how she would ever justify omitting this pertinent piece of evidence to our group while discussing the details of the case. It took every shred of restraint not to shout at Lauren.

"How could you forget about that? Wasn't that noteworthy?" Madison added sternly, puckering her lips into a stringent pout.

"Yes, Madison," Lauren stood up from her lab stool, frustration pervading her tone. "But he arrived about an hour before the murder happened."

This was even worse than I had expected. I could only stare, bewildered. I instantly thought Lauren was trying to hide something. Why would she try to cover for a homeless man that she didn't know? Madison abruptly stood up and stormed towards her, obviously not having the same self-control that I had mustered.

"Hellooooo, Lauren! Did you just wake up from a coma? A transient shows up, and an hour later, the owner of the house is killed. Hmmm, seems cut and dry to me that you shouldn't leave that minor detail out when discussing the details of a murder case!" Madison told her in a hard voice. "Don't know why you'd think for a minute to not mention that yesterday during the meeting."

Lauren shrugged her shoulders as she dropped her head, staring in deep thought at the lab counter for a long minute. Her massive curls framed her face like a tablecloth.

"I didn't think. He was quiet and showed up without warning. I first thought he was Mr. Foster's friend, but then it became apparent that they didn't know each other. He kept thanking Mr. Foster for allowing him to stay for the night. He just sat there eating and watching us do our thing. He didn't really speak to us, and honestly, so much was going on; I forgot he was even there!" Lauren pleaded apologetically, wiping a tear from her cheek.

Willow Walker hurried by Lauren's side. She bequeathed a snarl to each one of us, contorting her eyelids in repugnance.

"I can understand how you could miss it, Lauren. Fiona, stop being so harsh!" Willow muttered, rubbing Lauren's back to comfort her.

"Can't we all just get along?" Wolfe sang playfully and snickered as he straightened the navy blue knit beanie on his head.

I marched toward Lauren and Willow. "Look, we don't mean to come down hard on you, Lauren. But as forensic investigators, leaving out a detail as large as that could one day mean that your carelessness allows a murderer to walk free. As an investigator, every minor detail, no matter how insignificant you might think it is—*matters*," I added sympathetically.

Lauren relaxed her stance and gestured for Willow to take a seat next to her.

"I'm sorry, Fiona. It will never happen again," Lauren mumbled as she plopped down on the lab stool.

"You don't have to apologize, Lauren," Willow retorted, slamming her palm on the lab counter.

"Lauren, you're our friend and a great investigator. You are the best with numbers in our group. We need you. Not only for your friendship but also for what you contribute to our program. I don't want you to feel as though we are ganging up on you, but I do need to emphasize that we all need to be careful and diligent when it comes to investigating," I lectured. "No detail is insignificant."

"Understood, Fiona. Thank you," Lauren countered delicately, waving off the utterly disturbed Willow Walker.

I needed to be a strong leader. I had to continue the meeting and cover the evidence as outlined by Detective Chase. Glancing out of the lab window, I saw a handful of students walking toward the school. I knew we had limited time left so I gave a few moments of silence for everybody to settle in and refocus before I abruptly continued.

"Here is the list of evidence from Detective Chase. This is what they have collected and what analyses are currently being done as I speak," I reported, holding my clipboard that was armed with my hand scrawled bullet-pointed notes.

The group madly jotted notes as I methodically covered the evidence collected at the crime scene. I detailed the fingerprints, glass shards, hairs, dirt samples, and carpet fibers found at the crime scene. I explained to the group that the amount of evidence was massive and would take time to sift through what was real and what mattered to the case.

The Godley Grove CSI team as well as Lauren had noted that a blue vase was found smashed into pieces at the site of the victim's body. We reasoned it was most likely knocked over by the victim as he fell to the ground. Detective Chase had reported that blood samples were collected from the victim. We understood that these would take some time for the full report to be released, especially since the serology section manager had left her position without notice only two months prior. Addie Coleman, the rookie of the crime lab, was running things in the serology section and was in charge of doing all toxicological analyses on blood samples. This young forensic tech had only worked in the lab a year out of college. Detective Chase had to spend countless hours making sure Addie's lab techniques were sound, as he didn't want there to be any problems in the courtroom. The previous manager of the serology section had been in her position for over twenty years so this was an unexpected quandary for Detective Chase. Godley Grove Crime Lab was a small lab as far as forensic labs went, and he didn't have the manpower to cover anybody's section while they were out.

"Fiona, I have a question," Wolfe Nero sparked as he raised his enormous hand derisively.

"Yes, Wolfe. No need to raise your hand," I smiled, trying to hide my appeal to him. His stunning gray eyes always threw me off balance.

"You mentioned that there was a smoldering fire in a metal barrel behind the main house, correct?"

"Yes, correct. They have no idea what was burned. They can only assume that the murderer might have been burning evidence given that it was done the night of the murder," I responded and checked my report for additional details.

Wolfe appeared perplexed. The prey of an epiphany, he excitedly pushed up from the lab counter.

"Well, can't they swipe everybody's hands and look for accelerant residue? Case solved, right?" Wolfe offered, shrugging his broad shoulders.

I nodded slightly, smiling. I pursed my lips, hesitating for a moment before I answered.

"Detective Chase and I spoke about this, and yes, that might have been helpful evidence, but it wasn't done at the scene of the crime. The burning barrel was found after the suspects had been released. Cedric Otto, the arson expert with the Silver Springs lab, is investigating this lead, and Detective Chase said he'll have the report soon," I stated flatly.

Madison cleared her throat and locked into a stern gaze with me.

"Fiona, why don't we assign sections of the case evidence to each club member, investigate our individual parts of the case separately, and then meet to discuss our findings. There's no need for all of us to work on all of it," she suggested.

I noticed the club member's faces were in a simultaneous harmony. It seemed as though everybody agreed with Madison, including me.

"Exactly, Maddie. Agreed. We've never had this much evidence in a case, and we need to be organized. Quality over quantity. One more thing I must add that I reluctantly have to say," I hedged, wearing tension on my face. "Duncan Doyle and Ralph Boomer are adamant that a paranormal entity be included as a suspect. The Chair of the new Paranormal Science Department at Hartford University is backing up Duncan and Ralph and has already released a statement to the local media. This is more than annoying that the Godley Grove Police Department would even have to *consider* this as a viable lead, but since it is in the media now, we'll have to address this, even if it is only for the future jury's sake. The jury sometimes can be very gullible, and Detective Chase needs to cover all bases – as silly as they may be."

Lauren's face lit up like a New York City Christmas tree on Christmas Eve. I was more than annoyed at having to divulge this information.

"Uh, you're right. Now that it is out there, if anybody is arrested for this and goes to trial, the defense will use that in their favor! The jury can sometimes be gullible, and often the members can be uneducated," Madison added reluctantly.

"A paranormal investigation team from Ohio are on their way, and they will spend the night at the Foster Manor and either confirm or refute Duncan and Ralph's report that the manor is indeed, seething with paranormal activity," I hissed through my teeth. I was wallowing.

"What? Are you joking, Fiona?" Wolfe shrieked.

I sighed, staring out of the window of the lab as if that would ease my irritation.

"I wished that I was. I've had it cleared. We are going along with this team from Ohio this Saturday so clear your schedules, people."

# 5 FOLLOW UP

After school, Madison rushed over to my house to discuss the case, and Janice set us up with warm sugar cookies and milkshakes on TV trays in my bedroom.

"Did Janice really decorate these cookies with strands of DNA using tube frosting and sprinkles?" Madison chuckled as she took a bite of her cookie and plopped down on my fluffy pink memory foam chair.

"Yes. I like it better when she draws microscopes on them!" I laughed as I pushed my furry bed pillows aside, took a seat on the bed, and sorted through the papers in my lap.

"I love Janice! I wish I had a Janice!" Madison countered.

I had assigned Madison to the fingerprint analysis, and I was working on the carpet fiber analysis. However, I couldn't stand to stay away from the entire array of data so

I had already somewhat analyzed each piece of evidence in Detective Chase's report.

"Fiona, there were so many fingerprints taken all over that place that it's impossible for me to sort through it to determine any sense of it. The suspects were obviously in the manor so what do their fingerprints matter, anyway?"

Luminal was barking incessantly to have a cookie so I put my plate on the distressed wood floor for him, figuring it was the path of least resistance to a quiet room. I definitely would have made a horrible parent at my age.

"Maddie, it's not about having their fingerprints there to establish they were there, but rather to see what they touched compared to what they had no business touching. For example, if we find out that the victim was murdered with rat poison, the prints on any box of rat poison points to a good suspect."

Maddie immediately fumbled through her list of fingerprints, dragging her pointer finger down the page, stopping at the words *bottle of drain opener.*

"I see. They did dust for prints on anything suspicious of poison. Got it, Fiona."

Without warning, my cousin, Haley Frost, rudely swung open my door and popped her curly platinum blonde locks inside, gawking at Madison and me with her fierce blue eyes. My stomach churned in disgust.

"Let me borrow five bucks," she grumbled boorishly.

I flushed red, cursing silently in my head. I had always been a single child. I preferred it that way.

"Haley, why would you need five dollars? My parents give you everything you could ever want, unfortunately."

"I need cigarettes, and your stupid mom wouldn't give me any money this morning," her tone was pungent with disrespect.

Madison tightened her lips, watching for my next move. Her jaw muscles flexed as she gritted her teeth together, most likely to hold back a rage on Haley. Madison didn't quite have the same control of her emotions as I did.

"Haley, please leave my room. You are too young to be smoking cigarettes, and they will kill you, anyway. You don't need five dollars, and my mom is probably the furthest from stupid as you'll ever know, and I hope that one day you'll find a shred of gratitude for my parents for taking you in."

"I can't stand your parents, Fiona. They are so lame and have ruined my life. I'd rather be home in Jersey. I don't understand why I'm here, anyway. This is hell!"

"That will do, Haley. Let's go," Janice snapped from the hallway.

Haley groaned and slammed my door shut. I heard Janice scold her and soon after, Haley's door slammed, vibrating my walls. I had to count to ten to prevent an outburst.

"Seriously, Fiona. I have no idea—

"I know, Maddie. Thank you for not going off on her, it only makes it worse. And I get it – you have no idea how I put up with that behavior or maybe why my parents would ever take on that New Jersey demon seed."

We laughed in unison, and my aura faded from rage to contentment in seconds. Madison Christie could instantly yank me from the dredges of emotional mire.

"I've been thinking. Remember when we assisted Detective Chase with the missing diamond earrings case, and we found that crazy ransom letter from Mrs. Krickbaum?"

Madison giggled for a moment before she responded.

"Yes, and they would have never known that Crazy Krickbaum had lost her last marble if we hadn't found that note. They would probably still be investigating that case had we not found that she tried to hold them for ransom in response to believing that her neighbor stole her dog!"

I busted into a fit of uncontrolled laughter. Madison followed my lead.

"Yea, the dog that had died nearly ten years prior!" I could barely choke the words out as I snorted, desperately trying to catch my breath.

We fell into a spasm of mirth for a moment before Madison furrowed her brows and looked at me with a serious facade, "So what brought that up, Fiona?"

I composed myself, reaching down to grab the last bite of cookie from my plate on the floor. I raised an index finger to hold her attention.

"Well, if the police can miss something on a silly case, they can certainly miss something on a bigger case. I asked Detective Chase if the crime scene was cleared, and he said it was, and that we could go out there and do our own investigation if we wanted to do so."

Madison nodded as a sheepish grin spread across her face.

"Was Mr. Foster the last living heir of the estate?" Madison trailed off, shaking her head in wonder.

"No, he was married to Glenda Foster. She is a 65-year-old retired chemist from Hartford University. She actually worked with my mother in the same department for a year or two when my mother started working at the university. Ms. Foster is at the manor and is expecting us."

"You certainly are thorough, Fiona. Was she there the night of the murder?"

Madison tilted her head back, dumping the final swig of milkshake down her throat.

"Yes, and she is listed as a potential suspect by default. The spouse is always an automatic suspect, but we must not treat her as one, all right? At least not until some evidence points her way."

"I'm in. Let's pack up the crime scene kits, load them into the car, and get out of here. How long does it take to get there?"

"Probably about fifteen to twenty minutes. It is southeast of the Southfork Hills."

"I've never been down there in my life. Do you know where you are going, Fiona?"

As if Luminal knew I was leaving, he jumped on the bed and compulsively licked my cheek.

"Ha! Of course. I've mapped it out via Google. No worries!"

We packed our equipment, popped our heads in at Maddie's house next door to fill her mom in on our plans and jumped in my VW. We set out on our way to Foster Manor.

During the fifteen-minute car ride, we discussed the plans for the paranormal investigation with the Ohio team that would take place the following night. I knew that Lauren Hope was probably more than ecstatic that she would be involved in yet another paranormal investigation and this time, with her own club members. This is exactly what I wanted to avoid since I didn't believe that paranormal science was a real science. I certainly didn't want my club members' impressionable minds to be clouded with such things, but since the Godley Grove Crime Lab was endorsing this silly investigation for the benefit of the future jury in the trial, we had to comply and play along.

"I didn't mention it to the group earlier at the meeting, Maddie, because I think if you know too much house history, and you do a paranormal investigation, you may sway your own opinion on things about what you see and hear – especially as you grow tired in the wee hours of the night. For example, if you know that a ten-year-old boy drowned in a bathtub, you might interpret a shadow that you see at 3 AM as an image of the little boy dripping in water. The less that the group knows about the history, the more of a clear mind they can have when they witness the Ohio team collect data at the house."

Madison turned down the radio slightly, her forehead creased in anticipation.

"I agree with you one hundred percent. But since you know that I don't believe in ghosts as well, please tell me what you know about the house!"

I narrowed my eyes as I stared blankly at the road in front of me, taking into consideration the consequence of divulging what I knew about the manor to Madison. I wanted her to have an unbiased opinion of the Ohio investigators, but at the same time, she was my best friend, and I didn't like keeping things from her.

"The details on the internet are sketchy to say the least. We will have to go to the courthouse and sift through the birth and death records as well as newspaper archives to get the full picture," I begrudgingly reported.

"Great, sounds like a blast!" Madison added, turning the radio back up slightly.

I wanted to tell her more. I paused as I strained to remember the details in my notes. I turned the radio knob to the off position.

"Here's what I can remember, Maddie. Richard Foster built the Manor in the mid 1800s. Soon after, he married a woman named Eleanor, and they had two children, Albert and George. From there, I can't confirm much of what happened other than Gilroy Foster was the last blood relative alive in the lineage. Glenda Foster, Gilroy's wife, is now the heir of the estate. There are a few articles about the house having paranormal activity or being cursed and another about how nearly every person who has ever lived in the home since it was built has either committed suicide or been murdered. However, any house that's been around that long will have made up legends and old wives' tales so I don't put much stock into those stories. We will have to go to the courthouse and look up the official records when we get some time."

"That would be horrible if that were true, Fiona. Hey, did Gilroy and Glenda have any children?" Madison inquired.

"Yes, I found out from Detective Chase. They had two sons."

"Well, where are they?"

"Godley Grove Cemetery. They died from unknown causes when they were only ten years old," I said, a little breathless from the thought.

"Unknown causes? They died at the same time?" Madison exclaimed, her hands on her knees and face contorted into a heartrending mask.

"Yes. Disturbing, isn't it? Both found dead in their beds on the same day. The autopsy report on both children says *unknown causes*. I hate to say this, but all of this *is* evidence toward Duncan and Ralph's claims of a paranormal murder or maybe some type of a curse if you believe in that stuff," I admitted feebly, it sounded as something was stuck in my throat.

Madison sighed arduously before slumping back into her seat.

"You don't believe that for a second, Fiona."

"I know."

We both laughed as I turned onto the street of the manor.

"Here we are!" I said, guiding the VW underneath a rusted black iron archway that read *Foster Manor* in old world lettering. "Foster Manor."

"I can definitely see why they say this place is haunted. It looks like a cemetery from here!" Madison said wearily, fear flickering on her face.

I parked the VW on the circular drive in front of the manor. Large, unevenly trimmed hedges and potted plant sculptures lined the drive. We jumped out of the car and cautiously treaded toward the front door.

Perched on the overhang, a family of owls caught my attention. They locked their sizeable eyes onto every move we made as a gust of wind funneled in behind us. The concrete walkway was riddled with jagged cracks, and I dodged the weeds bursting through and spilling onto the ground. The smell of old, musty wood invaded my senses. Carefully swiping away a cobweb, I grabbed the discolored brass handle of an over-sized doorknocker. I gently struck the base of the lion's mouth two times. The knock echoed throughout the manor.

"Yea, like I said, creepy," Madison whispered, taking a deep breath and a cautious step backward.

Within moments, I knew someone was coming as it sounded like the clinking of high-heeled shoes across a hard surface. The bulky wooden door swung open with scathing creaks, causing Madison and me to cringe in trepidation. An elderly woman stood before us with the door half-ajar. She was a very peculiar looking older woman. She was only 65 years old but appeared much older than her age. I knew that it had to be Glenda Foster, and she was as frail as a paper doll. Her diminutive size stunned me as she stood next to the huge door, wearing a satin pink nightgown under a white feather boa adorned floor-length robe. Her aged hair was thrown carelessly into a tomato-colored braided bun, obviously dyed, with one-inch gray roots jetting from her pasty white scalp. Her skin was limp, withered, and folded into a thousand pleats that clung to the skeleton below. Ms. Foster stood in silence as she held her bony hand awkwardly on the edge of the door and surveyed us with her vivid blue eyes, staring through her red-rimmed glasses. After examining Madison and me from head to toe, she spoke in a crackling, high-pitched voice.

"Hello, young ladies. Please, come on in. I'm Mrs. Foster," Glenda gestured for us to enter the huge marbled floored foyer, "I understand you two want to be crime scientists one day and have asked to pretend to investigate my husband's death?" Glenda grumbled with a tinge of sarcasm hidden in her voice.

She stuffed a skinny cigarette into a long, opalescent pearl and gold cigarette holder that she grabbed off a gold-trimmed table in the foyer. Using a diamond-encrusted lighter shaped as a small revolver, she lit the end of the cigarette and inhaled deeply, coughing as she let out the smoke. I loathed smoking and couldn't stand how it made my hair smell after being around it. This is when I realized why she looked so much older than her age. Smoking certainly doesn't do a body good.

I absorbed her words and thought carefully about how to respond. Reasoning Ms. Foster was mourning over the death of her husband, I didn't want to disturb the balance of her potentially unstable emotional state so I remained cordial. I knew the best route would be to go along with her story.

"Yes Ma'am. We would like to have a mock investigation. We understand that the police have already cleared the scene, and you've probably had the place cleaned up. We'd like to have some practice, if you don't mind."

"It is fine. I always like to help our youth. Even if you're completely wasting your time."

I thought it seemed like a great time to pull out the mom card. I needed something to ease the tension between Ms. Foster and us.

"I heard you used to work at Hartford University? In the Chemistry Department?"

I changed the subject, each word distinct and calculated. Ms. Foster twirled around and sneered at me, the tip of her cigarette spewing smoke in a fury. She huffed and reddened before lifting the cigarette filter to her thin lips, her crimson lipstick bleeding into the tiny folds that outlined her lips. After an exaggerated exhale of smoke, she arched an eyebrow and glared into my eyes.

"Yes, I did. Are you pretending that I am a suspect? Did you do a background investigation on me, young lady? If so, you can leave now," Glenda stammered, her mood was thrown onto ice.

I had to do some damage control immediately. Detective Chase would not be impressed if Maddie and I were kicked out of a crime scene we were about to investigate.

"Oh, no Ma'am! I remember you! My mother's a chemist, and she started in the department while you were there. Her name is Dr. Frost. Dr. Emma Frost."

Glenda Foster cocked her head to the side as if to contemplate her next move. A mask of warmth invaded her face, and she smiled out of the corner of her slender mouth.

She threw her feathered robe to the side and strutted across the marbled floor toward the kitchen.

"Yes, I remember Emma. How is she doing? She was always so...spunky."

I silently sighed with relief, and Madison and I trailed her steps underneath the huge, crystal chandelier hovering from the second story above the foyer.

"She is great, Ms. Foster. I mean, *Dr.* Foster."

"Oh, I never went for my PhD. I stopped at a Masters degree. Always wished I had finished out but didn't see the reason to bother."

Ms. Foster snuffed her cigarette in a golden ashtray on another golden-trimmed table in the hallway and placed her filter beside it.

"Understandable, ma'am. Do you mind taking us to where the murder occurred?"

"Keep following me, we're nearly there. So you think that he was murdered? I think his ticker finally gave out, but that's my opinion on it. You know he was on heart medication, right? Or are the police not sharing information with their junior scientists?"

"Well, they share a small portion with us. We are in a training program. I actually wrote a grant and have my own forensic training laboratory at the high school."

Glenda took in a deep breath as she stopped in her tracks, turning around once again to study me, untwisting her feathered gown from her silky robe.

"Your own lab at the high school? I am impressed! I should have known a child of Emma's would have that kind of ambition. Here we are...the kitchen. The old coot dropped right over there," Glenda pointed a skeletal finger toward the floor in the middle of the kitchen. "And I see my cleaning lady didn't do that great of a job," Glenda mumbled angrily as she picked up a splinter of blue glass off the floor and went to toss it into the trash bin.

"Wait! Can I have that, please?" I pleaded, ripping out an evidence bag from my forensic kit and holding it out in front of Glenda Foster.

Glenda studied the evidence bag and smirked.

"Of course. Here ya go. It's no news, though. The timeworn codger knocked over my expensive Grecian vase on his way down. The real police lab collected all the pieces. But I suppose they missed some of it."

"Thanks, Ms. Foster. Well, we will have a look around here and collect what we can, keeping everything in order the way we found it. Also, do you mind if we look in the other parts of the house and maybe around the estate?" I said, gazing out the back window, "I see you have another house in the back."

"Knock yourselves out. I made some lemonade tea in the refrigerator if you want some, but I haven't tasted it, so I'm not sure how strong it is. I don't usually make the stuff, Mr. Foster always did, but he drank it hot. I always wanted it cold. Those are servant quarters in the back. Walter Hargrove lives there. You should knock if you go back there. There's also a gentleman staying here in the main home for a few days. His name is Kosmo. He's in the third bedroom on the right down the main hallway. You should knock on his door too; never know what you'll walk in on if you don't."

My heart raced as she spoke the name Kosmo. He was the primary suspect in the murder. If he was a nomadic homeless man with a broken down car, why was he still at the manor? This would definitely be information that Detective Chase would find interesting.

"Thank you, Ms. Foster. We won't be long."

"Oh, and watch out for ghosts. They can be nasty sometimes," Glenda warned as her heels clinked down the marbled floor of the hallway.

Spinning around to Madison, I rolled my eyes and withdrew a pair of purple nitrile examination gloves from my forensic kit.

"Here we go with the ghost story again," I shook my head in repulsion, pulling the glove over my bandage on my palm and snapping the wristband of the glove onto my wrist.

Madison cracked a huge smile and reached for her gloves.

"Fiona, look at this place. If there ever were a haunted house, this is it!" Madison whispered as she shimmied on her gloves and pulled her fingerprinting supplies from her forensic kit. She sorted through the camel hair and fiberglass fingerprint brushes to choose the appropriate one.

"She mentioned lemonade tea, Madison. Make sure you dust for prints on all tea boxes, canisters and maybe anything used to make lemonade and tea. It would be great to have her prints as a reference."

"I'm sure Detective Chase took a sample of fingerprints from the people at the crime scene. I know Lauren told me she was fingerprinted."

I didn't like to be second-guessed when it came to the direction I was giving. Madison was my best friend, but this was a job, and I was in charge. This was a crime scene and business was business.

"Be a good investigator, Madison. Leave no stone unturned, and just do it," I ordered sternly as I picked up another piece of blue glass with my tweezers from the travertine tile of the kitchen. "Ms. Foster's cleaning lady needs to be fired."

# 6 ENVELOPE

The next few hours, we worked silently yet diligently, collecting as much evidence as we thought would have the slightest possibility of being relevant. The crime lab had investigated; the scene was cleared, and the Foster's weekly house-cleaning service had come and went. We realized that our efforts were most likely futile, but in the end, Ms. Foster had even recognized that this would be a good training exercise, nonetheless. We packed up, thanked Ms. Foster, and headed to the school laboratory to drop off the evidence. Madison and I sorted through the evidence we collected, and I called an early Saturday morning meeting at the lab to discuss our findings. Exhausted, I fell asleep the moment my head hit my pillow.

Saturday morning couldn't come fast enough as Madison and I sped off in the VW to my lab. Using my master key to the school, I opened the side door, and Madison grabbed the rubber wedge doorstopper to hold the door ajar so the rest of the club members could get into the school. We scurried through the halls and passed the bank of charred lockers.

"I see they took the door off your locker, Fiona," Madison said quietly and pointed to my locker that was still burnt from the blast.

"I'm sure it was a hazard. The door was so mangled; there were crispy sharp points all over it."

I inspected the inside of the locker. It contained baked on char, and the metal walls had been bent by the blast. A slight hint of accelerant lingered at the scene; most likely, it had been spilled on the carpet or in the adjacent lockers by the perpetrator. Shaking my head, we entered the lab and awaited the remaining club members' arrival. Lauren and Willow arrived soon after and within ten minutes, Wolfe and Carden Doyle had joined the group, and we began the meeting.

"Thank you all for being here on a Saturday," I announced, standing at the front of the lab. "First, I want to introduce Carden Doyle. I think you all know each other already."

An assortment of *welcomes* and *hellos* sounded as Carden's cheeks blushed a bright crimson as he fervently nodded his head.

"Carden is our first lab trainee. As you are well aware, our lab supports five students a year. We are all graduating in May, and Carden will be one of our replacements. That is, if I get my grant reviewed. Fingers crossed!"

"No doubt!" Madison chirped.

"Carden could very well be the one running things next year if he wins the job this summer. He's going to start observing how we run things here in the lab, and this summer, he'll actually get to work on cases with us before we officially move on to college. Plus, the renewal might actually include funding and support for more than five members. I suppose if all ends well with us this year," I gave a shamefaced grin.

"Will he go to Foster Manor with us?" Lauren asked candidly.

"No, unfortunately he cannot. Due to the grant, only the original five can attend field trips or go to the police station on business. Carden is allowed to assist us, attend meetings and train with us here at the lab only," I said frankly.

Carden Doyle was sitting at the back of the group, overtly nervous to be among us in the lab as he fidgeted with a string hanging from his sleeve. He was a carbon copy of his older brother Duncan with both having an odd combination of chocolate brown eyes and pale blonde hair. Athletically built, they stood nearly six foot tall with dark olive skin. Both had a peculiar bounce to their steps and strong ties with the local rodeo.

Duncan had been at the crime scene the night of the murder, and I hoped Carden would be an important asset to our investigation. However, I knew that Carden excelled in his science classes, and that is why I selected him in the first place. Having a brother at the crime scene was only an added bonus for our group.

"I hope you are all packed and ready to observe the Ohio Paranormal Investigation Team tonight at Foster Manor. Yesterday, Madison and I went to the Foster Manor to see if we could find anything that the Godley Grove Police Department might have missed."

Lauren slammed her hand on her notebook, startling the club members.

"What!" Lauren shrieked, obviously surprised by my announcement. "Are we not supposed to be a team?"

I gave a defiant stare to Lauren before I responded. This was my program. I was the leader of the group and shouldn't be questioned in that manner. "Yes, Lauren. We are a team, and that is why Madison and I went to the manor to collect the evidence, and now we are meeting as a team to discuss our findings."

Madison interrupted, "Fiona, you don't have to explain yourself—

"It's okay, Madison. I knew I couldn't get everybody to go on such short notice. I decided to go, Detective Chase cleared it, and we left within ten minutes. As it turned out, Ms. Foster would not have appreciated our whole group going to her home," and then the prickliness of rage set in as my lungs picked up the pace to keep up with my rapidly increasing heart beats, "Please, don't forget that *I* founded this program, and *I* am the leader of this program. If you question me, you will no doubt question your future supervisors, and that's not the way to build professional relationships. Great followers made great leaders," I huffed, releasing an onerous sigh. "May I continue with my report?"

My capillaries flushed blood to my face that recoiled against my skin as the heat of restrained fury radiated from my pores.

"Absolutely," Wolfe Nero shouted.

"Go for it," Willow snapped, rolling her eyes toward Lauren, as if I couldn't see her.

Carden Doyle nodded shyly as he avoided to make eye contact with me. Lauren shrugged her shoulders in a sarcastic fashion before she dropped her elbows on her desk and grimaced.

"I guess so, Fiona. Nevertheless, I don't see why you wouldn't at least call us to see if we wanted to go on the mission to the manor. I would have gone, and I know that Willow would have gone. We didn't have plans last night."

Wolfe added, "I actually had plans, Fiona. Thanks for not calling me. I'm already giving up my Saturday night for this ghost hunting malarkey."

"Thanks, Wolfe. Lauren, it simply wasn't necessary to have us all there," I maintained, openly frustrated.

"Fiona's right, Lauren," Madison rasped with a stern hand gripping a hip. "Ms. Foster wouldn't have been receptive to all of us showing up. She barely allowed Fiona and me to investigate. She thinks we were just pretending and didn't take us seriously at all. She has no idea that we can actually influence the crime lab with our findings."

Lauren slumped over onto the lab countertop, rolling her eyes toward Willow. Willow returned with a one-shoulder shrug, followed by a slow headshake.

"Enough of the ego strains. I'm going to continue. Madison and I arrived to the manor at 5:30 PM. As you will see for yourselves tonight, the manor is everything you'd expect it to be as a suspected haunted house. You all know my stance on that. However, I will say that the manor is creepy in itself – ghosts or not. Ms. Glenda Foster, the victim's widow, is still living there and so is the groundskeeper, Walter Hargrove."

"Walter Hargrove? That's a new one. Why was he not mentioned before?" Wolfe interjected.

"He is an employee; he's been there since he was sixteen, like in 1960. He was hired by Victoria Radley Foster, Gilroy's mother. She actually died that same year," I added.

"How did Gilroy Foster's mother die?" Willow inquired brusquely.

"Supposedly, she shot herself," I reminded myself that I didn't want to give the group the history of the manor as I had researched. I didn't want them to have preconceived ideas during the upcoming paranormal investigation with the Ohio team. "Glenda Foster told us that the manor was cursed but didn't want to give details. We're going to take a trip to the courthouse and comb through the news articles and birth and death certificates to try to outline a pedigree with birth and death dates and causes of death. We get pieces of information here and there, and it would be helpful to see what has gone on in this house since it was built in 1845. Maybe we can find some articles about this crazy curse. Not that I believe in any curses, but it would be helpful to know the psyche of the people living in the home."

"As well as to know the propaganda that the defense attorney will dig up to muddle the jury once they find a viable suspect and go to trial," Madison added.

"Well, I would like to tag along when you go, Fiona. I want to help with this investigation, not just be fed the evidence. I was there when it happened and do feel an obligation, at the very least, to the victim," Lauren said coldly, looking to Willow for back up.

"Me too," Willow said, her voice a monotone.

"That's great. In that instance, we'll need as many people to help as possible. We will most likely go to the courthouse on Monday after school so mark your calendars," I instructed.

"Done. Doc and I are there," Lauren snapped, grabbing her cell phone and inputting the appointment into her calendar.

Madison added with hesitation riddled in her voice, "Ms. Foster is, uh, rather difficult to deal with. Just a heads up."

"Agreed, you'll see when we arrive tonight. Hopefully she will be in a more pleasant mood," I added.

"Great, so she's a hag," Wolfe said boldly.

The group collectively snickered. Wolfe knew how to break the tension and get everybody to lighten up.

"She is grieving, give the lady a break!" Willow howled, punching Wolfe playfully in the shoulder.

"Well, team. We have many fingerprints and pieces of evidence to analyze. As you know, the Godley Grove Crime Lab can't actually use our evidence, but they certainly can listen and use any leads we give them. Stay diligent. Also, read the evidence analysis that they have shared with us to try to make sense of the evidence that Madison and I collected yesterday. We found some fingerprints and some glass vase splinters as the police lab did. However, we found some additional carpet fibers, a hair and other various trace evidence. Ms. Foster's cleaning service isn't that diligent, I must say. They left a lot of evidence behind."

Madison stood up from her lab stool.

"We also met with Mr. Walter Hargrove. He wasn't a big story with the initial report, but his fingerprints are all over the manor. This makes sense, however, since he is the groundskeeper and has been there for most of his life. I must ask, was Walter in the main house the night of the murder, Lauren?"

Lauren's eyes rolled to the top right corner of her lids, and she stared at the ceiling for a quick moment in thought.

"No, I never saw him nor knew he existed."

"Well, it's probably nothing, but we'll definitely keep him on the suspect list. Anybody that was there that night should be investigated," I noted carefully as I slowly turned to gaze at Lauren.

Madison noticed my gesture and thought quickly to change the subject into a different direction to deflect the attention from Lauren. She was correct; we didn't need to conjure any hard feelings at this time. However, Lauren had to know that she was a viable suspect in this case. Even if she was only a teen with no motive to murder an elderly man, she was at the scene of an unsolved crime. As a budding investigator, she had to realize the seriousness of the situation.

"Mr. Hargrove has a very nice greenhouse, by the way. He has tons of exotic flowers such as poinsettias, orchids, rhizomes and some others that look like upside down tulips. There are also some ginormous sunflowers."

"Fiona, did you guys see any ghosts while you were there?" Wolfe mused, exposing his perfectly sculpted teeth.

I couldn't help but snicker. I knew Wolfe was trying to get under my skin.

"Obviously not. Didn't think that we would, either."

"Fiona, tell them about the locker evidence!" Madison added, changing the topic once again.

"Oh yes. The locker," I countered, clearing my throat.

In my peripheral field of vision, I detected motion from the hallway and twisted around to face the door. I listened carefully, looking out the door window. I perceived faint footsteps sounding like ballet shoes on carpet. I pulled my index finger to my lips to signal silence as I tiptoed toward the door. I yanked the door open, peered out into the hallway, and saw a silhouette bustling around the corner. Not many people had permission or a reason to be inside of the school on the weekends.

"Hey!" I dashed out into the hall. The club members rushed out after me. I shouted again, "Hey! Come back here!"

I spun around to face the club members as a bright red envelope inside of my charred locker caught my attention. I was certain it hadn't been in there when I arrived to the lab.

"They must have left this in here. Wolfe, go after them!" I screamed as I lunged closer to view the envelope in my burned locker.

"On it," Wolfe yelled as his long legs tore off down the hallway.

"What the heck is that?" I said with resignation, racing back into the lab to grab a pair of nitrile gloves and a sterile pair of tweezers from the autoclave cabinet.

I cautiously slipped on the gloves over the bandages covering my palms. The slight pressure on the bandages ignited tiny sparks of pain down my forearms. My injuries were healing rapidly, but little spells of pain kept reminding me they existed.

"Careful, Fiona," Madison warned, gently pulling my arm toward the laboratory door.

"Of course, Maddie. It's me you are talking to!" I snapped abruptly, holding the envelope tightly with the tweezers.

We rushed back into the lab and laid the envelope on the desk on top of an evidence bag that Madison grabbed from the shelf of the lab.

"I hope Wolfe catches them so we don't have a mystery. I'm sure whomever it was in the hallway was the one who put this envelope in the locker. I walked by that locker on my way in this morning, and it definitely wasn't there before!" Willow sighed.

"Maybe it's an invitation to a party, Fiona!" Lauren howled.

The group let out a nervous fit of laughter.

"I know it wasn't there as well, by the way. I nearly put my head inside of your locker because I thought the damage was so cool looking," Lauren admitted with a grin.

"She totally did," Willow chuckled.

"Madison and I had a conversation about the missing door. We both inspected the entire bank of lockers at that time. Therefore, this envelope had to have been put inside of the locker—most likely by that person in the hallway during our meeting," I told them.

I was shocked to see my name written on the front of the envelope in a childlike, handwritten print. I could immediately tell that this person was attempting to hide their handwriting. I grabbed a sterile probe from the autoclave cabinet and carefully slid open the flap, removing the folded paper from inside the envelope. It was notebook paper. I carefully unfolded it as the club members gasped in unison, all eyes landing on the glued on, cut out letters.

"Drop the case or you will suffer," I read the cryptic cutout words aloud. My eyes filmed as I found it impossible to look away, mesmerized in a disturbed manner.

The letters had been individually cut out from what appeared to be a newspaper. I immediately took the paper and envelope, inserted them into the evidence bag, and filled out the front label with a permanent marker.

"Well, I guess I will drop this off at the Godley Grove Crime Lab. We wouldn't want to risk analyzing it here and not having it included as official evidence with the police. Especially since it might be involved with the actual murder case now that the locker and the case have been linked—

even if it is a coincidence. I'll drop this off and meet you guys back here at 6 PM. The Ohio team will be at the manor by 7 PM so we'll have plenty of time," I instructed as I waited for the members to exit the lab so I could lock the door.

The moment that we entered the hallway, Wolfe, out of breath, jogged back towards us.

"I couldn't find them. They got away," Wolfe panted, hanging his head low as he grabbed my shoulder and gave it a gentle squeeze.

"Darn!" I shrieked, momentarily distracted by his touch.

"What about the parking lot? Certainly you saw a car or at least a car driving away?" Madison pleaded.

Wolfe's expression turned more remorseful.

"Nope, nothing. I took off down the hallway and into the parking lot and there was nobody, not a soul, not a car, nothing."

"What's done is done. They had a good head start, it isn't Wolfe's fault. Thanks for trying, though," I lamented, openly disappointed.

I adjourned the meeting and raced my VW to the Godley Grove Police Department. Not that getting the evidence to the crime lab a few minutes faster would make a difference, I simply felt compelled to have it in safe hands as soon as possible. We had never submitted official evidence to them before, and I didn't want anything to go wrong. I whirled the car into a front parking spot and donned a new pair of nitrile gloves as I held the evidence bag tightly. Wearing gloves was going beyond what was expected as the evidence was already protected from contamination inside of the evidence bag. I just wanted to be sure. I jogged at a steady pace to the front entrance. It was Saturday, and the front of the station was buzzing with activity. The uniformed Ms. Spinks was on the phone with her orange acrylic nails clinking away on her computer keyboard. Her reading glasses were propped dangerously at the tip of her bony nose. She noticed us and placed her call on hold.

"Hello, Miss Fiona. What can we do for you today?" The white haired Ms. Spinks echoed throughout the lobby.

The police station always smelled like dirty, musty feet. I didn't understand where the smell originated from, but it always caught me off guard for the first thirty seconds of entering the lobby. Ms. Spinks used multiple plug-in air fresheners in attempts to cover the stench, but it only served to make it smell like dirty feet soaked in strawberry cream. We never had the heart to tell her that her air freshening efforts were pointless.

"Hi Ms. Spinks. I have official evidence. Can I go back to the crime lab?" I responded, holding up the evidence bag.

"Official evidence? Wow, Fiona! You're really becoming part of that lab, huh?"

"Yea, I guess so. This evidence just kind of stumbled into my lap, though."

Ms. Spinks pushed a button underneath the counter, and the bright green door to my right clicked open.

As I walked toward the door, Ms. Spinks pointed out, "I'm not sure how many of the lab techs are here today since it's Saturday. I know Detective Chase is in a meeting until 3:30 PM. Go on back, Fiona. Ring the bell at the evidence collection desk if nobody answers in the lab. Have a great day!"

"Thanks, Ms. Spinks," I uttered, dashing through the door and down the concrete industrialized hallway and around the corner to another bright green door of the crime laboratory.

I pushed the buzzer abruptly, sounding the high-pitched chimes inside of the laboratory. I stood on the tips of my toes to look inside, but I couldn't see any movement even though the light was on. I waited a few seconds before pushing the buzzer again. Looking on my phone, I saw that it was 12:01 PM.

"Lunch. Great," I whispered in frustration to myself. My shoulders slumped as I dredged over to the evidence collection desk.

I hit the bell with my left palm, forgetting about the injury under my bandage. The pain made me wince and hold my breath until the throbbing subsided.

"Coming!" a familiar voice sounded from the evidence room.

I felt reassured to hear a voice. It sounded familiar, but I couldn't match it with the face in my memory. Moments later, a young, brown-eyed girl with black shaggy hair framing her round face emerged from the shadows and strolled up to the counter. It was Addie Coleman, the twenty-two year old serology technician. I had never gotten along with her too well, but it wasn't from a lack of effort on my end. I had always tried to be her friend, but she never seemed interested in building a working relationship with me.

"Hello Fiona," she smirked, openly irritated at being disturbed.

"Addie, I have some evidence. Are you the one in charge of evidence processing today?"

One grizzled eyebrow rose as folds surfaced on her previously smooth forehead.

"Fiona, get real. I know you went to the manor and collected whatever kind of evidence you think you collected but you know the deal. We can't take evidence from you on a scene we've already cleared. You are not allowed to submit evidence on any official open case or you will hand the defense mistrials and allow criminals to walk free. Have a good day," Addie snarled in a condescending manner as she swirled around toward the door.

"Addie, wait! This is new evidence but not for the Foster murder case. It's an envelope with a note in it—it was in my locker at school. Did you hear about the bomb that exploded? The one that nearly killed me."

Addie stopped in her tracks, still facing the doorway.

"Yea, so what does this evidence have to do with it?" Addie slowly turned around to face me before she continued coldly, "We already sent someone over for that. In fact, the Silver Springs bomb squad was there and collected all of the evidence. I get it, Fiona. You want a job here. You'll have to graduate high school and go to college first. *Then*, you can get a job here and become an investigator. Why don't you go get a prom date or something? You should just enjoy high school."

I clenched my fists reflexively as I shuddered; gritting my teeth to suppress the impending fit of rage trying to evade my voice of reason. I repeated her words in my head a few times, searching for their true intent. Everybody at the police station had always welcomed my endeavors - especially given who my father was, and because I was only seventeen with a federal grant. Addie was the exception. I took a deep, calming breath before I gently tapped the bell on the desk. Addie spun around and glared at me, her eyes burned with an intensity that was overwhelming.

"Addie, this is *new* evidence. I was at school this morning in my lab, and somebody slipped this in my locker. The locker was open, burned into a crisp and didn't even have a door. My friends saw it before and after, and we are certain it was placed in there this morning. It's a threat! It needs to be analyzed immediately!"

Addie's face was suddenly serious again, and she engaged in an awkward period of silence. I wondered if she was coming around to see my point.

"There will most likely be residue from the locker on the envelope so that should be noted. Can you please check this in as evidence on the bomb case and forward to the document analyst at the Silver Springs Police Department?" I paused as I surveyed Addie's next move. The silence encouraged me to continue, "I would greatly appreciate it. If I need Detective Chase or maybe my father to contact you to give you further instruction on how to do so, I will definitely oblige," my words came out stronger than I intended.

Addie's face turned resentful as I watched her fight an outburst. Thinking better of it, she decided to remain civil.

"Not needed, Fiona. I misunderstood you," she drew in a long breath as if it were riddled with nails, "I will check this in and get it to who it needs to go to at Silver Springs. The courier should be coming soon."

"Thank you, Addie," I replied serenely, exhausted from the confrontation.

"Fiona," Addie said, voice breathless with irritation.

"Yes, Addie?" I cautiously awaited her reply.

"The tire evidence from the Foster Manor was analyzed. Here's a copy of the report," she retrieved a document from the printer and extended it to me from across the desk. "And can you please pass it along to Detective Chase that I helped your investigation by giving you a copy of this report?"

"Sure, thank you."

Her expression melted into a pleasant look, and she continued, "Thank you. Almost forgot—we heard from the Silver Springs bomb squad that investigated the locker bomb at your school. There were tool marks on your locker. The perp used a crowbar, and it left many distinctive impressions. They're sending the report over to us tomorrow. We find the crowbar, we find the bomber," Addie stated bluntly.

She spun around and disappeared through the doorway.

# 7 VISITORS

Later that evening, the club members arrived at my house as planned. Janice packed each one of us a *care kit*, as she called it, that was filled with cookies shaped like ghosts and a juice that was called Boo-Berry. We set out in a two-car caravan toward the Foster Manor to meet up with the Ohio Paranormal Investigation Team. The Ohio team had certified many locations as sites for known paranormal activity, but they were also infamous for refuting claims of paranormal activity. Because of that, I was tolerable about the pending collaboration.

Madison jumped in the front seat, and Wolfe Nero's bulky body filled up my small backseat. I wondered why he chose to ride with me when Lauren's Acura had a much larger backseat. I didn't mind, so I didn't mention it. I overcompensated during the drive by not looking into my rearview mirror at all. I figured that if I did look and accidently connected with his icy-gray eyes, it would be an even more dangerous distraction than not looking into it at all.

"Oh, guys, I got a tire tread report from the night of the murder. All of the cars are accounted for besides two unknown treads that don't match up to the known cars at the scene. They'll keep the records until they need to match a suspect's vehicle with the treads. It doesn't mean the tires belonged to the murderer's car, but it might be useful to later establish a suspect was at the manor at some point, however."

"The more evidence available, the better," Madison said, pointing ahead. "We are almost there!"

"This place is out in the middle of nowhere," Wolfe wailed, his deep voice seeming even more powerful in the small space.

The two-car caravan trekked underneath the Foster Manor archway and down the dirt pathway lined with barren trees and into the circle drive behind two large black vans. I killed the engine, and we piled out of the car as Lauren's burgundy Acura pulled in close behind. I was startled as a large black raven landed on the hood of my VW. It turned its head slowly to gaze directly into each one of our eyes.

"What is it with weirdo birds gawking at us, Fiona?" Madison shrieked.

"Coincidence, Maddie. Hello, we are in the country! There's wildlife."

"Swag bird," Wolfe chuckled as he gawked at the raven.

"Swag bird?" I laughed as I smiled at Wolfe.

"Good point, Fiona. Maddie, watch out, there's probably killer squirrels here too," Wolfe added lightheartedly.

"Okay, I've had enough. This place is already creeping me out," tiny Willow yelped as she stood beside Lauren's car. She attempted to climb back into the passenger's seat. "You guys have fun, I'm staying here."

Lauren, bright green mangled straw hanging out of the side of her mouth, gently pulled Willow by the arm. Lauren and Willow were nearly opposites in appearance, and when I looked at them as a pair, I was always obsessed with comparing their drastic differences. Lauren was of average height with a full build, tanned skin, with dark, massive curly hair. Willow was barely five foot, maybe a hundred pounds with bright-green eyes and brownish-blonde, shoulder-length hair. Lauren had a thing for military-inspired clothing, and Willow chose blazers and slacks—as if she were already a practicing physician. I had heard a teacher refer to the duo as *Frick and Frack* before, but I was never sure what that was all about. Willow reluctantly ambled onto the broken concrete driveway.

"Be a big girl, Willow. You're going to be a doctor, and you'll see and experience much worse than this," Lauren smirked as held her best friends arm tightly and guided her around the large black vans. The vans had Ohio license plates. They obviously belonged to the Ohio team.

"At least those guys will know what to do when we find the ghosts," Willow whispered, finally cracking the resemblance of a smile as she surveyed her surroundings in a fluster. "Why is that black bird staring at me like that?"

"Willow, he's just curious! He's a wild animal, and we're in his territory!" I responded, laughing silently.

We reached the front door, and I grabbed the brass handle of the door knocker and struck it against the base. Quick footsteps sounded from inside seconds before a young man with spiked platinum hair swung the heavy wooden door open; the speed of the swing minimized the creakiness of the door from when Ms. Foster had opened it earlier. He was wearing an Ohio Paranormal Investigation Team polo shirt tucked into tight-fitting skinny jeans. Untied industrial boots rounded out his casual attire.

"You must be the famous Fiona and friends?"

"Yes, sir. Are you Justin?" I inquired, strolling into the marbled foyer, motioning for my group to follow me.

The slightly sweet and acrid smell of electronics overcame my senses, and the hairs on my skin stood on end from the electricity filling the air. The manor certainly didn't smell like that earlier in the day. I reasoned immediately how the energy alone could give a false impression of paranormal activity.

"That's me! Justin Long at your service!" Justin burst into an array of laughter, sounding as if it came from ten men as it changed tone and pitch.

"Wow, what a laugh," Madison whispered softly into my neck so only I could hear her.

"I heard that!" a voice behind Justin squeaked, holding a skinny microphone in the air. It was Lance Jefferson, another member of the Ohio team. He was smaller in stature with vivid green eyes that contrasted with his wiry strawberry blonde hair.

"Sorry, I didn't mean to be rude," Madison apologized, flushed red from embarrassment.

"That's what I deal with, guys. Glad to be working with some dudes, finally," Wolfe returned. He grinned wildly as he extended a massive hand to Justin.

"No doubt," Justin countered Wolfe.

Justin shook Wolfe's hand, and he and Lance burst into another fit of laughter before turning back toward me. Wolfe immediately melted into a face of sincerity as soon as his silver eyes met mine. I smirked in response, shaking my head.

"Lance hears everything, even your stomach growling! He's the audio guy. He collects the EMF data," Justin said. He swished around toward the massive amounts of crates and tables that they were setting up in the main living area. "And over there is Lady Mia. She's a work horse."

Mia was the female member of the team, probably mid-forties. Dressed in every color of the rainbow, she stopped unfolding cables to tie back her colorful dreadlocks with a wrinkled rainbow-inspired skull bandana. She was diligently placing the cables across the tables. She obviously loved color but definitely wasn't as social as Justin and Lance. I was afraid to bother her and decided to allow her to approach our group when she was ready.

"Is Ms. Foster here?" I quietly asked the ginger-topped Lance.

"The creepy lady that lives here? With the bright pumpkin-colored hair?"

"You're one to talk about pumpkin-colored hair, Lance." Justin shouted playfully from the tables.

"My hair is called strawberry blonde. It's more like a ripened squash than a pumpkin. Plus, I don't dye my strands like that haggy old woman," Lance squeaked, brushing his undersized fingers though his bristly hair.

Justin skipped over toward me.

"I apologize for Lance's rudeness about Ms. Foster. It's unprofessional, and we shouldn't act that way. However, Lance and Ms. Foster exchanged some heated *words* when we first got here. Ms. Foster doesn't want us here and was more than rude about explaining that to us. Ms. Foster went out for a bit, but I'm sure she will return soon enough," Justin said, catching me gazing at his white spiky locks on his head. I became instantly embarrassed and tasted panic in the back of my throat. "If you are wondering about my hair, well, go ahead and ask."

Justin framed his unique tresses with his hands, waiting for me to respond.

"Sorry for staring. Yea, I was wondering why you seem so young but have pure white hair. I wasn't going to say anything but since you offered," I asked with a nervous giggle.

"I get bleached. *Major* bleached—make my stylist leave it on until there's not a spot of pigment left. I'm not prematurely gray or anything. I like it this color, makes me look distinguished."

"Makes you look like a freak, Justin!" Lance shrieked jokingly.

"Ha! Look at you carrot crown! However, I'm just used to new people sitting around wondering for hours about it and then they finally get the nerve to ask. I noticed you staring at it in a wonder and thought I'd get it out of the way," he said good-naturedly. A slow smile spread across his face.

"Gosh, Fiona! Way to call a dude out," Wolfe Nero added as he smiled.

My face flushed red once again.

"Good to know! I like the color, actually. Maybe after I turn eighteen, and my mother doesn't lord over my hair color, I can venture out to something like that?"

"That will never happen, Fiona. Your mother will always have control," Madison cackled.

"True, Maddie," my lips turned up in a private smile. I turned back to Justin, "Ms. Foster seemed unfriendly to us too, but then she warmed up. She certainly is different," I stated flatly. "By the way, is Kosmo here?"

"Who's Kosmo?" Justin inquired without hesitation, lifting a large monitor onto a foldable table and punching a power cord into the back of it.

"He's a homeless man with a broken down car that showed up the night of the murder. Ms. Foster told us that he was still staying here, but we never actually saw him. I guess Ms. Foster feels bad for kicking him out into the street with nowhere to go when she has a huge house like this. Maybe she doesn't want to be alone, even if it is with a transient," I explained, shrugging one shoulder and raising the opposing eyebrow.

Justin scratched his head as he looked at Lance for answers.

"That might've been what she said when she stormed out of here earlier. Now it makes sense. I think that Lance thought she was going to have a *Cosmopolitan*."

Confusion took over my face like a neon sign. Justin nodded with a chuckle.

"A Cosmopolitan is a cocktail. Maybe she was referring to her houseguest *Kosmo*. Even Lance didn't catch what she said clearly, but he didn't have his audio equipment running yet."

We laughed for a moment, and then my club members and I integrated ourselves into assisting the Ohio team with whatever they needed with their set up. It looked like an awful amount of work just to disprove there were ghosts in the house, but I figured I'd go along with it for the experience. I also figured that Detective Chase might need more witnesses to attest the house was not seething with paranormal activity.

As the sun dropped from the sky, everybody scattered toward their places in front of their respective monitors and assorted outputs. I could tell they had done this many times prior. They were professionals, manipulating their equipment like drones, routinely scanning the room. They monitored the surrounding rooms with meters and checked the video surveillance of the entire manor in regular intervals, making notes into their composition notebooks. Wolfe Nero was more than excited to be an integral part of the paranormal investigation circus, but Willow, sitting straight on the stately couch in the middle of the living room, looked as uneasy as a cricket in a pesticide factory. Lauren was walking around the Ohio team, boasting about being part of the previous Hartford University investigation at the manor. I rolled my eyes to Madison each time she bragged about her previous experience as if one night made her a paranormal expert. Willow was feeding her ego, but to Maddie and me, she was nearly intolerable.

The living room furniture was Victorian style, designed for the owner to appear rich and pompous. The pieces had golden-sculpted frames with white textured silk covering the taught cushions. The silk glistened in the moonlight streaming in from the huge front window. The carved cherry wood finish grandfather clock chimed on the hour and startled us as we settled into our positions.

As the room drew quiet and still, the front door creaked open unexpectedly. Ms. Foster stomped inside, shopping bags in hand. Without a word, she marched toward the hallway leading to the master quarters. She had refused to allow the Ohio team to put any surveillance equipment in the master bedroom suite, and the team reluctantly complied. Her heels clinked on the marbled hallway floor all the way to her bedroom suite. She slammed the door, which sounded throughout the bottom floor, vibrating the walls.

"Was that necessary?" Lance mocked quietly to Justin.

Within seconds, the coat closet door across the foyer slammed shut.

"Here we go," Justin exclaimed, grabbing a meter and cautiously scanning the room surrounding the coat closet.

Mia jumped up and leaned over to read the numbers on a monitor closely.

"Was that open before?" I grumbled as I scampered over to Justin. "Or did it open and shut back again?"

"It was closed, and it did it on its own, Fiona. Nobody was over there," Maddie exclaimed.

"Not sure what happened," Justin suggested as he jogged across the foyer.

"There has to be an explanation!" I gasped.

Justin reached the door and carefully examined it.

"The door doesn't appear to catch the lock. The piece that fits inside of the lock doesn't protrude enough so this door will never officially close," Justin said clearly, as he moved to inspect the inside of the dark closet. He waved his meter in a methodical manner starting at the top of the closet and working his way to the floor. "I do detect a cold spot in the closet here."

"A cold spot?" Wolfe Nero shouted. "What the heck is a cold spot, and can this cold spot attack us?"

The rainbow-dreadlocked Mia finally chose to engage in the conversation as she glided toward Justin, responding to Wolfe in an arctic voice, "Warm air rises, and cold air sinks. This is normal. When there is an anomalous paranormal occurrence, you can detect a pocket of ionized air, a bioelectric charge, by using an infrared meter. An infrared meter is essentially a thermographic camera, detecting parts of the electromagnetic spectrum including infrared waves."

I struggled to understand exactly what she was explaining, but she was clearly speaking over our heads. I could minimally understand her, and that is because I had read many journal articles from the *Skeptical Inquirer* – a publication from the *National Committee for Skeptical*

*Inquiry.* This organization, founded by scientists in 1976, refuted all paranormal claims. I stood still, cogitating her words.

Wolfe jumped up from the couch and followed me. I spun around to identify the owner of the footsteps and locked into a gaze with his exquisite features. Seconds passed before I realized I was awkwardly staring at him. I abruptly snapped to my senses and turned around before I was caught gazing at a boy twice in one night. Being caught by Wolfe would be even more humiliating because I was beginning to realize my growing attraction for him was genuine. Nevertheless, I could never openly show it or let him know.

"I am somewhat following you, Miss. But aren't closets normally colder than the room they're in because they aren't heated?" Wolfe cautiously added. He looked down at me and smiled shyly.

I knew by his expression that he had caught my stare. I shut my eyes briefly, hoping it would make me invisible so he would forget about it. I silently took in the largest breath of air I had ever filled my lungs with before holding it tightly, expanding my lungs to new horizons.

"You are correct, young man. But we have experience and know what a normal cold spot in a closet looks like versus an anomalous one," Mia countered abruptly.

I exhaled silently. Wolfe had decided to pretend he didn't notice.

"By the way, I'd like to formally introduce myself. My name is Mia Tipper. I am the founder of this team. I've been around this business essentially my whole life," Mia explained, swishing her colored dreads onto her back as she approached the closet with another meter. "But I let Justin run things because he's more of a talker."

Intrigued, I followed her toward the closet and continued, "Well, isn't it right that an infrared meter only tests surface temperature and not ambient temperature? How can you be sure that is a pocket of ionized air if you are only testing on the surface? It seems fallible to me. Please, I mean no disrespect."

"Looks like you have been reading the *Skeptical Inquirer*, Fiona. Doing your homework, huh?" Mia antagonized, her eyes flickering between Wolfe and me.

"I'm going to be a scientist. I like to read all sides of an issue. I happen to be a fan of the scientific method and Ockham's razor. You know, a science experiment with tangible data, choosing the hypothesis with the fewest assumptions. Paranormal *science* is based upon too many assumptions."

I felt a lump forming at the back of my throat. The lump was my passion for the refutation of paranormal science. Mia was my antagonist, and I was ready and poised for a debate, but knew that I had more than a worthy opponent.

"Wow, I like your attitude. If I could convince you to open your mind, I'd like to maybe hire you one day. You are very thorough," Mia continued, holding up a meter to the top of the closet.

"No thank you. I respect you for what you do, but I do not respect your field. I am only here in case you try to make a claim that there are ridiculous ghosts here. Again, no disrespect intended."

"None taken. I'm used to that," Mia hissed through her teeth.

"Get her, Fiona," Wolfe whispered in a tight voice as he strolled back to the while silk couches.

"Hey, Fiona. I'll change your mind about ghosts," Justin promised with a smile.

My phone rang, and I fought to retrieve it from my pocket. I shot an apologetic plead towards Lance who was cringing at the volume projected into his ears from his sensitive audio recording equipment. He speedily typed away on his equipment, probably marking the occurrence for what it was on the output so they didn't later think it was a ghostly outburst.

"Hello?" I whispered gently, holding the phone to my ear tightly to minimize Lance's audio equipment detecting the conversation.

*"Hello, Fiona. Glad I caught you. Figured you would be busy catching ghosts and not have your phone on,"* Detective Chase's voice reverberated into my ear.

I quickly dashed onto the front porch to have a private conversation with Detective Chase.

"Yea, I should have had it silenced, but I forgot. Oops. I think I blasted the audio guy's eardrums with my ringer. It was set on loud, and he has sensitive equipment."

*"Unfortunate."* Detective Chase laughed for a moment and continued, *"I have some interesting findings to share with you."*

"Let's hear it!"

*"The Silver Springs arson investigator located a match right outside of the smoldering barrel at the manor the night of the murder. Match heads are made up of little animal's shells called diatoms. These diatoms are easily traceable. Well, we recovered a matchbook from Glenda Foster's kitchen junk drawer the night of the murder with one match missing, and the diatom evidence matches perfectly. It is a match, no pun intended, with over 99.999 percent certainty."*

"What does that mean? She burned something in the barrel that night? What did she burn?"

*"She struck the match is all that we know. There was a partial fingerprint on the match and a full fingerprint on the matchbook. Both were matches to Glenda Foster. There were documents burned in that barrel. It is going to take some time to ascertain what the documents might have been, but we do know there were documents that were burned by Ms. Foster the night of the murder."*

"Shocking. Well, not really, actually. Ms. Foster has acted strangely since yesterday when Maddie and I came here to investigate. Today, she got into an argument with the Ohio Paranormal Investigation Team about them being here to investigate."

*"Really? From what I recall, she wanted this alibi to stick. She wanted them to prove there was paranormal activity in the house. It's strange she wouldn't be cooperative."*

"Well, their data is used quite often in the *Skeptical Inquirer*, you know. They're the number one refutation team in the nation. I don't know why I'm telling you as I'm sure you selected them for that reason, Detective Chase," I giggled ever so slightly.

*"You are perceptive, my friend,"* Detective Chase chuckled.

"On another note, did you see that I brought in an envelope today? And did you look at the note that was inside of it or was it sent off to Silver Springs before you had a chance?"

*"No, I don't know what you are talking about, Fiona. You came to the station today?"*

"Yes, I was at my lab, and somebody had slipped a red envelope in my locker at school. You know, the one that was blown up. Well, the note was a threat for me to get off the case or suffer, whatever that means. The only case I'm working on is the Foster Manor case unless they are referring to the locker bomber case. I have no idea? I bagged it under proper protocol and took it immediately to the police station, and Addie Coleman was the one working the evidence desk. I gave it to her, in a sealed and labeled evidence bag, and she said she would forward it to the document analyst at Silver Springs."

*"Well, I'm looking at my computer right now, and there is no such evidence checked into our system. If she sent it over there, she broke the chain of evidence, as she is required to immediately input the evidence into our system upon acceptance. I will ask her about it, don't worry. Not that it would be acceptable, but maybe she just hasn't entered it yet."*

"Oh, okay. Wow. I hope she doesn't forget about it. I think it is somewhat important that I've been threatened about working on a case. I am sure it's just a school bully that is messing around, trying to scare me. It's probably nothing."

*"Well, it isn't nothing if you've been threatened. That is serious and not to be ignored for any reason. Fiona, I'm going to go check on it now."*

"Thanks, Detective Chase. I'll talk to you in a bit."

I strolled back into the living area with the others, noticing that there was a new face among them. He appeared demure as a dog that had just been scolded for ripping up trash, and he was a very small man. His salt-and-peppered straggled hair was void of style. His hollow hazel eyes confessed a history of malnutrition. Justin escorted me back onto the front porch and explained that while I was on the phone, a lot had happened.

While I had been on the porch speaking to Detective Chase, they had detected creaking noises from the second floor, right above the living room. He and Mia rushed upstairs to investigate and ran into none other than the homeless resident of the Foster Manor, Kosmo Wilder. Kosmo had explained to them that he was trying to stay out of the way of the investigation and didn't mean to cause any trouble. He pleaded with them not to mention his disturbance of the investigation to Glenda Foster. He didn't want to anger her. He didn't have anywhere else to go as his car had broken down, he didn't have a dime, and hence, he didn't have a way to get a job to earn money. Kosmo explained that Glenda Foster had only recently hired him as a handy man for the manor, but he hadn't collected any money from her as of yet and thought if she became incensed, she might forego payment and ask him to leave.

The investigators, being sympathetic, obliged and asked him to sit in the main living area so he wouldn't interfere with their recordings for the duration of the investigation. Kosmo amiably agreed and sat quietly on the couch by the tables.

I was stunned and couldn't believe that all of that happened while I was on the porch. As I strolled back into the living area, I surveyed the room and noticed that Willow's expression was sullen. She looked as if she could fold up like a Swiss army knife and put herself away.

"Oh my gosh!" Madison shrieked as she scrambled to jump onto the couch.

I lunged to look at what Madison was screaming about and instantly followed her lead, balancing myself on one of the foldable tables amidst the equipment.

"Holy crap! That looks like a rattlesnake! Everybody get up! Get as high as you can! I'll try to grab this sucker," Lance shouted as he dashed toward the kitchen, rushing back a few seconds later with a pair of barbecue tongs.

Kosmo Wilder didn't move a muscle and remained in his initial position on one of the white silk couches. Wolfe Nero calmly took a spot in the middle of the golden-sculpted coffee table, and Willow cried uncontrollably as she jumped on a foldable table, scooting the monitor over to the edge to make room for both of her legs.

The snake's rattle echoed throughout the living room of the manor as panic hung thick in the air.

"There are two of them!" Justin screamed, lunging out of the room.

# 8 CODE

Lauren's scream pierced my eardrums. I crouched, cupping my ears as I clambered around the equipment to get a better view. Lauren violently tossed her body to the ground, screaming as she thrashed about. Her military-style cap fell from her head, as her curls expanded and sprawled out onto the floor in a mad pile. We scampered on top of the couches and tables to see what was going on with Lauren, while avoiding the snake pit on the ground. I grabbed my phone from my pocket, pushing the numbers 9-1-1 as I balanced myself on the wobbly foldable table.

"It bit me! The snake bit me!" Lauren screamed as she held her thigh. She was writhing in obvious agony; she stared at the ceiling in horror as she lost her grip on her chewed straw, and it slid to the floor. Wolfe jumped down from the coffee table and dove over to Lauren. Willow let out a blood-curdling scream as she tried to climb the furniture to get to Lauren.

Shouting over the chaos, I gave the address of the manor to the 9-1-1 operator, and after confirming the ambulance was on its way, I jumped off the table to assist Wolfe in getting Lauren to safety and into the open air. One of the snakes was coiled in the corner of the room and raised it's torso into an *S* shape as it watched our every move. I could hear Lance on the other side of the room attempting to capture the second snake. Justin had disappeared from the room, but I knew we had to get Lauren out of there immediately.

"It. Hurts. So. Bad!" Lauren wailed, fighting for her breath as she screamed.

"Calm down, Lauren. You need to focus on breathing, try to ignore the pain. I know it is hard, but you can't get too excited for your own good," I warned, trying to comfort Lauren by pushing her dark curly locks away from her bronzed face.

Willow let out another panicked squeal as Maddie tried to quiet her.

"Found a bucket!" Justin shouted as he dashed back into the living room.

I opened the door for Wolfe who carried Lauren in his arms over the threshold into the night air. As we ambled to the front porch, he carefully placed her onto the ground. I took her head in my lap, trying to console her, as she convulsed from the pain. Madison and Willow had managed to conjure enough courage to jump off the furniture and soon joined us on the front porch around Lauren who continued to squirm in agony.

"Lauren, you don't want to increase your metabolic rate as that will circulate the poison through your system faster. Remain calm!" Willow instructed sternly, hurrying by her side.

"K, Doc," Lauren mumbled, wincing in anguish.

"She okay?" Justin asked, poking his head out of the door.

"She will be okay as long as the ambulance makes it here," I replied.

"I think Justin and Lance have had some experience with snakes before. They already caught one of them and are working on the second," Willow reported in a shaky voice, taking over for me as she put Lauren's head into her lap.

"Where in the heck did the snakes come from?" I shrieked, as my frustration intensified.

The front door creaked open wider, and Kosmo Wilder sauntered slowly around Justin and stood next to me on the porch. Justin lunged back into the manor.

"I've been here a few days and ain't never seen a snake. That girl all right?" Kosmo asked calmly.

I turned to face Kosmo and was shocked that he was much shorter than I was. His awkwardly frail physique made him appear even shorter.

"Well, she's in pain and needs medical attention, but other than that, she'll be fine," Willow snapped, rolling her eyes in disgust at Kosmo.

"Can I ask you something, Mr. Wilder," I said, gazing downward into his sunken hazel eyes.

"This might be off topic given the happenings of tonight, but when we were here yesterday, we didn't see you. Where were you?"

Kosmo's eyes darted to the top left corner inside his eyelids. He stared blankly in this direction for an uncomfortable period before he responded.

"I was here. I was in the third bedroom on the right down that main hallway. I didn't hear you knock," Kosmo responded, openly nervous as he brushed his tangled, grayed hair away from his face.

"I never said I knocked," I retorted sharply, slanting my head to the side as I waited anxiously for his reply.

"Uh, sorry," he stumbled, avoiding further eye contact with me as he went on, "I figured you might have had to knock since my door was locked, and Ms. Foster said you visited the house earlier that day. My apologies for not letting you in."

He took two steps back from me and gazed out into the courtyard toward the black vans.

"You were there the night of the murder, correct?" I pressed diligently.

"Yea. I ended up here that night. My car broke down right outside them gates. I've lost my job, my family, and my home. That car was all I had left. If you're tryin' to pin me as a suspect, lady. I s'pose I'm offended."

"No, of course not. I'm just trying to get all of the facts straight as to who was here and what was where, you know, the entire picture of what happened."

"Fair enough," Kosmo responded, still facing the courtyard.

Lauren let out a laborious moan as the sirens sounded in the distance. A wave of soothing relief made its way through my body, as I knew my friend was soon to be in able hands. I dashed over for a final check over Lauren before the paramedics arrived.

"Lauren, you're going to be all right. Rattlesnake bites are hardly fatal if you get treatment in time. And you'll be treated very soon," I assured, tapping her shoulder to comfort her.

"She's right, Lauren," Willow assured as she rubbed Lauren's shoulders.

The ambulance pulled up in the circle drive, and two paramedics rushed over to Lauren. After taking her vital signs and hooking her up to an IV, the brazen paramedic added, "She's in for a night of screamin' and hollerin' 'cause the last poor chap that I picked up with a rattlesnake bite didn't get over the pain for about three days. He just kept carryin' on and on."

"I think that story should have been kept to yourself!" I shouted, looking at the paramedic with a caustic expression. "Lauren will be fine. I can tell her pain is already subsiding. She isn't thrashing about anymore."

Lauren gazed at me with hazy eyes and muttered, "Because I'm too tired to thrash."

"Sorry, Lauren. I'm so sorry you have to go through this. We love you," I said softly, dropping my head in remorse. I hated nothing more than my friend to have to go through pain.

The brazen paramedic lifted Lauren into the back of the ambulance and situated the IV bag beside her on the rack.

Lauren, wearing a mask of unadulterated torment, waved a solemn goodbye to us before the paramedic slammed the door shut. As if cued by movie producers, the ambulance pulled out of the circular drive, and a silver SAAB pulled into its place. Madison gave me a peculiar look as I eased toward the car. The driver's side door creaked opened slowly, and a plump, undersized man scooted out of the driver's seat clumsily. The moonlight reflected on the top of his scalp, encircled by his thinning gray hair. I approached him as he tossed the butt of a lit cigar on the driveway.

"Hi, my name is Fiona Frost. And you are?"

The middle-aged man surveyed the cars in the circle drive. He turned to analyze me for a moment before he decided to respond. I remembered there were two unknown sets of tire treads in the report that Addie Coleman had given me when I went to the crime lab. I noted the make and model of the car into my notepad on my phone. I'd get this information to Detective Chase later.

"I am Nic Dalton. I am the attorney for the Foster family. I am here to see Ms. Foster."

"Hello, Mr. Dalton, but there are poisonous snakes in the house right now. You should stay out here until we've been cleared to re-enter. One of our friends was bit and had to be taken to the hospital. That's why the ambulance was here."

Mr. Dalton seemed utterly calm and his accompanying grimace was limp. I found it odd that upon seeing an ambulance leaving his client's house and hearing bizarre news such as the house had been evacuated for snakes, he didn't have the slightest reaction or concern.

"Who exactly are you, young lady? I've never seen you before, and you look rather young."

"I am in training with the Godley Grove Crime Laboratory. I not only shadow the lab during investigations, but I also follow up with any ancillary protocols such as this one, with the Ohio Paranormal Investigation Team. I'm a high school student. A senior."

Mr. Dalton's grimace wavered into a smile that invaded his pudgy cheeks as his nostrils flared.

"The crime lab is sending high school students to investigate this supposed *murder*? With a ghost hunting team?"

"Supposed murder?" I repeated crossly, my brows furrowed.

"Yes, I didn't stutter. I think the old man kicked the bucket of natural causes. He had a bad blood pumper. This is a sham by the insurance company. They don't want to pay Ms. Foster the money she rightfully is owed," Nic Dalton scoffed as he looked back to the black vans in the driveway, taking a moment to read the small lettering on the side of the van. "Why are paranormal investigators here, anyway? Did Ms. Foster approve them being here?"

"Yes, sir. She did. I think she might be a little upset at them right now for some reason. I don't know why."

"And it wouldn't be your business to know why, either. I have no time to wait on rattlesnake wranglers. I'm going in to see my client. You can't stop me, child," Nic shouted as he waddled toward the front door and swung it open.

My eyes burned with indignation at the word *child*. Immediately as Nic Dalton opened the front door, Justin Long was there, holding a mop bucket with a platter over it, fastened with duct tape.

"Got the snakes!" Justin shouted, moving out of Nic Dalton's way as he barged into the foyer.

Justin cocked his head at me, shrugging shoulders of curiosity, as he sauntered out onto the porch. He obviously didn't know who Nic Dalton was either. Justin put the bucket down on the circle drive and checked the duct tape. I could hear the snake rattles and random hissing from within the bucket that sent chills down my limbs. The group stood around me, and I outlined the details of the conversation between Nic Dalton and me.

"His name is Nic Dalton. He is Ms. Foster's attorney," I spouted as something caught my eye on the front porch.

It was a red envelope, lying on the ground. It wasn't there before as I had just sat down there with Lauren's head in my lap. This envelope looked just like the one I found in my locker and had dropped off at the lab with Addie Coleman. In the same childlike lettering as the one before, it read *Fiona* on the front.

"Hold on!" I shouted, dashing to my car to retrieve my forensic kit.

I decided to remove the bandages from my palms and noticed I had healed quite nicely. I only had a bit of residual redness, and the stinging was at a minimum. I carefully pulled on a pair of gloves and cautiously picked up the envelope from the ground of the front porch. It was the same type of red envelope that was placed inside of my charred locker. They would definitely be able to make a match to the envelope and link them if they came from the same source. I surveyed the club members' expressions.

My heart pounded inside of my chest like a lunatic as I carefully slipped open the flap to find another folded piece of notebook paper. I gritted my teeth and fought to steady my hands as they trembled. I withdrew the notebook paper from the envelope and unfolded it. I wasn't surprised to see that the perpetrator had used the same type of cutout newspaper lettering as before. Everybody froze as they watched intently. I winced, pulling my eyebrows together as I focused on the note. This time, the cutout message wasn't words. It didn't make sense. It was five lines of random numbers.

*1-7-3-9-5-22-7-5-9*
*2-21-3-16-5-25-7-15-11-21-13-18-17*
*4-17-9-21-16-5-25-19-36-20-49*
*2-15-4-18-6*
*10-2-9-25-8-5-7-8-6-1-5-12-4-5-3-25-2*

"Fiona, what's it say?" Madison Christie eagerly inquired, peering around my shoulder at the note.

"Numbers. It is a series of numbers."

I examined the numbers furiously, trying to make something pop out in my mind—a code or a pattern. My mind drew blank, and I stared at random numbers. Meaningless, frustrating numbers. I needed Lauren. She was the one who lived for puzzles and codes such as these.

She was brilliant when it came to math and number puzzles. She would have made short work of it in no time.

"Well, you have to get it to the lab immediately. They can dust for fingerprints. They can analyze the handwriting on the front and possibly make a match for the envelope or paper to the store it was bought from. Time is our enemy, let's go," Madison ordered firmly.

"Let me call Detective Chase. Maddie, please grab an evidence bag for me out of my kit over there on the drive," I snapped out of my daze.

"Yes, of course," Madison said and yanked a brown paper evidence bag from my forensic kit. She fumbled inside the case, eventually pulling out a permanent marker.

Figuring I could start working on the code, I snapped a picture of the note with my cell phone camera before I placed it carefully into the evidence bag with the envelope. After completing the form on the front of the evidence bag, I tore off my right glove first, and the night air convected the moisture from my exposed palm, leaving a faint stinging sensation behind. The adrenaline routing through my veins made me forget the pain, and I pulled off the other glove and thumbed Detective Chase's number. I tapped my foot chaotically while listening to the ring tones and raised my shoulders in excitement as I heard him answer.

"Detective Chase!" I shrieked, trying my best to remain calm enough to communicate effectively.

*"Fiona. I am so sorry. I have some bad news,"* Detective Chase's voice was somber.

I cautiously responded, hurling the new envelope news to the back of my thought line. "What is it?"

*"I have checked everywhere, and the evidence bag that you brought in earlier to Addie Coleman is missing. She said that she checked it in and sent it to the Silver Springs lab with the courier. I checked with Silver Springs, and they never received it. I have spoken with the courier, it is not in the vehicle, and he doesn't recall ever seeing it. I gave Addie an official warning for not checking it into our computer system immediately. She said she was going to do it when she got the chance, but she swears she handed the evidence over to the driver along with some other evidence from a different case. The other evidence she sent did make it to the Silver Springs lab."*

I took a deep breath and stared at the ground for a long moment. I shook my head slowly.

"Well, that is a nightmare. I suppose it might be a moot point since I just got another envelope with another letter. Here at the Foster Manor."

*"You did? What does it say?"*

"Donno. It is all numbers. I really need Lauren to solve this one, but she was bitten by a rattlesnake tonight, went to the hospital."

*"Fiona, you are good with numbers too. You can solve it, I have confidence in you. However, you need to get the evidence to the lab so we can send it to the document analyst at Silver Springs. They'll dust for prints; analyze the handwriting, paper sources, all that stuff."*

"The only writing is on the front of the envelope. Hand written, and it says *Fiona*, just like the last one. You can tell it doesn't look like anybody's handwriting. It's unnatural. On the notebook paper inside of the envelope, there were glued newspaper cutouts as with the previous letter from my locker."

*"They can definitely analyze pen pressure on the handwriting as well as the handwriting itself, there's a lot that you can't hide, even when you are trying to. Come up to the lab to check it in. How is the paranormal investigation going? Wait!"* Detective Chase shrieked. *"Did you say that Lauren was bitten by a snake? Were you all tooling around on the grounds of the estate at dark?"*

"Out of nowhere, two rattlesnakes appeared in the main living area where the Ohio team's equipment was set up."

*"What? Are you serious? Inside the manor?"*

"Dead serious. Obviously, somebody put them there. Rattlesnakes just don't appear in a living room. And definitely not two of them, they don't travel in packs."

*"Whoa. I'm so sorry that I sent you guys out there. I feel responsible! Are they still in there? Did you guys leave?"*

"We are all still here. Justin and Lance from the Ohio team captured them; the snakes are in a bucket in the driveway. Nevertheless, how could you have known that we'd have to deal with that? It's not your fault. As far as how the investigation is going, I'm not sure. They thought they had found something earlier with noises on the second floor, but it was just that homeless man, Kosmo Wilder, trying to stay out of our way. There was also a cold spot in the closet, but most closets are nothing but big cold spots due to not having vents. No surprise there."

*"I shouldn't have sent you guys there. Why don't you pack up your group and get out of there, drop off the evidence at the lab, go home and get whatever sleep you can."*

"We're fine, Detective Chase. I will send Wolfe to the lab to drop off the evidence. I'll sign it over to him on the bag, just as I am supposed to do. I will ask him to take Lauren's car since he only lives a street over. Look for him in about fifteen minutes or so."

Detective Chase let out a sigh and continued, *"Okay. I suppose you are safe with Justin and Lance. Take care of yourself, and I'll see you soon. Call me if you need anything."*

I reported the make and model of Nic Dalton's car to Detective Chase before hanging up the call.

"Wolfe, would you mind taking the evidence to the crime lab?"

"Sure, Fiona. I didn't bring my skateboard, though, and it's long to walk. Your car?"

I surveyed the cars in the driveway and pointed to Lauren's Acura.

"Fiona, Wolfe should take Lauren's car to the station and then to her house. I can ride back with you and Maddie. He lives right by Lauren so he can drop her car off at her house and then walk home a block to his house," Willow said.

"Exactly what I was thinking, Willow," I added.

"Sounds like a plan," Wolfe held out his hand to catch the keys as Willow hurled them his way.

"Let's get back to it!" Justin shouted, opening the manor door.

"Fiona, be careful," Wolfe said as he gave me a secret grin and inclined his head toward me, arching a perfect eyebrow. He awkwardly froze and waited for me to respond, his steel eyes flickering from my eyes to my lips.

He was so tall and massive through the shoulders. His size reminded me of a professional football player, and it overwhelmed me.

I glanced over my shoulder, and everybody had followed Justin back inside of the manor. Wolfe and I were alone in the driveway. My heart entered a flurry, and I took a sharp intake of air. I had to remain the leader of this group. I couldn't let my emotions control my actions. My thoughts bounced from working in the lab with him to me climbing into a limo with him to go to our senior prom and spending hours talking on the phone about nothing.

Which made more sense? Was I ridiculous to think this way? Was I allowing my emotions to alter reason? I hadn't had a boyfriend other than a silly romance in fourth grade that lasted two days. I had no idea what Wolfe was truly thinking. Was he having the same impulse for me? All he said was to *be careful*. I would tell any of my friends the same without it meaning I was romantically interested. I'd be a fool if I acted on this urge, and it would ruin the harmony of our group if I even so much as misread his intentions. It could make it awkward between us forever.

Wolfe took a step toward me, gauging my expression. Nevertheless, he was flawless, so charming and treated every girl as if she were a princess. At an instant, my subconscious chose to remain the authority. It was the right thing to do and the safest course of action.

"We will, Wolfe. Thank you," I stumbled as I took two steps back from him, breaking the eye contact and pointing to the evidence bag. "You'll need to fill out the chain of evidence on the front of the evidence bag. The evidence is now officially transferred from me to you. The more links in the chain, the worse it is, so get this to the crime lab as soon as possible."

I looked up. His grin altered into an expression of uncertainty and settled into a pokerfaced straight line. His demeanor became solemn and mine followed suit. He pulled his striped beanie down, swishing his hair around the rim. I instantly fought the regret that overcame me. I realized I had passed the perfect opportunity to cross the forbidden line. Would he give up that easily? I needed him to. Some things were meant to be.

"Got it. Going straight there. Bye, Fiona," Wolfe said as he jogged to the car and slowly climbed into the driver's seat.

# 9 PENDULUM

With my shoulders slumped, and feeling as bad as I would if my dog had run away, I forged back into the manor. With Wolfe on the way to the lab to drop off the note evidence, the rest of us gathered in the main living area of the Foster Manor to resume the paranormal investigation. It took a few minutes to put the equipment back in order since we had wrecked the foldable tables to escape the snakes on the floor. Lance and Justin were in high spirits as if the snake disturbance boosted their energy levels. Mia remained quiet, monitoring the video surveillance like a robot. Willow, Madison and I scuttled around, trying to be of help to the Ohio team in any way that we could. Kosmo Wilder took his shiftless position on one of the golden-framed, white silk couches. I just wanted to void my mind of Wolfe so I did anything I could to stay busy such as engaging in idle conversation.

"Did any of you see Nic Dalton leave? I don't see his car here anymore," I said, gazing out the window onto the circle drive.

Looking around the room, I saw everybody shaking their head *no*.

"Lance, why was Glenda Foster so upset with you guys earlier? I thought the Fosters wanted this place to be certified as a haunted house. Wouldn't she welcome you guys here if she thought this house was truly haunted?" I whispered softly as I watched the green-lit displays on the screens in front of Lance.

Lance raised his ginger eyebrows, crinkling his forehead as he nodded eagerly.

"Yes, she does want it certified. Justin opened his big mouth and told her that we were also the number one refute team in the world and if this is a hoax, we'd sniff it out in no time. She didn't like that one bit."

"I bet not!"

"We bust hoaxes and people take our word for it, end of story."

"I know, that's why I agreed to be here with you guys. I subscribe to the *Skeptical Inquirer*. The scientists that publish in that journal cite your research projects quite often," I hesitated to ask the next question, but I had to know the answer, "Do you *believe* that you've actually found paranormal activity before or do you just give up on trying to disprove some cases?"

Lance smiled, exposing his jagged teeth. Once again, he nodded eagerly. He knew my stance on the paranormal, and I could tell that he agreed with my line of thinking.

"We simply collect data, Fiona. If we can explain the data, it is refuted. If we can't explain the data, that is what we report, and it is open to the scientific community to discuss, analyze and even counter our investigation. We are all scientists too. Justin and I have master's degrees in physics, and Mia has a doctorate in biomechanical engineering."

I sighed silently. A glowing happiness radiated through my cells as I smiled, realizing that Justin and Lance weren't radical swindlers claiming the intangible, but rather they were legitimate scientists collecting data. It suddenly made more sense to me why Detective Chase was backing their role in the investigation of the case.

"Well, that makes sense. I am sorry I talked so much smack about your team. I just thought you were a bunch of crazy ghost busters taking people for their money."

"We refute about 90% of the houses we investigate. Glenda Foster was furious when Mia added that statistic into the conversation. I think that is when she turned sour on us, nearly kicking us out."

"Really? Well, it seems as though Ms. Foster doesn't want you guys to report that there's no paranormal activity here," I paused to soak in the concept, "That's interesting."

The green lights on Lance's main monitor screen jumped wildly. He grabbed a meter and set off for the adjacent room.

"Excuse me, Fiona," he whispered loudly.

I followed silently and watched as he took measurements from corner to corner, ceiling to floor. Justin popped into the scene with a different style of monitor and engaged in his routine. This routine continued for most of the night, and I eventually passed out on a couch next to a table of monitors.

Hearing mumbling of voices in the distance of my consciousness, I opened my eyes, and the sunlight streamed through my pupils, searing my retina. Lance and Justin were busily packing their equipment. They appeared haggard and mentioned that they had collected enough data to where they were satisfied there was no paranormal activity in the house. Knowing Glenda Foster would be furious with their findings; Justin mentioned that he wanted to leave the manor before she confronted them. Kosmo Kramer was asleep on the couch in the same upright position as I had seen in him prior. I supposed he had nothing better to do with his time. I gasped as I heard Ms. Foster's high heels clinking on the marbled floor of the hallway.

"Crap!" Justin shrieked as he slipped the monitor into the padded case.

Justin froze in his tracks; shoulders flaccid in defeat as he moved slowly to the foyer of the manor to greet her. She stood before him, donning a new shimmering red satin robe, adorned with sequins. Her crimson hair was fastened into a bright red bun on the top of her head, roots still white as snow.

"Well?" Glenda Foster shrieked with one bony hand on her hip.

"Ms. Foster. We collected data until sun up, and we did not find any evidence of paranormal activity in your home.

You should feel safe and secure," Justin reluctantly reported.

I cowered as Ms. Foster let out a high-pitched scream that reverberated into the walls. Madison and Willow crouched and covered their ears, their eyes looking to me for assurance that we should not flee the scene. I nodded ever so slightly and waved my hand as to gesture them to remain in their positions. Ms. Foster was harmless for the most part, and we would be safest staying with Justin and Lance.

"I knew your rickety team was not credible. If you were *real* investigators, you would know that this house has ghosts! I live here. I see them! Mr. Foster knew there were here. Everybody that has ever lived here knows there are ghosts here, you fools. You can't come into my home for one night and say that the century-old history of ghosts is false! I demand that you stay another night or send a more reputable team! I DEMAND IT!"

Glenda's frail frame shook vehemently as she screeched every word, her pale face burned red, matching her bun and satin robe. Willow dashed for the door and rushed out into the courtyard. I shot a look of alarm to Madison, urging her to stay with me in the living area so we could hear the conversation between Ms. Foster and Justin. Ms. Foster, after all, was a still a suspect in the case we were investigating, and this was evidence unraveling before us.

With the sound of Ms. Foster's shrieking, Kosmo Kramer awoke from the couch and treaded softly into his room down the hallway. Madison and I exchanged grins as we found it funny that he was avoiding Ms. Foster during her tirade. I conferred a smirk to Madison who returned with a silent giggle.

Lance stepped in front of Justin and calmly responded, "Ms. Foster, my team has the most experience of anybody in the world with paranormal investigations. We are actually respected in the scientific community, unlike those television show teams that do it for the production value. We don't need to be here another night. If there were paranormal activity in this home, it would have manifested last night while we were here. We would have detected it with our top of the line equipment."

"Lies! Deceit! THIS IS A SHAM!" Glenda Foster screamed as she stormed down the hallway, heels clinking with fury against the marbled floor. Within seconds, the master bedroom door slammed shut, vibrating the walls in the foyer.

A dainty noise manifested above me. I looked up and saw hundreds of Swarovski crystals moving above my head. The foyer boasted a nine-tiered crystal chandelier, gracefully suspended in the middle of the foyer from the second floor ceiling. The dazzling crystals swayed slowly, clinking together ever so gently as the chandelier changed direction. No way would the slamming of a door down the hallway cause a chandelier of this size to move, much less - swing like a pendulum.

"Look, watch out!" Lance shrieked, yanking Justin by the arm and pointing up to the chandelier.

Lance dragged a bag of equipment out of the way and motioned for everybody to stand back, away from the chandelier's circumference."

"One of those crystal pieces can dislodge and give you a good whack on the head. Be careful to not stand under that," Justin said, spiking up his white hair through his visor.

I stood in awe as the chandelier picked up momentum. The gentle clinks turned into controlled crashes as the crystals collided. We all froze, brows furrowed in confusion, as we looked up at this lively chandelier. The base of the chandelier squeaked ferociously as it pulled away from the sheetrock of the ceiling. Fragments of sheetrock plunged to the marbled floor, each shadowed by a vapor trail of dust.

"What the heck?" Justin yelled, stepping back a few feet as he examined the view.

The chandelier continued to gain speed, as the crystals clanked together like angry wind chimes. The swinging pattern transformed from a bi-directional sway to a full circular action. Larger pieces of sheetrock took a nosedive to the floor. Simultaneously, we all stepped back to avoid the chandelier's span.

"That can't be happening from Ms. Foster slamming her door. Look, it's getting faster!" Mia exclaimed.

"Yea, I have no idea," Justin replied with angst, grabbing one of his meters from a table in the living area.

The last cable holding the chandelier snapped, and it broke free from the ceiling. As a graceful jellyfish, it descended toward the ground, breaking the two seconds of nail-biting silence with an enormous collision. The crash thundered within the manor, violently distressing the structure of the building. I felt the floor beneath my feet quiver as if there was an earthquake. Pictures rumbled against the walls before unhinging and smashing onto the floor, tiny glass shards scattering about in disarray. The debris of dust, crystal fragments, and sheetrock coated the room, and I covered my mouth with my shirt to keep from inhaling the particles in the air. Through the haze, I could see the chandelier, demolished into pieces. Willow swung open the front door and released a scream of horror.

"Doc, stay outside, we'll be there in a minute," I cautioned, waving the dust away from my face.

"C'mon!" Justin screamed, motioning for his team to follow him up the winding staircase.

I figured they were going to the source of the accident. Most likely, it would be the attic. Madison and I were also investigators. We were at the scene of a potential crime. We had to go as well.

"Let's go," I motioned for Madison to follow me as I trailed the members of the Ohio team up the staircase.

"This way!" Justin commanded, pointing toward the attic door. "This leads to the attic above the chandelier. Hurry!"

I wondered why they didn't grab their meters. Maybe it was because they didn't want to waste a second of time. Maybe they forgot?

"Fiona, certainly they don't think it's a ghost that did that, right? If so, are they going to fight in *hand to orb* combat?" Madison gasped, snickering as she climbed the stairs.

We arrived hastily to the attic door as Justin turned the knob.

"I guess we all are!" I shrieked.

Justin blasted through the attic and lunged to the hole where the chandelier base had broken free. He inspected a pair of wire cutters on the plank next to the hole. A window slammed, echoing throughout the open space. Lance gestured toward the only source of sunlight in the attic and Justin nodded, following his lead. Mia arrived on the scene, inspecting the hole for additional clues.

Justin and Lance made their way across the boards of the attic, being careful to not step in between and fall through the ceiling. Madison and I carefully followed behind, tracing their steps.

"Here it is! They went out this way," Justin shouted, making his way to the window.

Justin pushed the window open and poked his head out onto the roof. Footsteps sounded from the rooftop. Justin and Lance both lunged out onto the roof and took off in opposing directions, chasing the stealthy owner of the footsteps. Madison and I joined them in the search, looking over the edge to see if the perpetrator was escaping across the grounds. Nothing. We saw nobody and the footsteps had ended. After thirty minutes of searching the rooftop, we didn't find a soul.

"Well, we know it wasn't a ghost, at least," Lance huffed, out of breath from the chase.

"You can say that. Now, we need to find who that was so we can assign some attempted murder charges on them," Justin panted, climbing through the window and placing a careful foot on an attic board.

"I'll say!" I added, thinking of what would have happened if one of us had been under that chandelier. "Although, I'm not sure what was more dangerous. The chandelier or the race to catch them."

"No doubt," Maddie chimed.

Mia's investigation of the scene of the crime in the attic was also futile. The wire cutters were the only piece of evidence that we uncovered.

"Well, maybe there will be some prints on the handle of the cutters?" Madison inquired.

"Probably not, they most likely wore gloves, but we can take them anyway," I said.

As we returned to the living area to finish packing the equipment, I noticed Kosmo Wilder was once again on the white silk couch. I was certain that he escaped the living area and went to his room when Ms. Foster started screaming, but like Mia Tipper, Kosmo had the knack for blending into the environment easily. I couldn't remember where he was the moment the chandelier fell from the ceiling. Willow had eased into the foyer and was inspecting the scene; the dust had settled and created a whitish film on every surface within its reach.

"Hey, guys," I called for Madison and Willow to follow me away from the rubble pile. "Was Kosmo there the whole time?" I whispered softly, my back facing Kosmo.

Madison and Willow nonchalantly peered over at Kosmo Wilder's position in the living area. Madison's eyes darted to the corner of her eyelids as if to retrieve a stored memory before she responded quietly, "I think so. I mean, I remember him there earlier when Ms. Foster first came down to speak with Justin and Lance, but then after that, I'm fuzzy."

Willow pouted her lips and shrugged a shoulder.

"I left before the crash, but I thought he was on that couch all night. He never moves! But then again, he creeps me out so I'm not trying to remember seeing him," Willow giggled silently.

"I remember him going to his room when Ms. Foster started screaming at the guys," I added.

"Oh yea, that was hysterical," Madison responded with a grin.

"I just can't remember when he came back into the living room," I added in a dreary tone.

My phone sounded in my front pocket, and I scrambled to retrieve it. I accidentally swiped my palm inside of my pocket, reminding me of my injuries. It was Detective Chase. I slid my finger across the screen to answer the call, my palm throbbing delicately.

"Hi Detective Chase! There's been more drama here at Foster Manor! Did the evidence make it to the lab?"

*"Yes, we received it from Wolfe last night. Sending it immediately to Silver Springs as soon as the courier gets here for the morning pick up."*

"Awesome news!"

*"I wanted to share something else with you. First, I checked in with Lauren at the hospital, and her prognosis is 100%. She's in pain, and they are treating her for that so she'll be out of it for at least 24 more hours. Unfortunately, I know she's your numbers girl, but you'll have to work on the code, Fiona."*

I sighed arduously. This was horrible news. I despised coded messages. Hated to play scramble puzzles, number riddles, and word games as well. I was more into hard evidence like DNA, fibers and blood splatter analysis. Lauren was the one with the talent for codes.

"All right, I'll put my math hat on, no problem. I'm going straight to the hospital to check on Lauren as soon as I leave here."

*"No need. She is knocked out and will never know you are there. Spend your time wisely, Fiona. Send her some flowers or something."*

"Will do, Cap'n," I laughed anxiously, still feeling remnants of stress.

Madison and Willow anxiously scrutinized my every word, trying to decipher the other end of the conversation.

*"I heard something else disturbing. The Paranormal Science Program at Hartford University is in jeopardy. I'm not sure why, but the newspaper has a blurb in it about the program potentially being shut down. I think I'm going to speak to Duncan Doyle later today to see what is going on. He'll probably be the most honest about it. I have his contact information in the murder case file. The Chair of the Department at Hartford probably will give me canned politically correct answers, and I need the truth."*

My façade morphed into perplexity, and my restless audience grew concerned.

"Wow! That is shocking. I thought a donor gave a huge donation to start that program not too long ago. What have they done so horrible to already be shut down?"

*"Maybe it was because they didn't consider Foster Manor to be haunted? You know who the donor that started the program was, right?"*

I stared down the hallway of the manor for a prolonged moment, scowling at the bedroom door of Glenda Foster, my face hard and bitter. I was surprised that she didn't even come out of the master bedroom suite to see what the commotion was in the foyer. Willow and Madison followed my eyes to see what I was glaring at, and then Madison mouthed the words: *what is wrong?* I held up an index finger and mouthed back at her panic-stricken face: *hold on.*

"No way. It was the Fosters?"

*"You are correct."*

# 10 GONE

Viewing the picture I had taken with my phone, I played with the code for most of the night and the entire next morning at school. I copied it countless times, nearly filling up an entire notepad. I felt awful for not paying attention to my teachers for I loved to learn and felt compelled to respect those in authority. Ignoring studies was my pet peeve, but I also felt compelled to decipher the code. I was very worried that the message could have been time-sensitive. What if the perpetrator knew details of my group and assumed Lauren would be there to decipher the code? As my frustration grew, I searched for Madison once the bell released my class. I soon found her in the hallway.

"Maddie. I'm going nuts! I can't figure out this code, it's too complex!" I shrieked, looking into Madison's brown eyes to boost my self-confidence, my hands clenched into fists of frustration.

Comprehension flickered in Madison's face as she spoke. "Have you tried the alphabet code? You know A equals 1, B equals 2, all that?"

"Of course, and it would make for very long words, and I tried an unscrambler, and it comes up with nonsense. We need Lauren!"

I drew in a deep breath while Madison seemed to gauge my emotional status.

"I know, Fiona. I heard she is still knocked out. Willow went to the hospital to see her before school today and didn't even get to see her. Lauren got a secondary infection from the bite, and it spread to her body. Supposedly, she is on major antibiotics and will have to be in the hospital a little longer."

I grunted. We had our differences, but Lauren was my friend; this was the last thing I wanted to hear.

"Oh no. That is horrid. I'll keep her in my prayers all day, I'm sure she'll be fine, but it will be a hard road ahead of her. I'll see ya at lunch, Maddie."

"I know, I feel for her. See ya!"

I trudged off to Calculus with a foreboding expression. This was the class where I sat next to Wolfe Nero. Even though I had remained *business as usual* with Wolfe the night before, I felt an awkward tension between us. I didn't like it. I had to get things right in my head, Wolfe was far too important to me.

"Hello, Fiona," Wolfe whispered loudly, not one trace of awkwardness on his chiseled face. I knew at that moment that it was going to be all right.

"Hi Wolfe," I struggled to look normal. I told myself to not smile too big or seem awkward. I must have looked like a broken robot as I fought through my expressions. He slanted his head to the side and nearly burst into a fit of laughter.

My face flushed, and I slumped into my chair and grudgingly stared ahead to Mrs. Garcia as she commenced class. Figuring I needed a break from the code, I paid attention to Mrs. Garcia's lecture for the first ten minutes, trying to forget the ever so distracting Wolfe Nero across the aisle. I found myself hoping she would give me the slightest hint in the right direction of how to solve the code. Nothing. She was lecturing about proofs. I didn't think the code was anything of that nature so I phased my attention back into the abyss, pulling out my notebook and rewriting the code on a fresh page. I studied it until I had it nearly memorized.

My phone vibrated. It was a text, a welcomed interruption. Wolfe glanced at me, watching me commit the classroom conduct crime as I nonchalantly opened the message, being wary of Mrs. Garcia as I drew my line of sight under my desk at the screen.

It was from Detective Chase. It was an update. He said that Ralph Booner, the one who assisted Duncan Doyle in the investigation at the Foster Manor, had a criminal history. The case against Ralph had been dismissed due to a technicality, but he had been accused of none other than *murder*. Detective Chase requested to meet with me at the station after school, and I was more than happy to do so. Beside from my father, Detective Chase was potentially one of the smartest men I knew. I felt bad for disappointing him by not solving the code, but at the same time, I felt assured that he could solve it, nonetheless.

In the hallway, I spotted Madison and dashed over to her.

"Maddie! Detective Chase wants to meet with me after school. He has news about Ralph Booner, you know, one of the suspects in the Foster murder case."

"I'm so going with you, Fiona!" she chipped, tugging on my shoulder.

"Of course. I have a favor to ask of you. Can you please take this darn code and work on it during your afternoon classes? I know you have computer tech next, and you obviously could teach that class better than your teacher!"

I handed her the notebook.

"Sure, tell me what you've ruled out."

I opened the notebook to the latest handwritten code and explained everything I had done with it thus far. I had ruled out most of the known codes. This one was different. It was an enigma to me. I trekked off to class. The next three hours of school seemed like an eternity as I daydreamed about Madison being in her class and solving the code. This fictional vision replayed in my mind.

"How did it go?" I shouted to Maddie across the courtyard.

Madison swung her head low, shaking it from side to side. She shrugged a shoulder as she handed the notebook back to me. She had written on the last white space of notebook paper. She now shared the same intimate frustration of the code.

"That's impossible. We need Lauren!"

My heart sank into the chasm of my abdomen. I was sickened that we were beaten by something that appeared so trivial.

"Darn! I know! Well, she should be out soon enough. Let's go see Detective Chase."

We jumped into the VW and jetted off to the station. We jogged into the lobby, and Ms. Spinks was humming a melodious tune, as she completed a telephone message form. The smell of strawberry cream-soaked dirty socks rang my senses as she looked up over her reading glasses and smiled.

"He knows you're coming so go on back!" she chimed, pushing the button under her desk and clicking the adjacent green door open.

"Thanks, Ms. Spinks!"

"Have a great day!" Madison added.

We darted through the concrete hallways and toward Detective Chase's office. His door was slightly ajar, and we could see was on the phone. I crept in and took the far seat in front of the desk; Madison sat in the adjacent seat. We smiled apologetically for interrupting his phone call. Detective Chase held up an index finger and smiled. He got off the phone within a few seconds.

"Hi Fiona. Hello Madison. That was the Silver Springs document analyst. They have received the red envelope evidence. Hoorah! We should hear something back shortly. In addition, one of the unknown tire treads found at the manor the day after the murder is consistent with the stock tires put on the model of SAAB that you gave me.

We can see if we can make a positive match, if needed, to the specific vehicle belonging to Mr. Nic Dalton. So how are you doing with the code?"

"Horribly," I lamented, passing the notebook to Detective Chase.

I felt like such a loser for not being able to crack it. Humiliated, I didn't feel worthy of being a colleague in any capacity to Detective Chase. This was the first time that I actually felt like a young, inexperienced child in comparison to him.

"I will take a look at it, but no guarantees," Detective Chase chuckled.

The man that sat before me, the one I revered as a God in my eyes had just shown a slight hint of mortality. He said that he might not be able to decipher the code. This was surprising as I thought he would do it in mere seconds, showing me how feeble-minded that I was. I sighed gently, feeling more at ease.

"Good luck, that thing is a monster. It doesn't make a lick of sense," Madison added brightly, tapping on her knee.

Madison obviously wasn't ashamed of her failure to solve it. Maybe I was being too hard on myself. I conjured a way to not to feel so humiliated.

"Great, should make for an evening of entertainment," Detective Chase chuckled and went on, "I went over to the manor this afternoon to speak to Glenda Foster about the report of her blasting the Ohio team and then of her withdrawing her gift to Hartford University to the Paranormal Program."

"Oh really? How did that go? She is a fireball!" I added bluntly, sitting straight in my chair.

"Not good, she wasn't there. However, I did run into Walter Hargrove. The groundskeeper."

"And?" I impatiently added, leaning forward, my elbows on Detective Chase's desk.

"He seems like an upfront character. He told it how it was. He said that Mr. and Ms. Foster despised each other, and it all seemed as though their feud began after their twin boys died in 1980. They were only ten years old, and both boys were found in their beds, dead of unknown causes. They blamed each other, they blamed the house, and they blamed anybody and everybody."

Hearing the news again of their loss made it hard to see Ms. Foster as a villain in my mind. I suddenly felt sorry for the lady.

"Wow. That would be so hard to lose your children. I can only imagine that could tear a family apart," I said softly, my expression was bleak.

"Exactly. Who can blame them for fighting about it?" Madison chimed in, her accompanying grimace was distant.

"Nobody. But when you have a spouse that dislikes their spouse that becomes a murder victim, well, that puts a bright and shiny *number one suspect* sign on their forehead." Detective Chase put an index finger to his forehead and scowled, his eyebrows pulled together at the bridge of his nose.

I nodded in agreement. I added, "It does all make sense. Did you ever hear back from what was being burned in that barrel; since we know that she struck the match?"

"Not yet, that will take a little time. I can't believe they got the match evidence back so quickly," Detective Chase added.

My cell phone rang, and I glanced at the screen before deciding to answer. It was my mother, Emma Frost.

"I am sorry, I need to get this. *My* mother doesn't call unless it is important," I said as I smirked at Maddie.

"Hey! Not fair, Fiona! My mom has trouble translating English, and I need to help her with customers at her restaurant," Maddie laughed.

Detective Chase chuckled and shook his head playfully.

I slid my finger across the screen to answer the phone.

"Hello, Mother!"

"Fiona, come home immediately! Don't speak to anybody on your way. Where are you now?"

"At the police station."

Madison and Detective Chase stared into space as I spoke on the phone.

"Have them watch you enter your car, and then you drive straight home. Anybody with you?"

"Maddie is, what's wrong?"

Detective Chase perked up, wearing curiosity as a mask and straining to hear my mother.

"Just do what I say. The FBI is on their way to the house. Hurry!"

I was stunned. This was a little too much to process. I poked the screen to end the call and then gazed into Detective Chase's eyes, turning slowly to Madison. I was unsure of what I could say, even to the both of them.

"Uh, I have to go home. Madison, are you ready? Detective Chase, can you watch us get into the car?"

"What happened, Fiona?" Detective Chase said bluntly.

"Donno. My mother said to get in the car and drive straight home, and do not talk to anybody," I said begrudgingly.

I had no comprehension why I was unable to tell the head of the crime lab the bit of news that was calling me to come home immediately. I had no idea why my mother didn't even tell *me* what was going on. My father was the district attorney of Godley Grove. Many hard-edged criminals had it out for him. I panicked over the news that the FBI was on their way to my home. I prayed it didn't have anything to do with my father.

"That is crazy, what happened?" Madison shrieked.

"No idea, but she was serious. She said FBI agents are on their way to our house. I wonder if one of dad's past criminal cases has come back to haunt him?"

My head throbbed, and my legs deadened, feeling like limp noodles.

"No way, Fiona. Your dad has more security around him than the President does. He's fine. Maybe he just received a threat, and they are taking it seriously. It's happened before, Fiona," Madison reported candidly.

Detective Chase appeared more than concerned as he rose from his desk, his dark eyes peered intensely into mine as if he were trying to figure out what had happened by my expression.

"True. Well, I better do what my mother says," I sounded, grabbing my keys.

"I will do better than watch you get into your car. I will give you an escort. I'll follow you myself," Detective Chase exclaimed, grabbing his jacket and keys and heading up the rear after us down the concrete hallway.

Detective Chase followed my VW in his beige, unmarked Chevrolet Impala all the way to my home on Nickale Street. As I pulled up to the house, I noticed multiple black Lincoln Town Cars parked in the front. These were not part of the *Frost fleet* as they had government issued license plates, multiple antennae and hidden red and blue lights on the grill. These cars must have belonged to the FBI agents. I bounded out of the car, Madison mimicked me, and we met on the driveway. Detective Chase parked his Impala behind my VW, vigilantly stepped out, and surveyed the cars parked in front.

"Looks like they are already here. Detective Chase, please come in. I'm sure you should hear what is going on, nonetheless."

"Certainly," he responded, following close behind.

We strolled guardedly toward the front door, and the tiny Emma Frost rushed out and hugged my neck. Tears streamed down her face; random wisps of her caramel hair stuck to the tears and framed her cheeks.

"Mom, please tell me what is going on!" I brushed the soaked hair tufts from her face.

Detective Chase and Madison closed in to hear.

"Haley. It's Haley!"

For a moment, I could only stare into my mother's topaz eyes, bewildered yet not surprised.

"She ran away, didn't she? Or, did she do something horrible? Robbery?"

"Fiona! No! This is your cousin you are talking about," Emma wailed, her body trembled as a frown stretched across her reddened face.

My mother was entirely too softhearted. Haley had done nothing but make us all miserable since she moved in with us the previous summer. I wanted to snap my mother out of being duped.

"Right, my fourteen year old cousin that's going on thirty years old that can't ever do the right thing. She gets in trouble at school nearly every day, and now I'm supposed to be surprised by this?" I scoffed, taking a step back from Emma in disgust.

I wasn't angry with my mother; I was only repulsed by her emotional display about my irresponsible, self-loathing cousin. This wasn't shocking. No matter what my cousin did, it wasn't going to be a shocker. Everybody that knew her would have guessed she'd be in jail by the time she was an adult. No matter what Haley had done, I would have expected worse.

"She has been kidnapped!" My mother screamed, revealing the maximum capacity of her lungs.

I took a few seconds to take in a deep breath as I decided how to proceed. I figured she ran away and made it look like a kidnapping. I rolled my eyes at Madison who in turn, shook her head in repugnance. Detective Chase's onyx eyes were peppered with concern. He stared at my mother with an apologetic façade.

"Unlikely. She ran away, don't believe the hype, mom," I turned to face Detective Chase, "I'm not sure if I ever mentioned this before, but my cousin is a juvenile delinquent. My parents rescued her from her downward spiral from my aunt and uncle in New Jersey. She's been nothing but trouble for us since she moved in with us last June. My mother obviously is buying into her game here. She has clearly run away, no surprise to me. Right, Madison?"

Madison pursed her lips and nodded ever so slightly, keeping a wary eye on my mother. She would never want to upset her.

"Fiona, let's hear the details before we make rash assumptions. I'm sure your mother has cause to believe it isn't a ruse," Detective Chase pleaded calmly, running his fingers to smooth the sides of his short brown hair.

My mother squared her shoulders to Detective Chase, drew in a huge breath and continued, "There was a note in her room. It was in an envelope. It said *Emma* on the front," she wailed, trying to gain composure.

This caught my attention. I stepped into my mother's view once again.

"Red envelope?" I whispered, glancing at Detective Chase. "Mom, what did the note look like?"

"Yes, it was a red envelope. There was a folded piece of notebook paper inside. It had strange newspaper letters on it, all glued, and it said, *'you are too late, drop the case or I drop Haley.* Dad feels so bad. He's been working on this case, the suspect is downright horrid, and so he called it in to the FBI as he's supposed to do.'"

Red envelope, notebook paper with glued on letters. This note was definitely linked to my notes in my locker and at the Foster Manor. Whoever left this note at my house was certainly in the same group that was terrorizing me.

"Mom, it's not *Dad's* case. At least I'd say it *probably* isn't his case. It's mine. I've received similar notes. I have one that is in a code, we're still working on it. Maybe it is a clue as to where Haley is?"

Emma's expression melted into fury as she scowled furiously.

"Share this with the agents, Fiona! Immediately!" Emma shouted, pulling me by the hand into the house. "Why have you not told me about this?"

"Mom, we'll talk later. I didn't want to worry you."

The living room was frenzied, FBI agents were scattered about as if they lived there. They were on the phone, typing on laptops, writing in notepads, and even one had his face pressed against the ocular lenses of a microscope. Detective Chase found the agent in charge and introduced us, taking a seat next to me on the couch. Emma stood right behind us.

"Go ahead, Fiona. Tell him about your notes," Detective Chase instructed.

I nodded and turned to the agent that was holding a tape recording device toward me. Another agent had a pen and pad ready to take notes. They all seemed alike, like honeybee workers, but the one in charge was the tallest, probably over six foot three. He had unique, pallid sapphire eyes, and his meticulously coiffed hair was the shiniest black I had ever seen. It looked like a wig that you could buy at a party store.

"I have received two threats. Both in red envelopes. Both on notebook paper with newspaper letters glued onto the paper. The first note was a message, a threat, and the second was in a code of numbers. I can't decipher it," I mumbled as I fumbled with my cell phone to locate the picture of the coded message. I handed the blue-eyed agent my phone.

He looked at the picture for a second and sent the picture via a text message to his office.

The agent continued, "We will have this deciphered in a few minutes. The first note was a threat to you personally?"

I flinched at his statement that they would solve the code in a few minutes. That seemed quite egotistical to me to make such a claim, but if they did decipher that masterpiece, I would have the utmost respect for them.

"Well, it was a threat to drop the case. It said *drop the case or you will suffer.*"

"What *case* are you working on? Aren't you in high school? Was this a school project?"

I explained about my federal grant and association with the police. The agent looked less than impressed and feverishly took notes on every word that left my lips about the program before asking to speak with Detective Chase privately. As I looked on at their conversation from afar, it appeared to me that Detective Chase was on the defense with this agent about something.

"Well, this isn't going well," I grieved.

# 11 AGENCY

The remainder of the night was hectic. The FBI agents were more than thorough as they questioned me, Madison, my mother and father for a good portion of the night. It seemed as if they asked the same questions repeatedly but with a slight twist or variation. Madison thought they were trying to wear us down to catch us telling lies. I couldn't see the reason in that. Why would we lie about details surrounding our family member being kidnapped – even if it were Haley? I couldn't pinpoint an answer to that question and simply thought they were disorganized.

Detective Chase left my home soon after the heated conversation with the head agent, and I hadn't heard from him since he left. I wondered why Detective Chase seemed he was arguing with the agent during their private conversation. It just didn't make any sense why the FBI agent would have a problem with the police in respect to my cousin's kidnapping.

I woke up the next morning and immediately grabbed my phone off my nightstand, hoping to see a message from Detective Chase. To my relief, there was one waiting for me.

*Come to my office at the station after school. Bring the club members with you.*

Great. No direction of what this was about. I was sure to go nuts all day at school as I anticipated what the topic of the meeting was going to be. Being a very detailed man, I realized that he didn't intend to give details in his text. I knew that if I inquired further, he wouldn't have divulged any further information so I didn't even bother. I simply returned his text with a message that I would be there. I contacted the club members to meet me after school in the parking lot so we could drive over the police station together.

After a very maddening day of anticipation at school, the final bell sounded, and I nearly jumped out of my skin as I scrambled to the parking lot to my VW. I waited in anguish for the others to arrive. Soon, we sped off to the police station, Madison and Wolfe rode in the VW with me, and since Wolfe took up most of the back seat, Willow followed close behind on her Moped Scooter. Her camel colored tresses spiked out randomly from her helmet, framing her head as they blew in the wind. Madison turned up the radio on our favorite station, and we enjoyed an amusing ride to the police station as Wolfe sang along with the songs. Wolfe wasn't a good singer at all, and Madison and I couldn't help but laughing silently. As we drew near to the station, I turned down the radio. Lauren popped into my mind.

"Have you heard anything about Lauren? I was going to go to the hospital after school today, but then we got summoned," I pointed out, turning the VW into the police station parking lot.

"I heard that Willow spoke to Lauren's mom this afternoon. She is starting to recover from the infection, and the rattlesnake bite pain is nearly over. She should get out of the hospital soon," Maddie reported confidently.

"Great. My mom sent over a ridiculous amount of balloons and flowers. I need to find time to get to the hospital to see her," I returned softly, guiding the VW into my usual parking spot.

"Why are we going to Chase's office, Fiona?" Wolfe shouted from the back seat, unlatching his seatbelt and letting it recoil against the seat.

"That is the mystery, Wolfe. I don't know. He's never been so enigmatic. It's as if somebody was there when he sent the text to me."

"Maybe there was?" Madison added guardedly, unlatching her seat beat.

I slammed the shifter in park and scrambled out of the car. A Lincoln Town Car immediately caught my eye. I stepped back to check the license plate before noticing that it wasn't the only one of its kind in the parking lot.

"Government plates. The FBI is here. Great," I gasped, my shoulders slumped at the thought of it.

We dredged into the lobby, and Ms. Spinks clanked open the green door with the button under her desk before we could even say hello.

"Go on through, they're waiting in the conference room on the right," Ms. Spinks said, her voice was blank with an ominous tone.

"They?" I remarked as I walked through the green door.

"Conference room? I thought we were meeting in his office?" Madison whispered.

We slowly walked down the concrete hallways and into the conference room. The door was wide open, and Detective Chase was sitting in his position at the head of the table. We entered the room, and he gestured for us to take our seats.

Before I could ask why we were meeting, a familiar federal agent sauntered in the room, shutting the door behind him. He strolled behind us and to the other side of the table, taking a seat next to Detective Chase and staring at each one of us directly in our eyes before he decided to speak. His blue eyes were intriguing to me, nearly non-human in color. His slicked back hair picked up the light in the darkened conference room, the blackness of the strands shined like onyx. His nose was slightly irregular, appearing to have been fractured once or twice before.

"Good afternoon, youngsters. My name is Special Agent Jonas. I am with the Federal Bureau of Investigation. I have met some of you prior to this meeting, and I remember that you," Agent Jonas turned his chiseled features toward me, "Miss Fiona Frost, are quite the little over achiever."

I stared at Agent Jonas squarely in the face, turning both shoulders to face him. I never did well with intimidation tactics, and I certainly was not feeling good about this agent's condescending demeanor. I was definitely one to respect authority as long as I was given the proper respect in return. I chose not to respond and allowed him to proceed with whatever he intended. He looked down at his notepad for a moment before popping his head up to continue with his monologue.

"I've read through all of the paperwork, the grant, the program and your affiliation with the crime lab. It's all great stuff, but it needs to be scaled back a bit. Your program is now hindering the progress of a federal investigation, and you are no longer allowed access to any of the data or other private information about the murder at Foster Manor or any affiliated cases. At this time, you no longer have access to the crime lab under the direction of Detective Chase. Do you understand, Miss Frost?"

My eyes widened uncontrollably as I sensed a huge gaping hole forming through my chest. Sharp, erratic pains radiated from this cavity to every fingertip and toe as my heart altered into an irregular rhythm. I was astonished.

I had never in my life been spoken to in this manner. I didn't feel as though I had the capability to deal with an adult of this stature talking to me as a common child. Adults always praised me and treated me as nearly their equal; never did they suppress me or talk down to me as if I couldn't understand what they were saying.

I gasped for air, pressing on my chest to force my heart back into a normal rhythm. I could feel Madison's deep brown eyes searing the side of my face. I fought to regain my composure. The phantom pain pulses streaked throughout my body as I blinked forcefully to stay focused on Agent Jonas's face. I mentally prepared for my calculated response.

"Sir, with no meaning of disrespect, my program has not hindered any part of this investigation," my voice throbbed with the depth of my rage. "Counter to that, I have assisted the investigation by delivering evidence to the police station immediately upon receipt of said evidence. My lab has also recovered pieces of evidence that the crime lab missed upon their initial investigation," as soon as the words left my lips, I regretted saying them.

I shot an apologetic gaze to Detective Chase who nodded accordingly.

"You did what? You contaminated the crime scene at Foster Manor?" Agent Jonas screeched, pounding a gigantic fist on the conference room table.

Madison and Willow gasped in unison at his display of aggression.

Detective Chase interjected, "it is common practice that once our team clears a crime scene, that we allow Fiona's team to come in and see if they can collect additional evidence as long as the owner of the location agrees. It is outlined as part of our training program, and as you can see, it is very successful."

"You know that is *hell* on our court system, Detective Chase. Only experts would ever be allowed as part of the chain of evidence. This is a defense attorney's dream to have high schoolers in charge of a murder case!"

I stood up. Agent Jonas had it all wrong. Detective Chase waved for me to sit back down. My expression was sullen as I stared in disbelief of what was happening.

"We can't use any data or evidence that Fiona's team collects. It is purely for training purposes. After the case is closed, we simply compare her analysis with our analysis to determine if she is on the right track. This is always done after the case is closed. No harm, no foul," Detective Chase assured, nodding at me.

Agent Jonas stood up and pushed his chair aside. He was massive, about the size of Wolfe Nero but thicker. I pictured him working out in the gym at least twice a day. He towered over Detective Chase as he stood behind him.

"I understand that the initial letter that was recovered from the locker at Godley Grove High School has disappeared. I also understand that Miss Frost was the first one in the chain of evidence and hence, last one in the chain of evidence. Tampering!"

I struggled to catch my breath before I came to Detective Chase's defense.

"Agent Jonas, I delivered the evidence as I received it in an official evidence bag, marked with the appropriate information on the front label of the bag and immediately took it to the Godley Grove Crime Lab evidence collection desk. It wasn't evidence in an official case, by the way. Or so we didn't think it was."

My fists clenched instinctively, reminding me that my palms had not fully healed.

"And I am sure you left it on the desk, walked off, and that's how it disappeared. Young lady, there is protocol.

You might learn this in college. That's why we have college degreed individuals working on murder cases, not high schoolers!"

Agent Jonas stormed over to face me across the conference room table. Madison squeezed my leg under the table as if it was going to help calm me. It served to give me confidence that I had back up in the room.

"No sir. I left the bag with Addie Coleman."

"There is no documentation of that transfer, Miss Frost."

Detective Chase rose his hand in my direction.

"I can explain that, Agent Jonas. I spoke to Ms. Coleman, and she did not deny that Miss Frost dropped off the evidence bag. She explained that she transferred the evidence bag to the courier along with other pieces of evidence for a different case. The driver has no recollection of the bag, and the bag supposedly disappeared on the way over. The break down was between Ms. Coleman and the driver or the driver and the Silver Springs lab. There's no way of pointing an exact finger. I did issue Ms. Coleman a warning about not following proper protocol when checking in evidence to the lab."

"You are the director. Every action that your employees do is a reflection upon you, Detective Chase," Agent Jonas snarled, dropping down into his seat next to Detective Chase.

"I know, I apologize. Ms. Coleman is young. She only graduated from college a year ago and was hired by my lab as her first job. She has always worked under a long time manager who left her position without a warning not long ago, so we are in a state of transition while I do a national search for a new manager of that section. I've got it under control."

"Well, I just realized, Detective Chase. Upon reviewing the results of the document analysis on the coded note evidence, it appears as though your Ms. Coleman's fingerprints were the only prints found on the note. Can you explain this? You allow your techs to handle evidence without gloves, do you?"

Agent Jonas sarcastically tapped on his notepad with his pen as he waited for Detective Chase to answer. I hadn't seen that document analysis report yet, but it had probably just got back from Silver Springs.

"No sir, of course not. I will speak to her about that as well. Obviously, she must have had a reason to handle it – maybe she dropped it or something? In any case, there's no excuse, and I will issue a second warning to Ms. Coleman," Detective Chase rasped, followed by an extensive sigh.

I gazed at Madison in an attempt to read her thoughts. I certainly didn't care for Addie Coleman, but I didn't like seeing the underdog lose the fight, either. I knew that one day; I'd be the new girl, the rookie in the lab. Seeing how it was so easy to make simple mistakes, I hoped to avoid such things.

We listened to Agent Jonas drone on about how he was going to ask that the funding agency, the *International Scientific Foundation*, reconsider my grant outline. This discussion more than set me into an internal rage, but I knew that I couldn't get anywhere today with Agent Jonas. I sat quietly as he continued about how my program was fallible and needed to be revamped completely. He also gave a stern warning to the members of my club not to even think about the murder at Foster Manor again. After about ten minutes, we were all drained, zapped of our life forces. We stumbled to the parking lot to my VW.

"Wow! What's wrong with that dude? Seriously! Did a cat pee in his cheerios?" Wolfe shouted, climbing into the backseat, his knees pushed up against the front seats.

"Obviously! Oh my gosh, he was rough!" Madison shouted.

"Serious psycho alert," Willow added, giggling as she climbed on her Moped Scooter and slipped the helmet over her shagged hair.

I loved venting sessions. I couldn't help but start to giggle.

"So we are off the case. What about your cousin, Fiona?" Madison became animated as she clicked on her seatbelt.

"Detective Chase just texted me, and he said they deciphered the code already. It was a random mathematical code with every other number being odd, or a prime number, a square root, or other pattern. Once they removed the patterned numbers, they decoded it with the simple A equals 1, B equals 2—

"I knew it!" Madison shouted, tapping on the dashboard in a celebratory dance.

"But you didn't know the rest of it, and we'd have never gotten anywhere with removing those numbers from the message," I laughed, smiling at Maddie.

I pulled my door shut and rolled my window down so we could still speak to Willow. Looking at the text from Detective Chase, I got the message straight.

"He says the message was decoded as, *Give up your quest or bye Haley.*"

"Man! If we'd had decoded it sooner!" Wolfe yelped from the backseat.

"No lie!" Willow said abruptly.

"He also said to not worry about anything. I suppose that means we're not off the case," I said with resignation, firing my engine.

Willow paused and rolled her Moped closer to my car to catch the details.

"You think that is what he means by telling us not to worry?" Madison murmured.

"After that meeting, that's all I would worry about, right?"

"Good point, Fiona. Well, see you guys later. I have to get home, I didn't tell my mother I was coming here. I'm going to go check in with Lauren and will tell you how she's doing. See you all tomorrow!" Willow shouted, starting her engine.

"Bye Willow!" We yelled in unison as I rolled up my window. We followed her out of the parking lot.

"Well, if we would have had Lauren, I am positive we would have known in advance of her kidnapping," I added, my voice gruff from my earlier high-energy conversation with Agent Jonas.

"Have you considered that Haley is in on this, Fiona?" Madison reluctantly added.

"You know this," Wolfe scoffed.

"Of course. I just didn't want to say it after how I acted when my mother told me she was missing. I was going to investigate her room for evidence of the envelopes, glue, notebook paper...something...anything."

"Let's do that when we get to your house!" Wolfe exclaimed from the backseat, tapping the back of my seat.

"Done deal. We can't let my mother know what we are doing. She will be angry that we are even thinking that Haley orchestrated this whole thing. She still sees her as an innocent little child. She has no idea!"

"We will be careful, Fiona. We definitely don't want to upset Dr. Frost with everything she is going through. Even though there's a 90% probability that Haley, at a minimum, has simply run away to be with her wild friends. Dr. Frost is still a member of the demon seed's family," Madison noted.

We enjoyed a laugh as I pulled the VW into the front drive. We scampered into my house through the front door. I decided to run interference and allow the others to investigate Haley's room while I distracted my parents. My father was in his office, and my mother was relaxing on the sofa, reading a book with classical music softly playing. Janice was at her weekly dice game with her friends in the neighborhood so I knew she wouldn't be home. I had a bigger chance of my father checking in on me so I decided to go to his office.

"Dad, do you think that Haley's disappearance could have anything to do with a case you are currently working on?" I asked, my voice unbiased.

Lewis Frost looked up from the papers on his desk, cleared his throat, and his strident voice boomed, "No, Fiona. The defendant in my case doesn't have family or connections to any larger organization. It would be unlikely that he could coordinate such a crime. I would say, given what you are going through with the crime lab, it is more likely that it has to do with your involvement in the Gilroy Foster murder case. Murder cases tend to bring out desperate actions from the suspects. People don't want to go to jail for murder. If you're going to be in the forensic lab, you might, on occasion, get a threat. Most of the time, it's just threats, words to scare you into not doing your job. They normally won't act upon it because they'll be the suspect automatically and the FBI will always jump to investigate threats on law enforcement officials."

My head dropped. Luminal entered the room and stood on two legs, putting his paws on my thigh, his stubby tail swished his long black locks back and forth. I cupped his ears, rubbing gently, and leaned down to give him a kiss on his little black nose.

"I'm sorry, Dad."

My father stood up to rub my back. He always knew how to make things right.

"Don't be, Fiona. You didn't know. You are just doing what you know is right, you are training yourself in the prime of your academic life and you will be the world's finest forensic investigator one day. You shall not be blamed for that. You didn't know what would happen to your cousin. We'll get her back. Haley is one strong young woman," my father smiled. He lightly tapped on his desk as he remembered something. "Oh! I spoke to your Uncle Peter, and he said that Haley ran away from home three times last year. I wouldn't rule that option out, either."

"Yea, that was kinda my first thoughts on it."

"Actually, mine as well."

He sat back down and thumbed through the papers in front of him.

"If she was kidnapped, I'm sure they'll *pay us* to take her back," I giggled softly, treading softly toward my room.

I hoped the others were finished with their investigation of Haley's room. I slowly opened my bedroom door, and Madison and Wolfe were waiting for me.

"Well?"

I surveyed their hands. They were empty. Madison shrugged a shoulder; an apologetic expression riddled her face.

"Nothing. Absolutely nothing. But we did find some cigarettes and a ticket stub for a concert that I know your parents would not have allowed her to go to!" Wolfe chimed, raising a flawless eyebrow.

I let out a sigh, "Well, that doesn't surprise me in the least. So no evidence on the envelopes, paper, newspaper or anything else?"

"Not a shred," Madison said dryly.

# 12 DATA

I called another club meeting the following morning to discuss the updates to the Foster Manor case. Agent Jonas had instructed me to remain clear of the case, but Detective Chase had emailed me the updated analysis report from his home email address late last night. I knew that nothing was official until it was in writing and with Detective Chase texting me not to worry about anything, I felt secure in my position. My federal grant and training program were still intact. The grant gave my group the right to analyze forensic evidence as part of our training program. If Agent Jonas found out we were still on the case, it would be his word against Detective Chase with my club as the only witnesses. However, it was unspoken that the club's further involvement would need to be incognito.

Willow, Madison, Wolfe and Carden assembled around the lab benches. I had hoped that Lauren would make it back to school, but Willow reported that it would be a couple of days before she was able to come back. She was home resting, still on antibiotics. Carden took the back row once again, keeping his status as an observer rather than an active member of the club.

"All right, let's get started. I have some rather interesting evidence to discuss. I really wished that Lauren was here because I don't want to make assumptions about anything."

I gazed at their faces, confusion flickering in their expressions. I grabbed my papers and cleared my throat.

"I'm going to start with the victim's cause of death. Mr. Foster died of an overdose of his medication. It is called digitalis. It's a heart medication."

I surveyed the group's faces; their expressions altered into confusion and settled on discontent. A collection of moans sounded in harmony as Willow slid her notepad into her backpack as if the meeting was about to be adjourned.

"Wait! It *was* murder. It wasn't an accident!" I yelped, slamming my palm onto the lab countertop. A singe of pain quickly reminded me that my palms were still raw from the burns.

"How? An elderly man overdosed on his prescription meds. Case closed. He had a heart condition and died of heart medication toxicity. Please let me hear how this is *murder!*" Willow argued, dropping her backpack on the ground in front of her, her emerald eyes glowing fierce.

"There was a tea cup right next to his body. Look," I held up a copy of a crime scene photo that Detective Chase had sent me.

Gilroy Foster was posed awkwardly on the floor; his limbs sprawled about in an unnatural position. It was obvious that he had fallen to his death. The teacup handle was draped across his little finger, a small amount of tea spilled out onto the floor surrounding his hand. A blue vase was shattered on the other side of his corpse; the colorful flowers from the vase were spread out on the floor as if they too had been murdered.

Looking at the picture again, I pondered about what death looked like. I had never seen death before. This was my first murder case, and honestly, I didn't know how I would handle it when I finally saw a dead body. At least my first case, I could see it through a picture and not in person. It was best if I could step my way into it. Mr. Foster appeared to be sleeping, but it was an irregular, awkward position. I noticed the strange marks across his neck, definitely an injury made prior to his death. I found myself feeling a powerful obligation to Mr. Foster to solve the case. A dominant emotion had grown stronger inside of me every passing day and with each new piece of evidence. My sixth sense was tied to him.

I was thankful that my first murder case was a poisoning and not something more graphic such as a brutal stabbing, which might have made me change my mind about being involved in a crime scene investigation. This was the ideal way to ease myself into this life, especially only being seventeen. Other girls my age were making Facebook pages and picking out prom dresses, and I was studying a picture of a dead man, discussing his untimely demise. I smirked at the contradiction, passing the photo to Madison. She initially winced but soon settled in and studied the picture.

"I see it, right by his hand as if he was holding onto it when he collapsed," Madison pointed out, passing the photo to Willow.

"The residue in the tea cup was tested, as well as the small amount of tea that spilled onto the floor. The results show that there was enough digitalis in this tea to kill over twenty men. This was no accident," I reported sternly, surveying the emotional responses from my club members.

"Is this how you normally take the medication? Dissolving it into tea?" Wolfe inquired, his brow furrowed in confusion.

"Absolutely not, and his physician was interviewed as well as Glenda Foster who confirmed that he didn't take his medication this way," I added, viewing my report as I read, "It was a cup of hot tea so the tea was made fresh. It comes down to who made the tea for him that night."

"Well, did he make it? Did they take fingerprints from the cup?" Willow inquired anxiously.

"That is why I wanted Lauren to be here. I hate talking about this evidence without her here to defend herself—

"Defend herself? Fiona, what are you saying? That *Lauren* of all people did it?" Willow's voice was laced with ferocity as she stood up to face me, anger glinting in her sea green eyes.

"All I am saying is the facts. Lauren's fingerprints were on the teacup and so were the victim's. Nobody else's fingerprints were on it."

Wolfe turned toward Willow and added, "Lauren was really diggin' those dudes from Hartford University. Possibly if they had a fight with Ms. Foster, and she obviously threatened pulling the money plug on the new Paranormal Science Program, well—

"Wolfe, stop it now! That is absurd to believe that! Fiona, duh! Lauren told me she was the first one to find him on the floor in the kitchen. She probably moved the teacup. I can't believe you people would even think for a second that Lauren, *our friend*, who is suffering right now, would be a murderer," Willow screeched, snatching her backpack from the floor.

Wearing a caustic mask on her face, she bolted for the laboratory door and stormed out into the hallway. We heard her illogical mantra as she faded down the corridor. I resisted the urge to run after her, knowing that her irrational emotions would wear off, and she would seek reason later in the day. The evidence was black and white. Lauren was the only one to explain what had happened.

I looked back and saw Carden's head was down, and he appeared to be reading the papers in front of him. I knew he wasn't equipped to be part of this drama. I studied the faces of Madison and Wolfe before I continued. I felt a wave of comfort as I observed ration through their eyes.

"One more thing. Wolfe, the fingerprints that Madison and I took from the Foster Manor included the tea canister. There was only one tea canister in the entire manor, and there were only two bags left inside. It was lemon tea, the same type of tea that was in Mr. Foster's teacup."

"Whose fingerprints were on the tea canister, Fiona?" Madison gushed.

Wolfe eagerly searched my poignant eyes.

"Lauren's and Glenda Foster's."

The room drew silent as we searched the crevices of our minds for a reasonable explanation for the evidence. Carden popped his head up at the news that Lauren had made the tea that killed Mr. Foster. Only Lauren and Mr. Foster's prints were on the teacup. After a minute, I released a labored sigh before I resumed.

"But I understood that Mr. Foster always made his own tea. Why would his prints not be on the canister?" Madison inquired.

"Good question. The canister might have been cleaned at some point by the maids or maybe somebody wiped it clean at some point in the past?" I said.

"It would make sense that Glenda Foster's prints would be on it, as she told us that she made some lemonade tea that day we were investigating there, and that she didn't normally do so," Madison added.

"You're right, Maddie. As you know, we can't submit that evidence of the fingerprints on the tea canister since we collected it after the crime scene was cleared, but we can let Detective Chase know about it. Obviously, Lauren had to have done it the night of the murder since that was the first and only time she was there before we collected the prints, but it still cannot be primary evidence."

"Good thing for Lauren, right?" Wolfe said curtly.

I nodded with a sly smile. After all, Lauren was my friend, and I didn't want to believe she was involved in the actual murder, even possibly by accident. There was an explanation for this; we just didn't know what it was.

"Is that all you have, Fiona?" Madison asked, tapping her pen gently on her notepad.

"Can I add something, Fiona?" Carden managed to choke out from the back of the lab.

"Certainly!"

"Doyle, my older brother, told me that he really thinks it's a paranormal murder. There has been a documented case of a paranormal murder in the 1800's at a farmhouse in Tennessee. If someone like Lauren, with no motive or prior history of violence, could be the only viable suspect in a case—

"Enough, Carden. If you want to take over next year as the head of this lab, you will have to get over your beliefs in fictional science. Please, don't follow your brother's footsteps. If you are interested in *real* science, you are in the right place. If you want to be a ghost catcher, please let me know now," I snapped, each word distinct.

"Get 'em, Fiona," Wolfe snickered, smiling, exposing his bright white teeth in contrast with the russet skin of his face. I returned the smile and then looked past to Carden for his response.

"Sorry, Fiona. I didn't mean that I agreed with my brother. I was just stating what he had told me," Carden dropped his head once again and pretended to read the papers in front of him.

"Carden, I don't want you to feel as if you can't contribute to our discussions. I just don't want to include any nonsense in a real investigation. I appreciate your input, and please continue to let us know the facts as you know them. It's noted that your brother thinks a ghost killed Mr. Foster. After we push through every scrap of evidence and can't make sense of it, we'll revisit that issue."

I grabbed my papers once again and scanned down to the next batch of evidence.

"There was a sample of dirt found next to the back door of the manor that doesn't match the dirt in the flower beds surrounding the manor or the soil from the courtyard. We assume there is a possibility that the murderer might have come in and left through that entrance as it was found to be unlocked and ever so slightly ajar the night of the murder. The sample was analyzed and found to be a potted plant soil mixture. A number of our suspects have potted plants so this one is going to take some time to find a match. They can definitely look at the microbes, soil composition and mineral content to find the exact match. Glenda Foster certainly has her share of potted plants."

"Until we hear about a match, I'm not considering that as evidence," Madison debated.

Wolfe nodded. Carden remained discouraged, head facing his tablet.

"Wasn't the burning barrel in the back yard? So if the murderer used that door from the kitchen to the back, isn't it linked to the person that burned something in the barrel?" Wolfe inquired.

"Not necessarily but it would be a possibility. The burning could have been done at any time before or after the murder," Madison responded. I agreed with her.

"Nevertheless, there's more evidence that is even more confusing. The lab processed the carpet fibers found at the scene. The groundskeeper, Walter Hargrove, had mentioned to Detective Chase to consider Nic Dalton, the Foster family attorney, as a suspect. Obviously, Walter had grown suspicious of the man for some reason. Detective Chase sent an officer to speak to him at his office and casually to collect any evidence such as hairs and carpet fibers – anything that the officer could find. Sure enough, they found a match to the office carpet of Nic Dalton in Foster Manor."

"By the victim's body the kitchen?" Madison said airily.

"Even better. By the medicine cabinet in the master bedroom. Where Mr. Foster's digitalis medication was kept!" I exclaimed, my tan eyes brightening.

"So how does Lauren fit into the equation? Are you thinking that Lauren was working with Nic Dalton?" Madison's voice was lifeless, her lips pursed into a straight line.

"Well, that is why I wanted Lauren here. There was no mention of Nic Dalton being at the Foster Manor the night of the crime. But there's another intriguing piece of evidence here."

"Can it get any better?" Madison said with false enthusiasm.

"Or more confusing!" Wolfe pointed out bluntly.

"More confusing. There were also a few animal hairs found in Nic Dalton's office. They were dog hairs. The breed is a Siberian Husky. The officer's notes included descriptions of Siberian Husky dogs posing with Nic in various pictures around his office."

"Please say that the dog hairs were found on the victim's body so we can close this case," Wolfe pleaded, hands clasped together as he shook them back and forth.

The school bell startled me as it echoed throughout the school throughout the overhead public address system. School was to begin in five minutes so we gathered up our belongings.

"Well, I told you that I'd chosen the path of confusion," I held open the lab door as everybody exited into the hallway. "There were matching dog hairs found in Kosmo Wilder's broken down vehicle in front of Foster Manor," I stated flatly, as I shoved the key into the laboratory door.

Wolfe and Madison's mouths dropped open; they were frozen and stared blankly at my face, bewildered.

# 13  CUSTODY

I found it difficult to focus during my morning classes. My mind drifted uncontrollably to the perplexing evidence of the case. Why did Lauren make Mr. Foster tea? How did the enormous amount of his medication get into the teacup? How were the homeless man and the Foster's lawyer related in this puzzle or were they? I reasoned that it was possible that Kosmo tracked the dog hairs from the manor back into his car after his arrival to the manor. I would need to ask Lauren if she recalled him leaving the manor to retrieve something from his car. Why would Nic Dalton be at the Foster's medicine cabinet?

After contemplating the murder, I pondered on my cousin and her involvement in this case. Was she truly kidnapped, and was it my fault for working on the case? I had only a glimmer of doubt that this was a possibility and that she didn't just run away. I knew Haley. She was destined to always do the wrong thing, know the wrong people.   However, how had she known about the red envelopes unless she was involved in it herself?  Maybe the red envelopes had absolutely nothing to do with the murder case at all, and it was a diversion to cause my parents to blame me for her disappearance.  I'd take the latter in a Vegas bet with a shady bookie.

It was finally time for lunch and Madison and I stood in line for the usual cardboard pizza and greasy crinkled fries. We often ventured into conversations about the minimal nutritional value of our choice in lunch plates, but the other options in the line were worse.  I vowed that one day, if I ever became a member of the school board, I would improve the quality and selection of cafeteria food in the Godley Grove School District.

"Maddie, I've been over it in my head a thousand times. There has to be something we are missing here.  It's so disjointed!"

I stared out into the lunchroom, trying to concentrate my way out of confusion.  Josh Coleman, the school bully, caught my attention as he glared hatred straight into my eyes.  Without blinking, he continued his glower in an outward attempt to intimidate me, rocking back and forth on the balls of his feet as he caught a fist with his opposing hand.  This wasn't unusual.  I supposed I was his victim of the day.  It seemed as though he was always choosing a new prey.  I wouldn't allow myself to be frightened by him.

"Madison, look over there, Josh Coleman."

Madison spun around and fixed a casual gaze upon Josh. His upper lip curled back over his teeth as he continued to glare at me.

"What is his deal? Is he looking at you, Fiona?"

"Yes. Have no idea what his problem is," I whispered faintly, refusing to look away and break the stare.

The room went still as Josh, wearing a dark blue hoodie and blue jeans, marched toward me from across the lunchroom; his pitch-black hair exposed his shiny scalp through the shortened bristles. His grin stretched the width of his rounded face, eyes burning into me with an overwhelming intensity. I couldn't fathom what the impending confrontation would entail. My body started to tremble with unrest as he advanced in his path. As he neared our table, I let out a sigh of relief as Principal Dinges intersected his path. Maddie tapped my wrist in respite and sighed softly.

"Mr. Coleman. I need you to come with me, to my office right now." Principal Dinges scoffed, grabbing Josh's elbow. He pulled a highly resistant Josh toward the entrance to the cafeteria.

They seemed like an even match, both being of above average size. Josh countered by jerking his elbow away from Principal Dinges who stopped in his tracks, spinning around to face him.

"You will only be in more trouble if you resist, Mr. Coleman. We're going to my office whether you come quietly or if I have to get security to convince you to do it."

Josh did a quick backward maneuver, twisting around to snarl at me once more before Principal Dinges countered with a stern grab of his arm, followed by a heave through the cafeteria entryway. Principal Dinges was poised with his large nose resting on his walkie-talkie as if he were about to call in for backup.

With the last tug on Josh's arm, I noticed a crumpled piece of notebook paper fall out of Josh's hoodie pocket. I lunged from my seat and rushed over, snatching it from the floor. Josh was attempting an escape with Principal Dinges who called on his walkie-talkie for assistance. Just as I stood up with the note, I saw two security officers round the corner. I smiled, knowing Josh was about to have a bad afternoon.

I carefully opened the paper, straightening it out as I took my seat next to Madison. As it came into view, my hands trembled as a wave of prickly ice traveled down my spine, causing my entire body to shake from inside as if I were flashed with an arctic blast.

"Madison. It's him," My throat was being strangled from the inside, I could barely speak. I dropped the paper to the floor.

Madison quickly scooped up the note from the floor and slid it into her folder in her backpack. In a stupor, I grabbed my phone and fumbled to locate Detective Chase in my contacts. After three rings, he answered the phone.

"Detective Chase," I stumbled. "I have some evidence that you need to consider. A student at my high school named Josh Coleman had a piece of notebook paper in his pocket with a few letters cut out from a newspaper glued to it. The note wasn't finished; it was crumpled as if he was going to throw it away."

*"Josh Coleman. Who is Josh, do you know him?"*

"He is the school bully. A senior. I actually thought of him as a suspect in my locker bomb case. He's the only one crazy enough to do such a thing here."

"*Coleman. That sounds familiar. Hold on a minute, Fiona. I will be back in a moment.*"

"That's fine, Detective Chase," I replied anxiously, straining to see the clock on the wall of the cafeteria.

There was only nine minutes until my next class. I looked over to see Madison texting in a fury. I assumed she was communicating with the club members. Our club was usually good about sharing information about cases in real time, at least for the most part. Madison and I had broken the assumed rule by going to the manor without the rest of the group. We realized it caused hard feelings, and so we had agreed to be open about all evidence as it unfolds.

After nearly eight minutes, Detective Chase returned to the line.

"*Fiona. I have some news. Josh Coleman is the younger brother of Addie Coleman from my lab. They live together, actually. I let Addie go on administrative leave until we can see how deep this involvement really is with this family.*"

"Won't she run, flee the country?" I spurted nervously.

Madison stopped mid-text to lean in to hear Detective Chase's response. I slipped it on speakerphone so she could hear.

"*No, she won't. I didn't give her any reason to believe that she was being suspected for anything other than having an eighteen-year-old school bully as a brother living as in resident in a shared home. I told her it was a formality, and she'd be back at work soon. She is being paid for it so I told her it was a free vacation that she is likely never to get again so she should enjoy herself. She seemed more than thrilled, Fiona."*

"You're brilliant, Detective Chase! Well, I have less than a minute; are there any updates to the case while I have you on the phone?"

*"The only thing is that Kosmo Wilder does not own a Siberian Husky and has no reason to have the animal hairs in his car. After interviewing the witnesses there the night of the murder, they all say that he never left the manor once he arrived. The only thing I can reason is that Nic Dalton broke into Kosmo's car for some reason; maybe thinking it belonged to somebody else. I have no idea, but we're going to talk to Nic Dalton about a few things. I'll keep you posted."*

"Thanks, Detective Chase!" I said eagerly, pushing the call to an end as I strolled out into the hallway. The school bell echoed annoyingly throughout the building.

Madison and I parted ways to our afternoon classes, agreeing to meet in the parking lot after school. I had a new sense of hope with the latest news from Detective Chase. I thought that I might actually be able to pay attention in my classes, and this energized me.

"Hello Mr. Hezzle!" I sang as I entered my English class.

"Why, hello, Fiona! You look exceptionally chipper today. Love it!" Mr. Hezzle sparked, as he pulled out a piece of chalk and set it on the chalkboard ledge.

I was right. My classes were more fruitful for me, as I was finally able to separate my school life from the case. It felt good to be back in learning mode. It made me feel normal again and definitely more sane.

The school hours breezed by, and the final bell buzzed diligently. I darted out to the black VW in the parking lot, and the moment I put the key in the driver's side door lock, I noticed a silver SAAB drive behind me and then exit the parking lot. I couldn't see the driver due to the tinted windows, but I knew I had seen that car before. Nic Dalton had a car like that, but he would have no reason to be at the high school. I climbed into the car and turned up the radio, as I waited for my best friend. After a few minutes, Madison swung the door open and climbed into the passenger seat.

"Fiona. I'm very bothered."

"Me too. I can't believe Josh is the kidnapper. You know, the more that I think about it, I'm not so sure if this *is* a kidnapping. I saw Josh talking to Haley a few weeks ago. I reprimanded Haley and told her to stay clear away from that jerk. He is way too old and too horrible of a person...even for her."

Maddie pursed her lips as she shrugged back her straight blackened locks.

"Fiona, I agree with you. Maybe I'm skewed, but as far as your cousin goes, I was certain it wasn't a kidnapping when I realized it was Josh Coleman that left the notes. She totally is skipping school and hanging out over at his house. I didn't want to say anything but I saw them making out in the hallway last week."

"Maddie! Why didn't you tell me?" I rasped, openly irritated that my best friend kept information from me all this time.

"Fiona, hello! You knew they were hanging out. However, what were you going to do about it? Tell Haley to stop? You see how much good your altercation with her about the jerk went the first time. She won't listen to you! She won't listen to anybody. Nevertheless, the cops will listen. He is eighteen years old, and she is only fourteen – busted! He's going to jail."

"Oh my gosh, maybe that is why he was giving me the evil eye at lunch?" I pondered.

"Hello, duh! Fiona, obviously, if he is the one leaving the notes, he has a bone to pick with you. And the bone's name is Haley!"

In total disgust, I revved up the engine and pulled out of the parking lot.

"Gross. That is so gross, Maddie. Yea, I'm sure Detective Chase has already sent a car over to his house to pick him up, and Haley is probably already home, crying her eyes out for being such a loser and putting everybody through this mess."

"But what is truly bothering me is *Lauren*. Lauren's fingerprints on the teacup and on the tea canister are strong evidence for a murder by poison when there was poison in the tea. Hey, did they ever analyze the actual tea bags?"

"No, remember? There were half of the tea bags in the canister when we dusted for prints."

"Crap! Tell Detective Chase to get over there, and get them. Wow, they should have analyzed the discarded tea bag from that night as well! It probably went out with the trash or something. Remember Ms. Foster asked us if we wanted some tea when we went to the manor to investigate?

She said there was a pitcher of lemon tea in the refrigerator. That should be tested! If she isn't the murderer, she might be in danger if the poison was in the tea bags!"

"Great point, Fiona. I'm texting him now," Madison replied quickly, thumbs in a fury on her phone's screen.

My phone rang from inside my backpack. I pulled over to the shoulder of the road, slammed the car into park and grabbed for it. Madison's expression was glazed with mystification before it amended into comprehension.

"Oh yea, your *anti-phone use while driving* movement," Maddie smirked as sent her text to Detective Chase.

"Exactly. I'm not a fan of being a hypocrite, my friend. When a fellow student dies from a car accident due to texting while driving, I'm not going to touch my phone while I'm driving. It's not difficult to simply pull over, and take your call or send your text."

I slid my finger across the screen to answer the call from Willow Walker.

"Hello Doc. Feeling better?"

*"No! Lauren. Has. Been. Arrested!"* Willow wailed into the phone hysterically. *"It is all your fault! You and Madison called Detective Chase and had her arrested because you think she is a murderer! She just got released from the hospital, you heartless witch!"*

"Calm down, Willow! I didn't even speak to Detective Chase," Madison dropped her phone in her lap and leaned over to listen to the call. I slipped it on speaker so we both could listen clearly. "If she was arrested, it is because they have evidence on her. We know that her fingerprints were on the teacup. We know the poison was in the teacup. We know the victim died from the poison in the teacup. They had no choice!"

"*But you think she is guilty! You said it yourself. You think she also put the marks on his neck? Really, Fiona? What about that little snippet of evidence? You were going to have her defend herself to us! She is our friend! You've known Lauren your entire life, and now you are going to treat her like a murderer!*"

"Willow, you are being irrational. Please calm down. Madison and I are on our way to your house right now. We need to talk this out," I commanded, hung up the call, and fired up the VW once again.

"Guess we are going to Willow Walker's house, huh?" Madison sneered, shaking her head slowly as we pulled back onto the street.

# 14 BRIDGE

Madison and I were speechless during the detour to Willow's home. I pulled the VW in the front driveway of the colossal estate, and we grudgingly piled out of the car and dredged down the flower-framed walkway to the front door.

"Madison, let's calm her down, and then I'll go talk to my father. If anybody can have her released immediately, it is him," I assured Madison.

"Jail is no place for Lauren. At least nearly everybody knows her there, so I'm sure she's eating cupcakes at Ms. Spinks' desk. There's no way she is behind bars. No way!"

"Of course not, Maddie. No worries!"

I pushed the doorbell, and we waited in awkward silence. I realized a verbal storm was coming as brusque footsteps stomped toward the door from inside. The door flew open, and the tiny Willow stood with a hand on her hip, her face reddened by tears, and her lips forced into a fierce line as she glared at us. Her home always smelled sterile, like a hospital. I guessed that her parents, both physicians, were using hospital sterilization techniques at home.

"You did this to her! She is my best friend. She is *sick*, for gosh sake!"

Willow widened the entrance for us to pass through as she grimaced; her caramel tresses were as equally disheveled as her mood.

"Willow, she was released to return to school, and I heard that her health is just fine," Madison added reluctantly.

"How can they arrest her? She didn't do anything! It's *Lauren*, Fiona! Your friend!" Willow cried, gasping for her next breath as she marched down the hallway toward her room.

We followed her, trying to be quiet as possible as we knew we were not alone in her home.

"Willow, please calm down. Of course, Lauren is our friend. I just want to be sure you are calmed down before I go speak with my father. I am certain that he can make a call to Chief Ranglo and straighten this out. I'm guessing this, but the FBI agents most likely have *everything* to do with this, as everybody at the station knows Lauren personally. Madison and I had absolutely nothing to do with this. You *have* to believe me. I would never put one of my friends in harm's way."

"Well, just because you know the police, doesn't mean that you can't be arrested. Chief Ranglo's own son was arrested when he didn't pay his traffic ticket on time," Madison said sternly.

"You are not helping, Maddie," I warned.

Madison bowed her head, openly remorseful to have fueled the fire. I suddenly felt compelled to speak to my father immediately. I didn't want Lauren at the police station another second, but knew that Willow was a loose cannon and needed somebody to watch over her.

"Madison, can you stay here with Willow? I'll come back to pick you up in a bit."

"Sure, Fiona. Are you going to visit the one and only Mr. Lewis Frost?"

"Yes, I don't want to waste anymore time. I'm sure Lauren is in good hands at the station, but I'm sure she'd rather be at home," I said sternly, swiftly scuttling toward the front door.

Knowing that Madison would diffuse the situation with Willow and keep her from doing anything irrational, I dashed into the VW, fired up the engine, and sped away toward my father's office. Always aware of my surroundings while driving, I noticed a suspicious looking car in my rearview mirror. It followed awkwardly close behind my VW, appearing as if it were attached to my bumper. I could make out that it was a deep army green color, a Honda Civic. The windows were very dark tinted, and the driver appeared as a shadowy silhouette.

I wanted to test the driver to see if they were following me so I made a right turn onto Astantine Street. The Honda followed. I shuddered, hoping it was a coincidence. I approached Francium Street and made a quick right turn.

The Honda followed. I gasped, my heart galloped in my chest. I reached Biscane Street and maneuvered a quick right turn. The Honda mimicked my actions and sped up to get beside me on my left. I shrieked, but my voice was dampened by the small leather-lined space inside of my car. Tears dewed up in the rims of my eyes. I felt so alone.

I peered into the Honda's passenger window, trying to discern who the driver was to no avail. All I saw was a shadow through the darkened windows. Breaking my own rule, I grabbed my phone and dialed 9-1-1. As I drove onto the bridge over the Seven Point River, the operator answered my call.

"My name is Fiona—

The Honda lunged in front of my car, striking the front panel, forcing my car to collide with the side rail of the bridge. The crash was deafening as my cell phone flew into the floorboard in front of the passenger's seat. It happened so quickly, it was hard to process what I was supposed to do. Within seconds, silence ensued. I shouted my location, my name, my car model and that I had been in an accident. Hoping the 9-1-1 operator had heard me, I panicked, feeling my face flush with blood as my pores released sweat to the surface. I clenched the wheel of my car and attempted to steer away from the railing. My tires spun, and the smell of burning rubber filled the inside of my car. My car wouldn't budge.

I stared through my side window in disbelief as the Honda backed up, and with tires spinning and smoke spewing, it propelled toward me again, ramming the backside of the driver's door, slamming the VW further into the side rail. I leaned over to look out of the passenger's window, and all I could see was the river, water crashing against the rocks on the sides. The railing was hugging the VW, and with another push, it would likely give way. My car was about to plummet from the bridge. I was unsure of how to get out of my car once it hit the water. The middle portion of the river was deep, and I knew that I would drown if I weren't killed upon impact of hitting the water. At this moment, I realized I was about to die. It was an odd, calming sensation for a few seconds as I came to the realization, but I quickly snapped back into survival mode. I wasn't going to die that day. My body wouldn't allow it. My physiological systems hurled themselves into overdrive as a new surge of adrenaline snapped my senses into a near superhero-like awareness. As the Honda backed up once again, I tried to open the driver's side door, figuring I had better odds if I tried to escape on foot. The door was crunched, twisted into a locked position, and I couldn't force it to open.

I unlatched my seatbelt and was about to climb into the passenger's seat when I glanced over my shoulder and saw a red Ford Focus pull up and stop behind my car. The Honda driver punched the gas and with tires spinning, peeled off down the bridge, the smell of combusted fuel, and burning rubber permeated relentlessly inside my car. Through the miasma left behind by the Honda, I discerned a familiar face with a sculpted goatee. It was Mr. Zuptus, the biology teacher from my high school, jogging toward my car.

"Fiona! Are you all right?" Mr. Zuptus screamed as he approached the VW. "Fiona!"

I made my way to the passenger's door, unrolled the window and climbed onto the roof. I tried not to look down, as the river was rushing directly below, water cascading and bounding off the rocks immediately beneath me. My right front tire was off the road completely, held in place by the bowed guardrail. I ambled to the shoulder of the bridge and surveyed the massive amount of damage to my car.

"Oh no! Did you get the license plate on that car?" I screamed as I cupped my elbow with my sore palm to ease the intense pain radiating upward to my shoulder.

Mr. Zuptus raised his bony hands, palms facing the sky, his straggly chin-length tresses flailed about with each wind gust as his '70s inspired satin paisley shirt glistened in the sun.

"I certainly did not. I had no idea the car would hit you and run. I was far too concerned with your well-being, young lady. We've got to stop meeting like this, Fiona!"

"Yea, Mr. Zuptus, I am starting to think you are my guardian angel," I laughed nervously, lifting up my arm to examine my throbbing elbow.

I stared cautiously down the street to ensure the Honda wasn't coming back my way to finish the job they had started.

"You all right? Are you injured? I'm going to call for an ambulance," Mr. Zuptus shouted, grabbing his cellular phone.

"I already called the police, I think. If they heard me, they should be here in a minute," I explained, realizing I had just made myself out to be a hypocrite. "Yea, I broke my *no using a cell phone while driving* rule," I admitted hesitantly.

"Oh yes, your campaign. Worthy cause, Fiona. You are correct, some rules should be broken in certain circumstances and traffic accidents are one of them. You can certainly still call for help."

"I should get my phone. It's in the floorboard of the passenger's side."

"You are not going anywhere near that car, Fiona! It's far too dangerous!"

"Okay, Mr. Zuptus. I'll get it when the tow truck gets here."

"That's more like it, Fiona."

"It wasn't an accident, Mr. Zuptus. That car was following me. It pulled up beside me and tried to run me off the road and into the river. The driver could have hit me at any time before, but they waited until I was on the bridge! I think they wanted to kill me!"

Mr. Zuptus shot a look of deep concern as he pondered the scene, stroking his goatee with his fingers.

"I did witness them hit your car, Fiona."

"Well, that was the second time. They hit me once and saw it wasn't good enough so they backed up and did it again! They were going for a third when you pulled up!"

"That is deplorable! If the police don't arrive in the next minute, I'll call them again. I'll stay and give the police an eyewitness account of the car hitting you and driving away.

Unfortunately, all I saw was that it was a dark green Honda Civic. The windows were tinted so dark, I didn't catch sight of the driver."

"Me either!" I howled, taking a seat on the railing next to Mr. Zuptus's car, holding my elbow in the only position that it didn't discharge intense shards of pain up toward my shoulder.

"Well, they must have heard you on the phone, here they come!" Mr. Zuptus sang, the police sirens resonating in the distance.

I felt a surge of comfort race through my body as the police sirens drew near and finally, the red and blue light flashing cars pulled up to the scene. The first officer took my statement, writing down every detail. He knew who I was, and I had spoken to him on occasion at the station. Mr. Zuptus refused to leave until he could ensure that my car would be towed to the most reputable place in town and that the paramedics looked after my elbow. The elbow was just bruised, and I told them it would be just fine. I didn't want to go to the hospital again. I figured that if it didn't heal quickly, I'd have my mother take me to the doctor later.

"Thank you more than words can say, Mr. Zuptus. You are like a second father to me, and I can't say how much I appreciate you."

"Just doing my job, Fiona. I'm a teacher at the high school, and my job doesn't end when the bell rings. I'm here in the community to make sure you kids are looked after. Take care of yourself, you are safe now. The officer over there said he knows your dad, and he'll take you home."

"Perfect. Thanks again. See ya at school."

Mr. Zuptus jumped into his Focus and drove away. For a moment, I felt guilty for all of the things he had been through to help me in my times of need. I needed to get my life straight so I could help him out with the textbook chapter and return the favor.

The officer bellowed, "Fiona, your father is at the police station. Jump in the back of my car, and I'll take you to him."

This was the newest officer to join the Godley Grove Police Force. I hadn't officially met him yet, but since he knew my father, I felt as if it was all right to trust him.

"He's at the station?"

"Yes, he's meeting with some people. Not sure what that's about, but he wanted you there. He said to have you looked at if you were injured. I saw you with the paramedic. You all right? Did the paramedic release you? I didn't think to double check."

"I'm absolutely fine, Officer," I lied. My elbow was pounding with pain.

The ride to the police station felt like a millennium as every neuron in my system galvanized, turning me into an edgy blob of flesh. There was nothing in the world that I despised more with a feverous craze than the *unknown* did. It drove me into utter madness not to know ahead of time what I was getting into. I thought to call my father to get a heads up, and soon realized that I had left my phone in the front floorboard of my car. I gasped for air as the butterflies in my stomach started a melee. I worried about not getting the phone back. It was a sore reminder that if I was to receive sensitive information in my phone from Detective Chase, I had to be diligent about deleting it upon receipt.

I could only hope that the person finding the phone wasn't nosy and was an honest person that would get it back to me without looking at any of Detective Chase's text messages or emails or any of the correspondence between the club members and me. Even if the documents were password protected, that wasn't a one hundred percent secure process. Detective Chase had warned me to delete all correspondence after reading it, but I was slow to do this, I knew there was some sensitive information in my phone.

"So you have no idea why my father is at the station?" I pleaded with the officer.

"Nope. I do what I'm told, Miss Frost. All I know is what I told you. He was in a meeting with some folks, and when I radioed back that it was *you* in the accident on the bridge, they immediately requested that you join them. That is, if you were not injured. You sure you are all right? You seem to be nursing that arm, Fiona. You know, I can't afford to get in trouble. I need my job."

"I'm fine, Sir. Thanks for asking. Just a little bumped up. The paramedic wrapped it and said if it didn't get better in a few days to go have it X-rayed. I might have minimized the injury to the guy just so I could avoid another ambulance trip, I hate hospitals! But I *was* officially released by him!"

My elbow was throbbing. The only sense of relief was to extend my arm in the air so it didn't touch anything. This was going to get tiresome.

"Don't blame you. As long as the medic released you, I'm safe. Well, we're here, you know where to go?"

"Yes, thank you."

I jumped out of the car and rushed into the foyer of the station. It seemed like the movie Ground Hog's Day as Ms. Spinks opened the door for me before I could say a word, shooting a glance of concern to me as I passed through the doorway into the concrete hallway.

I walked slowly. My mind threw me back to the last meeting in the conference room with Agent Jonas and Detective Chase. A rush of uneasiness scurried through my body, settling down in each of my cells, followed by a panic surge at the top of my skull that worked its way downward. I could hear my heart pounding through my ears as a mist of chaos clouded my thoughts. The heated voices became louder as I approached the door. I twisted the handle, and the voices stopped at an instant.

I slowly opened the door and locked in with my father's matching topaz eyes. He was sitting straight ahead with Detective Chase to his right, Detective Chase's receding brown hair looked like a before and after picture with my father's picture-perfect coif. There were dark-suited men and women scattered around the room, seemingly too important to have a seat in the chairs. I turned to see the distinctive blue eyes belonging to Agent Jonas. He was sitting at the head of the table, his arms folded.

"Come on in, Miss Frost. Please take a seat."

# 15 ENCOUNTER

I hesitated before I reluctantly took a seat across from my father and Detective Chase. I hunted their faces for any signs of a hint as to why I had been summoned there. They both appeared calm so I refrained from entering a full-blown panic attack. Disinclined, I gazed at Agent Jonas who met my eyes with an expression that grew more resentful by the second.

"Miss Frost, we received a report earlier today from a young lady, Miss Willow Walker, from Godley Grove High School. I understand she is a member of your little club at the high school, is that correct?"

I drew in a calming breath before responding. I tried to keep my bandaged elbow out of my father's sight. I didn't want him to worry. The words *little club* incited my inner fury, but I fought to ignore them and remain mature.

"She is a member of the Godley Grove High School Forensic Science Training Program which is under my direction so my answer is *yes* if that is what you are referred to by saying *little club*," my words came out more sarcastically than I intended.

Agent Jonas smiled in deep satisfaction. My lips pursed as I boiled with rage, fists tightened intuitively to absorb the energy that was building within my body. With the adrenaline rush, my elbow ceased throbbing, and I was able to masque the pain.

He continued, "She reported that you, Miss Fiona Frost, analyzed data that you collected at a cleared crime scene, the Foster Manor, and subsequently provided this analysis to the Godley Grove Police Department as official evidence on the case."

"What? That is not true!"

My father waved a stern hand in front of me from across the table, signaling me to control my emotions. My father was a brilliant man, and I always followed his direction. Detective Chase nodded every so slightly in agreement with him. I closed my eyes tightly, trying to harness as much control as I could muster; my hands trembled ever so slightly.

"As I was going to say, Miss Frost, I've spoken to Detective Chase about this incident, and he has assured me that you did not, in fact, submit evidence that you collected at the crime scene to Godley Grove Crime Lab," Agent Jonas said, his condescending voice low and tense.

"That is correct. I have never submitted any evidence that my training lab has collected as official evidence in any case the police department was currently investigating," my voice trembled with anger.

"Let me get to my point. Miss Frost, do you recall the last time we were in this room, and I asked you not to work on any further evidence nor have any further correspondence with Detective Chase about the Gilroy Foster murder case?"

I paused, gazing casually at Detective Chase who gave a nod as if to say it was all right to tell the truth.

"Well—

"Yes or no, Miss Frost," Agent Jonas fumed.

My father cleared his throat as he straightened up in his chair, plainly irritated by Agent Jonas's tone of voice with me.

"Fiona, it is all right to tell Agent Jonas. He has no right to tell you to not work in your federally-funded and school district-approved training lab," my father instructed, nodding once, chiseled face unperturbed.

I realized at that moment what my father was telling me. It was a *training* lab. I needed to choose my words carefully and focus on the training aspect. Lewis Frost was an utter genius.

"Excuse me, Mr. Frost. I have posed a question to Miss Fiona Frost, and if you need me to have you escorted out of the room if you find that you cannot refrain yourself from coaching the witness, I will do so."

I stood from my chair at the thought of my father, of all people, being escorted out of the room. Fury burned through my previously boiled blood as I awaited Agent Jonas's next move. His pallid eyes tracked me with bitter umbrage.

I collected my thoughts and responded to his question, "Agent Jonas, we routinely examine all evidence, both from real cases and from mock cases in our training laboratory. We get the most benefit from analyzing the real case evidence because once the case is closed; we can compare our analysis with the real crime lab's analysis to see how accurate we were. This is a valid and proven method of *training* which thereby is the crux of our federal grant. There are many papers published on this subject in peer-reviewed journals. I would be happy to get you some copies of these papers for your records, Agent Jonas."

My father's eyes widened as he smiled at me with a bottomless approval. The room went still. Agent Jonas stared forward into nothingness, dazed. His fellow agents' eyes were affixed to his face, waiting for him to respond. My father turned toward Agent Jonas with a confident grin.

"I might add, Agent Jonas, that my conversation this morning with the *International Scientific Foundation* was a very positive one, and they are excited with the progress of my daughter's training program," Lewis Frost reported sternly, facing me while he continued, "In fact, they've agreed to extend the grant for another four years, Fiona."

Upon hearing the news, I howled and jumped around my seat. It was one thing to obtain a grant but another to have the grant renewed, which signified that your work was appreciated and respected by the scientific community. A blissful fluster overcame my senses as I jumped up and down, throwing my hands carelessly in the air.

"They extended the grant? Wow, I didn't expect to hear back so soon!" I shouted, a huge grin lighting up my face.

My father gave me a private smile. Detective Chase waved a silent thumbs up in the air while a sheepish grin raided his face.

"Well, it's not official, but the director of the foundation gave me the unofficial decision," Mr. Frost said, arching a perfect eyebrow. He swiveled again to face Agent Jonas who was overtly maddened by the news, "See, the training program was a test program, a two year grant until Fiona graduated and into the summer beyond so she can train her replacement team. Now, with Fiona's help, Godley Grove High School will have the program for at least four more years!"

"Thank you, Daddy! I'm so excited!"

"That is the best news all year!" Detective Chase added brightly, smirking at Agent Jonas.

"I should add, Agent Jonas, that this is being written up in the local paper, a massive array of scientific journals across the world, Time Magazine, and I had a spot on CNN talking about the program earlier today via satellite. If I were you, I wouldn't try to mess with such a successful training program geared for today's youth. The American public wouldn't take so kindly to it," Mr. Frost sneered as he followed with a blank, intimidating stare into Agent Jonas's direction. A period of awkward silence ensued as the two men contemplated the recent conversation.

I marveled in awe of how my father handled the situation. I immediately realized why he was such a respected, successful district attorney.

"Thank you for your time," Agent Jonas scoffed as he abruptly exited the room, his fellow agents trailing immediately behind like lemmings headed for the river.

"Fiona, are you all right? I heard that you got into a fender bender, but I was told you were not injured," Lewis said, examining me thoroughly with his eyes, stopping at my bandaged elbow.

"I'm fine, dad. I was released by the paramedic. However, it was more than a fender bender. I can tell you about it later, they have all the information in the report. I just want to go home. But I wanted to talk to you about my friend, Lauren Hope."

"Great job, Mr. Frost. Congrats, Fiona," Detective Chase interrupted as he stood up.

My father shook hands with Detective Chase who in turn jetted toward his office down the hall. My father and I exited the conference room and headed out through the concrete hallway toward the parking lot.

"I had Lauren immediately released as soon as I heard that Agent Jonas had the audacity to arrest a teenage girl based purely upon circumstantial evidence because there is zero apparent motive nor criminal history. She is a teen, her parents signed papers that she won't flee the country, and that's that. The FBI was only here to investigate a threat made to me as the district attorney and not to investigate a local murder case. But they are stating the cases might be related, so they are injecting themselves into the murder investigation."

"Oh, I get it, Dad. Thanks for getting Lauren released so quickly! Have you heard any news about Haley?"

"Nothing new. It appears as though a senior from your school, Josh Coleman, might have had something to do with the threatening notes you and mother received. He is nowhere to be found. There is an A.P.B. out on him, and they'll catch him. I understand that this is the fellow that Haley was romantically involved with during the past few weeks. If so, I'm sure this is one of her stunts," Lewis Frost said grimly.

"Yes, I've seen them together firsthand, and very reliable sources have seen some actual romance between them."

"Your mother is eaten up by it, still believes it to be a kidnapping, but I know what's happened. I am furious with Haley. I'm going to discuss this with your Uncle Peter, and it's most likely going to be a locked-down New Zealand boarding school for her when she gets home."

I climbed into my father's *Frost 2* Lincoln Town Car, we drove home, his latest classical music compilation playing peacefully, settling into my subconscious. It was serene, and I took time to do nothing besides stare out the window into the cloudless sky.

My dad pulled into the garage in the back, and I jumped out, rushed to the house, and swung open the back door. The aroma of a full course dinner bombarded my nasal passageway. It smelled wonderful, but I was too mentally exhausted even to think about eating. Lewis headed my mother off at the kitchen as she tried to rush toward me; no doubt, she wanted to check my injuries. He assured her that I was fine, and I blew her a solemn kiss as I dredged to my room. Tossing my backpack on the floor, I grabbed a walkie-talkie from my desk. I pushed the button a few times and waited patiently for my neighbor and best friend to respond.

*"Hello Fiona! I'm dying to know! How did you get your dad to release Lauren so quickly?"*

"Madison, there's so much to catch up on, I'll talk to you in the morning. I just wanted to make sure you got home all right since I abandoned you at Willow's house. She's a traitor, by the way."

"What? A traitor? How?" Madison's voice grew more excited with every word.

It slipped out; I didn't mean to say it. I knew I couldn't send Maddie off to sleep with so many questions. It was my pet peeve to have to wait for information, and Madison was no different.

"I guess I shouldn't have said that if I wasn't going to give details. Come to the window, the walkies get annoying with the static."

Madison's bathroom window was directly across the skinny side yard from my bedroom window. Since we were small children, we communicated at night this way, after our bedtimes. That is, until cell phones came into play. Within moments, she pulled up the window, and stuck her head out into the night air.

"Where's your phone?"

"I left it in my car."

"Well, go get it!" Madison shrieked playfully, trying to lean out to see my VW.

"Uh, my car was wrecked. It's in the shop for a while."

"What!"

I detailed the events that happened with the army green Honda. Madison's expression turned bitter with anger and confusion. I knew that we had to get back to discussing Willow if I wanted to get to sleep.

"About Willow and why she's a traitor. Before we got to her house, she had called the police station and spoke to the FBI agents that are working the kidnapping and now the murder case."

"About Lauren? She couldn't wait for your father to get her released, or what?"

"She called them and told them that you and I collected, analyzed, and submitted evidence to the crime lab for the murder case! She lied! She knows we didn't do that, the police *can't* accept our evidence as official evidence on an open case! She was trying to get us into trouble so we wouldn't tell Detective Chase about the fingerprints on the tea canister!"

"Whoa, Fiona. That's heavy. I never would have thought Willow would do that. She definitely didn't mention that to me when I was over there with her earlier. We even started playing video games, and she stopped ranting about us soon after you left to go talk to your dad about Lauren. So is Agent Jonas shutting down the forensic program or what?"

"Not really. Our training program is very safe. My father took care of it so no worries."

"Your dad is the best, Fiona."

"Wouldn't trade him for the world," I smiled brightly, tilting my head toward my shoulder.

"So what about Haley. Any word?"

"I'm pretty sure that Haley was in on it with Josh Coleman, and now they've run off. Interesting enough, from what I understand, Josh lived with his older sister, Addie Coleman. You know, the younger lab tech that Detective Chase put on leave."

Madison grew animated, her forehead creased tightly, drawing up her eyebrows into an arch of excitement.

"Why haven't they arrested her for kidnapping then?" She yelled, slapping her hands against her window frame.

"No evidence! All they have is a link to Josh Coleman for the note threats to me and for the kidnapping and hearsay that Haley was involved with Josh. That doesn't tie to Addie Coleman."

"But Haley is a minor and was at Addie's house! Whether she was willing or not, it was portrayed as a kidnapping so she should be held accountable as the adult in the house!"

"She is only a sister, not a responsible guardian, and Josh is an adult. He's eighteen and isn't home. They can't do anything. Again, there is just no evidence of Haley being at Addie's home."

"Something is not right with that, I just feel it," Madison scoffed.

"Agreed, but there's nothing we can do about it until we find evidence. Well, Maddie, I'm going to speak to Principal Dinges in the morning when I get to school and see if they have any further evidence about the locker bombing. I'm sure it was Josh, but they should still be working on the case, nonetheless. I'll see ya tomorrow."

"K, Fiona. See ya tomorrow."

We both shut our windows and crawled into our beds. I had difficulty sleeping as the evidence raced through my mind about the locker bombing, the murder, the rattlesnakes, the notes and now the driver of the dark green Honda that apparently wanted me dead. I didn't know how these events were related or if they even were at all. Had I grown to be the unluckiest person the on planet or was I part of a massive, intertwined murder case with a dangerous web of criminals? Something else plagued me as well. Was my cousin, my own flesh and blood, a part of this intricate web of criminal activity or was she a victim?

# 16 SIGHTING

The sunbeams trickled in on my face, and I hurled out of bed, getting ready as fast as I could so I could meet with Principal Dinges the moment he arrived at school. Luminal's furry ears popped up as his head contorted from side to side with confusion as I rushed around my bedroom. I typically followed a rigid morning routine and wasn't one to vary anything.

I jumped into Madison's bright blue Mini Cooper. My VW would be at the service center for at least a week or two. The timing worked out perfectly as Madison had early morning soccer practice, and I wanted to get to school as soon as possible. Janice was to give me a ride to school in the *Frost 3* Lincoln Town Car until my car was repaired, but not that day, I was far too anxious. I was still annoyed that I didn't have my phone. I never realized that I was helpless without it.

"Hey Maddie! Good morning!" I snatched the seatbelt and buckled in.

"G'morning, Fiona. I couldn't really sleep last night, you know. I wanted to call Willow and ask her why she thought she had to lie to the FBI about us. Such a betrayal!" Madison screeched, pulling out into the street.

"I know, I know. Confronting her won't do any good. Try to see it from her side. Lauren is her best friend, and she was trying to keep her out of trouble at all costs. Think about it - if it was me, you might feel compelled to do the same, right?"

"Well...I'd *want* to...but I don't think I would stoop that low to betray our club," Madison relented. "If Lauren is innocent, it will be found out and that's that."

"I do agree with you there, but at least I can try to put myself in her shoes."

Maddie's phone rang from the console of her car. I lifted the console and saw Lauren Hope's picture plastered across the screen.

"Not sure if I want to deal with her right now, Maddie," I said sternly.

"You know it's for you. Just get it, I will if you won't," Madison demanded.

"Hi Lauren," I moaned.

*"Oh, Fiona. I expected to hear Maddie's voice, but I wanted to speak with you. You aren't answering your phone, and I figured you were avoiding me. I want to say thank you. I know you spoke to your father, and he took care of me. I appreciate it,"* Lauren sounded from the other end of the line.

I was surprised that she sounded so happy. I knew that Willow must have told her that Madison and I betrayed her and were the reason why she was arrested.

"You are welcome, and of course I am not avoiding you, silly. I had nothing to do with your release, though. By the time I asked my father to do it, he told me he had already taken care of it the moment he heard about it. How are you feeling, by the way? Have you been released to come back to school?"

*"I'm fine. It was pretty awful, but the antibiotics took care of it and no more pain from the stupid bite. I hate snakes, by the way,"* Lauren chuckled.

"Yea, me too. I can't believe a snake bite turned into all that mess. I'm glad you are feeling better," I couldn't stand the big obtrusive elephant in the room. I had to say it, "I'm assuming that you know what Willow did?"

*"Well, that was the second thing I was calling about. I wanted to apologize on behalf of my best friend. Doc didn't mean to get you in trouble or jeopardize the club in anyway. She let her emotions get the best of her and concocted this story in her head that you were out to get me and make me the murderer."*

"It just isn't rational. She had no right—

*"Agreed, and she will apologize to you the moment she sees you. She has been a wreck with my illness, and then with me going to the police station and possibly jail, she just couldn't handle it."*

"We will talk. Things will have to be worked out here if we are to continue working together in a professional manner. I have to know something, Lauren. Why did you make Gilroy Foster tea, and how do you think the enormous amount of digitalis medication got into the tea that you prepared for him? I am not accusing you nor do I think you are a suspect. I just want to know the logistics of how the poison got into the tea."

*"Well, I was going to the kitchen to get a glass of water, and Mr. Foster asked me if I wanted some hot tea. It seems stupid, but I was kind of getting bored, and I asked if I could make it. He showed me where everything was and then went back into the living room. I made the tea exactly how he instructed, put it into the cup and brought it to him in the living room. That's that,"* Lauren outlined directly.

"Did you put anything into the tea like sugar or honey?"

*"No, he didn't ask for anything to be put into it."*

"Then how long until he died?"

Madison pulled the Mini Cooper into the student parking lot and swerved into a space at the front by the soccer fields.

*"It wasn't that long, maybe within the hour. He acted sick for a while like I explained to you before. Then, he went to the kitchen and collapsed. We all looked at each other as if we didn't know what to think of the noise. A couple of minutes might have passed, and I think I was the first one on the scene, but the others came immediately after because I screamed."*

"Thanks, Lauren. I just wanted to hear your side of things. That's all I ever wanted. I was never going to prosecute you. I have no doubt that you are telling the complete truth. One more thing. Can you remember if the homeless man that showed up, Kosmo Wilder, ever went back outside to his car the night of the murder?"

*"Gosh, I wasn't really paying attention to him, but I don't recall him leaving. He got into a weird, seated position on the loveseat and never even flinched. However, I didn't watch him every second. I mean, he could have gone outside when I was making tea."*

"Thanks, Lauren. We're at school now; I'm going to meet with Principal Dinges about my locker bombing case. See ya later," I said, hanging up the phone, giving Madison a look of derision.

"Good luck with ole big snout, Fiona. I better get to the field before I'm late and have to run laps," Madison sparked, running off to the soccer fields.

I laughed so hard that I snorted as I jogged up to the front façade of the school. The foyer was silent, and the only light on inside of the school was in the main office. I darted inside and marched toward Principal Dinges' office.

I knocked on the door. It was slightly ajar with the light on, and I could see his hands fumbling through paper files on his cheap plywood desk.

"Come in," he sounded blankly.

I strolled in, taking the wooden guest chair directly across from him on the other side of his desk. I cleared my throat, looking around at his cluttered office.

"Mr. Dinges, I know that I don't have an appointment, but I felt as though this was important and cannot wait," I said, the words spewed out of my mouth faster than I could process what I was saying.

"Fiona, I figured you would be in to check on the bomb case soon enough. Hold on a minute, I have a message here about it," Principal Dinges scuffled through a stack of handwritten memos before stopping at one and examining it carefully. "It looks like Officer Ponch from Silver Springs is still working on the case and has very unique tool mark impressions, undoubtedly from a crowbar, that was used to pry open your locker."

"Yes, I remember they said the surveillance video showed the perpetrator using a crowbar to open the locker," I added.

"Correct, Fiona. By the striations on the locker door and frame, Officer Ponch feels they can make a strong match if they can locate the crowbar. That's about the entire story, Fiona. I hope they can find this crowbar and close the case. I have a feeling on who might be responsible, but I'm keeping my opinions to myself for now," Mr. Dinges said.

"Me too. Thanks, Mr. Dinges. I'll be in touch," I said with enthusiasm, prancing out of his office.

It seemed clear-cut to me. I find the crowbar, I solve the case. The more I thought about the case, the more it seemed as though the locker bombing and Gilroy Foster's murder were related. I just couldn't put the pieces together as I essentially had nothing to do with Gilroy Foster. That is, until we started investigating the case. I wanted to talk to Madison and work through it during lunch. My morning classes seemed eternal after I jotted down a list of bullet points to discuss with her.

The bell to lunch finally rang, and I scurried into the cafeteria, notebook in hand.

"Maddie! I met with Principal Dinges this morning, and it seems very clear cut that if we find the crowbar used in the crime, we solve the case," I huffed with angst.

"Uh, Fiona, that's easier said than done! If you were the criminal, would you keep the evidence around you or would you dispose of it somewhere far away?"

"Madison, keep a positive outlook. These are not brain surgeons we are dealing with, I promise. I'm sure I can find this crowbar. I think I want to go back to the manor. Something is definitely fishy with Ms. Foster," I said.

"What! You think Ms. Foster is the locker bomber?"

"No, Maddie, of course not. However, I do think that the murder, the locker bomb and the Honda driver are all related. There has to be a clue at the manor that we have overlooked. What if I find a crowbar on the grounds somewhere?"

"I think you are grasping at straws, but if you can clear it with Detective Chase, I'm in. Other than that, let's just work on the evidence we have. We've not even processed it all. Maybe if we find the murderer, we'll find the bomber? It goes both ways, right? And what about Josh Coleman, have you given up on him?"

"I think Josh Coleman was simply jabbing a poker into the fire. My belief is that he wanted a diversion to run away with my cousin. I don't really buy that he has anything to do with the murder. I mean, his older sister works at the crime lab, and she's not related to the Foster Manor in any way, at least that I know of."

"You have a good point there, Fiona."

At the conclusion of our lunch discussion, we had decided that the bombing, the car crash and the murder might possibly be related, and if so, the key evidence would be at the manor. We contacted Detective Chase who said that we could go to the manor, ring the doorbell, and if Ms. Foster agreed, we could have another look around. He wouldn't clear it with her, however, given the fragile state of the relationship between the police and the FBI agents involved with the case. Madison and I had built a somewhat cordial relationship with Ms. Foster and had a chance of her being amicable to us if we simply showed up at her home.

After school, we set out for Foster Manor in the blue Mini Cooper. After a ten-minute drive of relaxing silence, we drove through the iron archway and up to the circle drive. The manor appeared desolate, not a car in the driveway.

"Great, she's probably not home, Madison."

"Let's still try; maybe she parked in the back or something."

We scrambled to the front porch, and I grabbed the brass knocker, releasing it into the base of the lion's mouth three times. I leaned over and rang the doorbell for insurance.

We waited a few minutes and tried the routine again. Nothing. No clinking of high heels on the marble, no movement through the windows. I peered into the large window of the living room and noticed that the chandelier chaos had been cleaned up and the pictures were hung nicely back onto the wall in their places.

"Not home. Well, let's go. We're not supposed to be here and will be trespassing if we try to poke around without permission," Madison said bluntly.

As I walked to the passenger side door of the Mini Cooper, a shiny black triangular shard caught my eye on the driveway.

"Check this out, Madison," I mumbled, picking up the quarter-sized shaving of black paint.

"What's that, Fiona? A gigantic beetle?"

"No, Madison. It is a sliver of black paint. It might be a long shot, but this looks like it might have come off a car, it definitely doesn't look like house paint."

"Let's take it to the crime lab."

# 17 SALE

Detective Chase was more than happy to accept the paint chip evidence and said that he would unofficially analyze it himself immediately. Within an hour after my car accident, he had sent an officer to the service station to take a control paint sample from my car in the event we found the hit-and-run Honda. Detective Chase was always thinking of every angle when it came to crime.

After saying hello to everybody at the police station and getting my phone back that was retrieved from my car, we hopped in the Mini Cooper. The moment I strapped on the seatbelt, my phone rang. It was Emma Frost calling from her office line at the university.

"Hey, mom! I only have five percent battery power; the phone can shut off any second."

*"Oh, I'm so glad you got your phone back, I was going to try Maddie's phone if you didn't answer. I'll call her phone if we are cut off. Fiona, somebody broke in the house not too long*

*ago. They left another red envelope; the police are on their way. I know you told me you had some errands after school, but just in case you beat me there, I didn't want you to panic when you saw the police cars in front."*

"What! Is Janice all right? Was she there?"

*"Yes, but she's shaken up. She was in the kitchen, heard a noise and saw the front door open. She had to chase Luminal down the street. Then, Maddie's silly cat got into it with Luminal, and she had to spray them with the garden hose to break up the fight. Not a good afternoon for Janice."*

"Hold on a second, Mom," I leaned away from my phone to tell Madison somebody had broken into my house because she was more than flustered as she attempted to drive away from the station. "Mom, what did the note say in the envelope?"

"Another note!" Madison exclaimed. As we turned the car onto to Nickale Street, we saw the red and blue lights ahead.

I shook my head *yes*, pointing to the government-plated Lincoln Town Car and two police cars parked in front of my house.

*"Don't know. The police told Janice not to touch it. They're probably there by now—*

"Yea, we're pulling up, I see them. I will go right over and check it out."

I hung up the phone with my mother and dredged over to my house, checking out the scene. A few uniformed officers with familiar faces were scattered about the living room. Some were speaking with Janice while others were talking over their handheld radios or taking fingerprints.

White knuckled and frazzled in form, Janice rambled on about the intruder. Over in the corner of the room, Luminal was passed out on his pillow bed, probably exhausted from his joy run and catfight.

I plugged my phone in to charge and then found an officer that I had known since I started hanging around the police station years before. She was holding an evidence bag; I assumed it contained the envelope. A suited FBI agent, one that I had seen in the conference room, stood behind her with folded arms.

"Hi Officer Smythe. Did you open the envelope? Was it a red envelope?"

"Hi Fiona. Yes, it's a red envelope, and no, I didn't open it. I was instructed not to open it. He wants the document analyst at Silver Springs to analyze it in its entirety," she gestured to the agent standing behind her, "The more we handle it, the more we contaminate it, destroying the evidence. Unlike the first two envelopes that you submitted, they want this to be official evidence, as it is likely linked to the murder case. It's probably way beyond the locker bomb case, Fiona. The courier is waiting on it at the station, and the document analyst is expecting its arrival within the hour. He is going to travel with it and assist the document examiner," Officer Smythe said, secretly rolling her eyes in revulsion toward the agent behind her.

"I'm just worried that it might have another time sensitive message like the last one."

"We understand that, and that's why they'll have it within the hour. Everybody is on full alert, and your family is under surveillance. There are undercover officers right now watching your mother and father, and now you're with us," she pointed over her shoulder to a couple of uniformed officers on the couch with Janice, "Those officers are staying here for the evening, but I have to get this to the lab's courier now. G'bye, Fiona."

"Got it, thanks."

I meandered over to Janice on the couch, trying to comfort her by rubbing her rounded shoulders. Her normally flawless bun was in disarray, wisps of silver air jetting at ninety-degree angles from her face. Her cheeks, once rosy pink, were flushed dazzling red, her forehead beaded with perspiration. I decided to get her a cool towel to put on her neck. That always worked to calm my nerves when she did it for me.

"Here you go, Janice. I heard you had a bad afternoon, huh?"

"Thanks, doll," Janice moved in closer, a bothered expression invaded her crimson cherubic features, "Fiona, I am so glad that you were not here. You know that if you'd have come straight home from school, you'd have been here, and then what would have happened?" Janice said in a flustered southern drawl, cupping her hands over her mouth.

"Oh, Janice, they probably would've run away if they saw me. Please don't worry! We're all right, and that's all that matters. Those two officers are staying with us to be sure we are all safe, especially since they haven't opened the envelope and don't even know what it says!"

"Oh my, oh my. What if it's about Haley?"

"Janice, I don't have a doubt that Haley ran away with Josh, a senior at my school, and potentially one of the biggest trouble makers in town. Don't worry about Haley – the FBI agents are here working on the case, anyway."

Janice sighed, taking the towel from her neck and patting her forehead.

"When will things get back to normal around here, Fiona?"

"Ha! Soon enough, Janice," I said as my phone rang from across the room.

I rushed over to retrieve it from the charger. It was Detective Chase.

"Hello Detective Chase, did you hear the news?"

*"Yes, Fiona. It's very disheartening that there's another note, and that the perp broke into your home. I hope that we can extract some real evidence this time from the envelope. I understand the FBI agent on site is walking with it to Silver Springs?"*

"Yes, but he won't even let us open it to see what it says!"

*"No worries, Fiona. I understand you have some protection until we figure it out. But I have some very interesting news for you,"* Detective Chase changed his tone of voice from grimness to enthusiasm.

"What is it?"

*"The paint chip you brought to the lab is a match to your car. Whatever car attempted to run you off the bridge traveled to the manor some time after the accident. We have a link, now we just need to find that car."*

"Wow! That's crazy! Do you know what Ms. Foster drives?"

*"Yes, of course. She drives a new Cadillac, and her husband drove a very old Mercedes. She definitely doesn't own a Honda, but we're checking all of our suspects right now. Not one of the suspects own a title to a Honda, but that doesn't mean that they don't have one. I'm actually headed out to the manor right now."*

"We'll meet you there, Detective Chase. I'll get Maddie and be there in fifteen minutes."

*"Fiona, no. Wait there with the officers until the envelope is opened. I'm here now, anyway. Wait—*

"What's wrong?"

There was silence on the other end of the line.

"Detective Chase!"

*"Sorry about that, Fiona. There's a 'for sale' sign in the front of the manor, and a moving truck is here."*

"I'm on my way, Detective. Wait for me."

# 18 BARS

After a heated debate between Janice and the officers in charge of watching us, I talked one of the officers into driving Madison and me to the Foster Manor. I knew if one of my parents had come home, I wouldn't be going anywhere so it was a game against time. Having the officer drive seemed like a good compromise.

"Here we are, and there's the sign," I chanted, pointing at the *for sale* sign in the front of the manor.

"I thought the moving truck was here?" Madison added.

"I guess they're done, out of here already," I said, unbuckling my seatbelt and hopping out of the car.

Detective Chase was waiting for us beside his unmarked Chevrolet Impala with a somber expression.

"I spoke to Ms. Foster," Detective Chase lamented as we marched toward him.

"And?"

"She is selling the house, moving to Canada."

"Can she leave the country?"

"She isn't a suspect. We have no evidence on her."

"What? She was burning things the night of the murder! There was a match to the matchstick and matchbook used to burn the documents in the barrel behind the manor!"

"That doesn't make her guilty of murder. It isn't illegal. She said she doesn't have a document shredder, and she was getting rid of financial documents. She claimed that she burns things frequently."

I sighed. This was bad. I thought Ms. Foster was the number one suspect, and now she would be leaving out of the country.

"I requested a new serology analysis to be done by the Silver Springs lab. With what is going on with Addie Coleman, I figured if her younger brother is tied to the case, I shouldn't trust her analysis," Detective Chase reasoned.

"Good point. So did you find anything interesting?"

"No. She performed the analysis perfectly. The normal level of a patient on digitalis medication is 0.8 to 2.0 nanograms per milliliter. The victim had over ten times that amount, and that was the only abnormality in the blood. It is what killed Gilroy Foster. However, when I did the autopsy, I did see a reddened area on his throat that does resemble thumbprints in a way. There was no bruising, but if these injuries were sustained immediately upon death or immediately afterward, the victim wouldn't have bruised very much at all, as there's no more blood flow. It's consistent with somebody taking out an insurance policy that the victim wouldn't recover from the poisoning."

"Whoa. That's heavy. So you think the murderer was there in the kitchen when Mr. Foster fell and choked him to be sure he wasn't breathing anymore?"

"Yes, I'm pretty sure of it. It's just so slight; it wasn't the cause of death for sure. However, it was enough to make us open our eyes that this was a murder case so the murderer made a grave error in that sense. The choking wasn't necessary in the end because the amount of digitalis in Mr. Foster's blood was enough assurance that he wasn't going to make it."

Detective Chase's phone rang, and he immediately snatched it from his inner coat pocket.

"Excuse me, Fiona. It's the lab."

I watched Detective Chase's face absorb the news from the other end of the line and morph into a mask of distress. After a few minutes, he hung up the phone and strutted towards Madison and me.

"This is bad. That was the lab. They did a thorough background check on Kosmo Wilder - the drifter that showed up the night of the murder."

"Really?" I shouted, Madison grabbed my wrist in angst.

"Well, it appears as though he is not a drifter after all. I just realized his car is gone, and it doesn't appear as though he is still here at the manor either. I asked the movers if Ms. Foster was still here, and they said nobody was in the manor."

"How does a homeless man with no money get his car repaired so quickly?" I asked.

"There's more to the story," Detective Chase enlightened.

"Oh no. This is bad," Madison went on.

"It gets worse. He went to college with Nic Dalton, the Foster's attorney. Now it makes sense how the Siberian Husky hairs were in his car. They are working together on something, and now we just need to figure out what that is."

"And, Nic Dalton's fingerprints were on the medicine cabinet!" Madison shrieked, jumping in a controlled fashion.

"Let's get back to the lab. There's nothing we can do standing here," Detective Chase commanded, jumping into his beige Impala.

We rode with Detective Chase to the police station, and Madison and I outlined the new evidence in the case on the way. I felt a wave of exhilaration that was incomparable to anything I had felt before. This was my biggest case, and like pieces to a puzzle, they were all in front of me, waiting to be pushed together.

We scurried into Detective Chase's office and collected ourselves before we started to discuss the case. The blue-eyed Agent Jonas knocked on the door abruptly. Detective Chase instructed him to come inside of the office. Upon seeing Madison and me, he sneered at Detective Chase, avoiding eye contact with us.

"I suppose when your training session is done with the teens, I have some revelations to discuss with you, Detective

Chase," Agent Jonas said mockingly, pivoting around to exit the room.

"You can tell me with them present, Agent Jonas. Remember what Mr. Frost said about the federal grant program and all of the press involved. Fiona and Madison are totally aware of the confidentiality of investigations," Detective Chase said boldly.

"As a member of the Federal Bureau of Investigation, I will not and am not expected to divulge sensitive case information in the presence of minors. I will, however, meet with you in the conference room, Detective Chase. Alone."

Detective Chase rolled his eyes to the ceiling for a moment before deciding to follow Agent Jonas into the conference room.

"I'll be right back, girls. Hold tight."

I was more than irritated at Agent Jonas, but at the same time, I was surprised that he didn't try to kick us out of the police station. We had at least made some improvements to our rocky relationship.

"Fiona, I seriously dislike that man," Madison said, a grin invading her face.

"He's just misunderstood," I laughed, breaking the awkward tension left in the room.

After about five minutes, Detective Chase scuttled back behind his desk, peering at us through his stacks of files.

"The plot thickens. The envelope contained prints from a perp from another, completely unrelated case."

"Really? What case?"

"Your father's, Fiona. However, it was an older case. Three years ago, a man was sentenced to ten years in prison for burglary of a habitat. He was a nasty individual, vowed to get even with your dad because he was the district attorney on the case. He blamed your father for the reason why he had to go to jail."

"Are you kidding? So he is the kidnapper and not Josh?" Madison howled.

"All we know is that his prints were on the envelope this time. They were not found on the previous envelopes, however, and we didn't find any of his prints in your house or at Foster Manor. Not to say he couldn't have worn gloves when he broke into your house. But it doesn't make a whole lot of sense that he'd break into your house with gloves but touch the envelope without them."

"Criminals are not brain surgeons, Detective Chase," I lamented.

"But they usually know how to get away with things, and this is a blatant mistake. However, even more interesting is the fact that he was to be paroled yesterday. Everybody at the station was on high alert that he was being released because of the threats he initially made against your father the day he went to prison."

"Why was he being released after only three years if he was sentenced to ten years?"

"Good behavior. He was a model prisoner."

"Threatening my father is a model prisoner?"

"He never threatened again after the day in court when he was sentenced. He said that he found God. He ultimately became the prison's minister. That's why it doesn't really make sense that he would leave a note in your house that said *I've got Haley now. This is payment for what you've done to me the last three years.*"

"What! That is what the note said?" I screamed. "That is unbelievable! Are you guys going after him? Where is he living now?"

Emotions flushed through my system as I tried to switch gears from believing Haley was a selfish teen runaway to a defenseless victim of a hardened criminal. My protective instincts took over my senses. After all, she was a part of my family, no matter how horrible of a person she might have been.

"He is still in prison, Fiona. It was a shock to everybody that he wasn't released. We had heard through the grapevine that he was going to make parole and be released."

The room drew dead silent. This didn't make sense.

"I don't get it, Detective. Then how—

"We're going to the prison right now. Want to tag along? You can watch through the one-way mirror into the interrogation room."

Madison explained that she reluctantly had to get home to work on a history project. We decided that I would go with Detective Chase, and an officer would give Madison a ride and ensure she was home safely.

"Bye, Maddie. I'll see you later. If you're up when I get home, I'll text you."

"Bye, Fiona. Have fun in prison!" Madison's chuckle faded as she strolled down the hallway with the officer.

I had never been to the prison on the outskirts of the city. It was called Huntville Prison, and many of the people of Godley Grove worked there. I'd heard stories, but I'd never actually been there. I was slightly intimidated as we drove up to the complex; all surrounded by three layers of high-rising electrified fences, and topped with rows of intertwined razor wire. There were guard towers scattered throughout the compound, each staffed with a couple of snipers standing as lookouts. Detective Chase had to go through two guarded entrances, showing his identification, and our car was searched at the second guarded entrance before we could enter the main parking lot.

Once inside the main building, we walked through more security checkpoints. An awkward weakness overcame my legs as we drew near the prisoners. This was daunting. We arrived to the section where Gerald Smith, the prisoner who threatened my father and whose fingerprints were found on the envelope in my living room, was being held. After a short wait, Detective Chase was notified that Gerald was waiting for him in the interrogation room. I felt a slight suffocating tightness across my chest. I was sure it was an anxiety attack looming in the distant crevices of my mind. I fought to hold it back.

"In here, Fiona. Wait for me until I come to get you. You'll be able to hear through that speaker and look through the mirror to see what's going on. Take good notes," Detective Chase instructed as he escorted me to the one-way mirror.

I hesitated before looking into the mirror at Gerald Smith. This was a man who threatened my father three years before. My eyes focused on the corner of the room, catching Gerald's silhouette in my peripheral vision. I eased over to gaze at him, still wary that the one-way mirror was working properly. He looked like an average man of forty-years old, hair in a halo around his scalp, beard grown out into a scraggly mess underneath his chin. He wore a bright orange jumpsuit with large black numbering across his chest. I always imagined prisoners to wear the black and white striped uniforms that I had always seen in cartoons and movies. Detective Chase walked into the room and took a seat across the table from Gerald. A uniformed officer trailed in behind him, stepping into the corner of the room behind Gerald.

"Hello Mr. Smith. I'm sorry to take up your time, but I've got a few questions for you."

Gerald Smith nodded at Detective Chase slowly.

"Your fingerprints were found on an envelope today. This envelope was placed in the district attorney's living room and is involved in a kidnapping case and possibly a murder case south of Godley Grove."

Gerald slowly raised his head, gawking at Detective Chase with a malevolent leer.

"Well, Detective. It wouldn't take a rocket scientist to know that I didn't do it. I believe I have a pretty strong alibi," Gerald Smith mocked derisively, speaking each word very slowly. "We through here?"

"I realize that you have an alibi because you are incarcerated. But how can you explain your fingerprints on the envelope?"

Gerald crinkled his forehead, the creases unveiled deep furrows as he appeared to recall what might have happened.

"Was it a smaller, red colored envelope?"

My heart raced at his words. He was linked. No matter how, he was a link. He knew about the red envelopes.

"Yes, it was a red envelope, about four by five inches."

"Why don't you do what you do and look into the visitors here. I'm sure they list who the visitors are, right? Obviously, somebody tried to frame me for this. I'd never seen the kid b'fore, came in during visitin' hours, dropped an envelope he was holdin' and asked me to get it for him off the floor. Claimed he had a back injury and couldn't bend over. I didn't believe it, figured the kid was just lazy. But then he left without talkin' to anyone."

"A kid? What did he look like?" Detective Chase said, pen suspended over his notepad.

"Don't you got cameras in here watching us everywhere, Detective?"

"Please, Mr. Smith. Your cooperation will be noted in your file."

Gerald stared at Detective Chase for an unwieldy minute before he decided to comply with the request.

"A little under six foot, a buzz cut, dark. Probably late teen, early twenties or so."

"Do you recall what he was wearing, Mr. Smith?"

"Do I look like I give a care on what people wear?"

"I will take that as a *no*."

"Thank you for your time," Detective Chase folded his notepad shut and strolled toward the door.

"Detective," Gerald Smith crooned.

"Yes, Mr. Smith."

"Does this mean that I'll get my parole since I cooperated?"

"That reminds me. Why weren't you paroled? We all thought you were as good as released."

"Because I made a threat on that district attorney right before I went to my hearing. Thought that guard was my friend. Turns out, he ain't."

"Well, that would be enough to make sure you stay in here. There's nothing I can do to get you out when you say things like that, Mr. Smith. But I do appreciate you helping me today."

"You found God, Detective?" Gerald Smith inquired in a disturbing tone.

"I go to church every Sunday, Mr. Smith. Good day."

My heart dropped to the pit of my stomach as I heard Mr. Smith admitting to a recent threat against my father. I watched as Detective Chase walked out of the interrogation room.

"Let's go, Fiona," Detective Chase said, popping his head into the waiting area. "Sorry you had to hear that last part. He's a whack job, no doubt. Don't want to make you paranoid, but everybody that goes to jail says they're going to get even with the D.A. It happens in every city, nearly every time. You're dad isn't in real danger, it's all just talk."

"Yea, that was pretty shocking. I knew my dad has had some threats in the past. I'm a skilled eavesdropper."

"I've had my share as the director of the crime lab and medical examiner. You will get your share one day too,

Fiona, if you work in a crime lab or have anything to do with the criminals getting a guilty verdict."

"Great.   Lots to look forward to.   Detective, the envelope, what does that mean?  He was set up?"

"We will check the logs, but I'm assuming the perp wouldn't have used his real identity if he had an active brain cell.  It won't mean anything, especially if it was a busy day in the visiting room.  We'll have a look, nonetheless."

Detective Chase guided us to the reception desk of the visitation wing of the prison.  After showing his credentials, the lady behind the desk exited and returned moments later with a leather bound guest register in hand.  She thumbed through the pages to find the day before, when Gerald Smith reported the visitor had brought the envelope.  She handed it to Detective Chase who began writing each visitor's name down on the roster along with their driver's license numbers.  Detective Chase stopped on one name before slowly raising his head, facing me, staring into my eyes.

"Josh Coleman was here."

# 19 TRANSPLANT

Detective Chase drove me to my home, made sure I was in safely, and told me that he would send updates to the case via email. We had spoken about the case during the drive; he told me that there were officers watching the Coleman house, waiting for Josh's arrival. I was feeling anxious, almost manic.

I rushed into my bedroom, plopped on my pink palace of a bed, and sent Madison a text about Josh Coleman. She immediately sneaked over to my window and lightly tapped on it to get my attention.

"Fiona!" she said in a loud whisper as she lightly knocked on the glass with her knuckles.

I slid open the window, smiling.

"Hey Madison! Can you believe that? Josh was the biggest idiot and used his own name! Hello, how dumb can you be?"

Madison was openly giddy as she galloped in place.

"Isn't that *probable cause* to search their house now?"

"Yes, I think they are watching the house, trying to minimize suspicion for now. I suppose so much time has gone by, if there were any evidence there, it's already gone. Addie knows she is being investigated now, and she's a forensic tech. Unlike her brother, she's no dummy."

Madison calmed her legs and nodded her head, leaning on the windowsill.

"Good point, Fiona. Certainly, she won't allow any evidence to remain in her house."

"Well, now we are certain that Haley is with Josh. The question that remains, is she a *willing* participant?"

I grabbed my large black eight ball toy, shook it up, and the message in the window appeared that said: *definitely, it is a yes.*

We laughed in unison as I chunked it to the floor, waking Luminal from a dead sleep in the corner of the room on his fluffy pink dog bed.

"Let's have a meeting in the morning. Can you set that up? I'm sure it's not too late, and people will check their texts," I instructed as I tapped on the windowsill.

Luminal warily trotted across the room to see what Madison and I were doing at the window. He looked at both of us before his shaggy tail began to wag, and we giggled at the sight of it.

"Certainly. I think it's about time we get together to discuss all of this. So, what do you think, Fiona? Do you think the cases are linked? The locker bomb, kidnapping and murder?"

"Not sure, but I'm nearly sure the locker bomb and kidnapping both belong to Josh Coleman. Addie Coleman, however, has to be involved in this. I've just realized that she's the reason why Josh would have known that a man that threatened my father would be released and would have been a great scapegoat for the kidnapping. Duh!"

I shook my head in disbelief that I had missed that obvious detail.

"But he only would have been released yesterday. He couldn't have been responsible for the locker bomb or first notes, Fiona."

"That doesn't mean that if he is linked to the latest note, that he wasn't orchestrating the others. That would have thrown off the scent to Josh, you know. There was no link. He probably thought that if Gerald Smith was released and linked to the break in at my house, we'd never look at the visitor's log at the prison. He was a man that threatened my father, case closed."

"Yea, but that still makes Josh an idiot for using his real name."

"Josh is no brain surgeon. He's a dummy!"

"I agree!"

"So you think Addie Coleman told Josh to take the envelope to the prison and get Gerald Smith's fingerprints on it?"

"Does it make sense that dummy Josh Coleman would have knowledge of who Gerald Smith is, otherwise?" I asked.

Madison and I stood in a gaze for a moment while we cogitated the issue.

"Nope. Now we need to know Addie Coleman's motive. Maybe to save her brother from being arrested?"

"Makes perfect sense. I'll see you in the morning, Maddie. Let's discuss this with the others. Can you miss soccer practice so we can meet earlier?"

"Sure, I'm sure coach will understand, and if not, I'll just have to run more laps tomorrow. Whatever. Hey, Fiona. What about going to the county office to look up the Foster Manor death records?"

"We need to do that. It's good background story for our case. We'll fit it in sometime really soon."

"Good night!"

"Good night, Fiona! Good night, Luminal!" Madison said, running off across her front yard.

For the first night in a while, I slept like a log. I was finally able to exonerate my brain from trying to sift through evidence. Sensing daylight, I popped out of bed. Luminal was lying on the bed with me. He raised his lazy head up with one eyelid sluggishly struggling to open.

"Hello Luminal! I'm going to school early again today so don't freak out!" I said softly, stroking his back and untangling his fine, black hair.

Giving rushed kisses to my parents and one to Janice on the back of the head as she stood toward the stove, I dashed outside and made it to Maddie's Mini Cooper at the same time she did.

"I'm so excited to discuss the evidence! I can't wait to see what Willow, Lauren and Wolfe have to say about all of this!" I squealed, pulling on my seatbelt.

"I know. I couldn't sleep last night. It all seems so obvious but in a disorganized way, Fiona. I mean, it's clear that Haley ran away with Josh, and Addie tried to cover for him, but why would he bomb your locker in the first place?"

"Donno, maybe it was Haley's idea? I remember that was the morning that she wanted to go to school early and was upset that I was leaving her and would have to ride with my mom. She said there was somebody she wanted to hang out with before school."

"Interesting. Locker bombing seems like something Haley would do. She really doesn't like you, does she? I mean, it seems so dangerous to put a bomb in your locker. She must not have cared if you got hurt."

"Probably thought it was funny, maybe trying to impress Josh, if it was her idea? I don't know, but it makes sense to me. That girl never surprises me," I said, slipping my phone into my backpack.

"Did Detective Chase send you any updates?"

"Oh crap, forgot to check. I was so excited for the meeting, I didn't even think to check my email," I lamented, grabbing my phone, pulling up my email. "Here it is. I'll have to wait to open it from the lab computer. I can't open the password protected documents from my phone for some reason."

"When we have some time, Fiona, give me your phone, and I'll set it all up for you. Can't believe we've gone all this time, and you aren't using your phone to its potential!"

We were the first to arrive on campus. I used my master key to get in, and we briskly walked to the lab. I noticed the wall had been repainted, the carpet cleaned, and the entire bank of lockers had been replaced, including mine. I wondered if the same code applied to the lock. In haste, I decided to forego the locker and bring my backpack with me for the day. I was nearly scared to open the locker and find another envelope. Ignorance sometimes is bliss.

"Let me check my email, and you can pass out the notepads and pens. Everybody said they'd be here, right?"

"Yes, everybody seemed more than excited that we had new evidence to discuss."

I opened my email and clicked on the pdf document from Detective Chase. I scanned it, making additional copies for the club members.

"You won't believe this, Maddie. Detective Chase says that upon hearing our evidence about the tea canister, and Lauren's fingerprints being located on there, he immediately sent an officer to retrieve the tea canister. They did an analysis on the tea bags—

"Good morning you two!" Willow sang as she burst into the laboratory. Lauren was skipping right behind her.

"Hey, Willow! Hi Lauren! Hot off the press, here is the newest," I passed the documents from the printer to Willow and Lauren, the paper still warm.

The enchanting Wolfe Nero vaulted in the room from the hallway in an attempt to startle us. I just couldn't get angry with Wolfe, as he was far too handsome. I passed Wolfe a copy of the report, attempting to hide a scanty smile. The room grew silent as everybody studied the report from Detective Chase.

"Foxglove petals in the tea bags?" Willow chanted.

"Foxglove is a flower, correct?" Lauren said wearily.

"Is that normally found in tea bags?" Wolfe added.

"No, Wolfe. It says at the bottom that the analysis concluded that the teabag had been tampered with, as the staple at the top is not the original staple that the Harbor Tea Company ever uses. Rather, it is a Bostrich brand of staple that is typically found in office environments. Plus, foxglove is poisonous and would never be found in tea."

I rushed over to the internet and typed in the search field *foxglove digitalis*. Multiple sites came up and outlined that the foxglove flower, native to Europe, is also called *Deadman's Bells* or *Witch's Gloves* because it is highly toxic to humans. The medication digitalis is extracted from this flower, however. In low doses, this toxin is an effective heart medication. In a toxic dose, it is fatal. The symptoms of the foxglove toxicity were similar to the symptoms suffered by the victim on the night of his death.

"The poison was put in the teabags!" Lauren shrieked. "That makes sense then." Lauren released a colossal sigh as she released the paper onto the lab counter. "Ms. Foster's prints were also found on the tea canister, so case is solved!"

"Told you guys, Lauren was innocent," Willow remarked boldly.

"Never thought she wasn't innocent, Willow. But now it makes sense," I added sternly. "However, the evidence still stands. Lauren's prints were still found on the tea canister. The teabags were altered, but that doesn't put Lauren in the clear. In fact, now that we know the poison came from the tea canister, we desperately need more evidence to clear Lauren completely from this crime!"

Madison's face grew serious.

"Good point, Fiona. Don't start getting all dramatic, Willow. Look at the case with an unbiased eye. Lauren's fingerprints are on the murder weapon. Glenda Foster's were also on there but she has an alibi for her fingerprints to be on it, as she said she made tea for the first time that day we were there investigating at the manor."

"Maybe she said that to throw us off?" I inquired.

"Okay, then why were Gilroy Foster's prints not on the tea canister? He told Lauren that he made tea every night. Detective Chase's report stated that Glenda Foster was out of town two days prior to the murder and came back in town the night of the murder. The report stated that she went straight to the master bedroom suite and never came back out until Gilroy was discovered. Therefore, her prints were put on the canister after Lauren's prints got on there the night of the murder."

Wolfe Nero looked on pensively, deciding not to fuel the debate further.

# 20 REBORN

The bell rang, releasing my third class of the day. I sprung out into the hallway, and the gossip was more excitable than normal. I hadn't checked my phone since the meeting, so I was oblivious to what had happened.

"Fiona! Fiona!" Madison shouted amongst the crowded hallway.

I waited for her, allowing her to catch up with me before I continued my path to the lunchroom.

"Did you hear?"

"Did I hear what?"

"Josh and Addie Coleman were arrested this morning. They found Haley!"

"What! Is she all right?" I stammered, grabbing for my phone, noting that I had five missed calls and numerous text messages.

"Yes, she's fine. As you suspected, she was with Josh. She actually got arrested too, but your father immediately had her out on bail."

I let out a gigantic sigh; thoughts of my mother's relief flooded my senses. I felt exhilarated, but at the same time, my exhilaration was tinged with intense surges of anger toward Haley for putting my mother through the stress of it all.

"What an embarrassment to my family. What exactly did they get arrested for since it obviously wasn't kidnapping?"

"The FBI made a match to a crowbar that they found underneath Addie Coleman's bed. They got the search warrant, and as soon as they saw Haley and Josh sneaking into the house earlier this morning, they enforced it, rushed in and well, that's that. It was blasted all over the local news; my history teacher let us watch the report."

I shook my head in frustration. I wanted to call my mother back, but I knew I wouldn't be able to get off the phone and still have lunch. I knew my mother was all right and that I could talk to her later, but I did want to hear from Detective Chase.

"I can't believe I am the last one to know about it in school," I laughed, "this should teach me a lesson not to pay attention in my classes and keep checking my phone! Addie Coleman had the crowbar? Amazing," I stared blankly at the floor for a moment, bewildered. "Hey, Maddie, I'll meet you in the cafeteria at our table. I'm going to have to call Detective Chase very quick. Can you carry my tray too?"

"Sure, Fiona. I'll be there waiting for you."

I read a text from my mother who was more than apologetic for how she had treated me for not believing that Haley had been kidnapped. I texted her back and said she had *family goggles* on, and I didn't blame her. I said we'd catch up later and talk about the details.

My father also had text messaged me and said he wasn't surprised at the resolve of the situation and was glad it was over. He loved it when things were resolved, no matter what the outcome.

When I spoke to Detective Chase, his tone of voice seemed curious. He had uncovered evidence related to Ms. Foster that was puzzling him. After absorbing all of the details from him, I scurried into the buzzing lunchroom to find Madison, waiting for me with my tray of cafeteria pizza and French fries. The curious smell of a hundred different types of food was never appetizing, but I knew that I had to eat as we discussed the details.

"Well, if this case couldn't get any weirder, it just did," I sparked, taking my seat and tossing my backpack on the floor in front of me under the table.

"Let's hear it," Madison said, lifting a ketchup glazed French fry to her mouth.

"It's Ms. Foster. We were told she was moving to Canada. Well, this is not true. Guess who she moved in with?"

"Hmmmm," Madison pondered. "Kosmo the supposed homeless dude?"

"Nope! Nic Dalton, her attorney."

Madison paused, folding her bottom lip over her top lip. Her brows crinkled.

"Isn't Kosmo Wilder friends with him and wasn't he not really homeless?"

"Correct. So these three are somehow in cahoots together. Now, we find out how and why."

Madison raised a sculpted eyebrow and pursed her lips.

"It seems quite obvious at this point that one of them is guilty if they are romantically involved."

I took a bite of my factory made pizza and shook my head *yes*.

"They have already taken her in for questioning the moment they discovered that she was staying at Nic's home. Her story is that she had to move out of the manor because the house is haunted and nobody will listen to her. She says that she is in financial dire straights, and Nic Dalton is a family friend, and she is only staying there temporarily."

"I hate to say it, but it makes sense, Fiona," Madison lamented.

"Well, Kosmo Wilder is missing and Nic Dalton is denying that he knows him. The fact that they were in the same fraternity together at MSU and the fact that Nic Dalton's dog hairs were in Kosmo's car reads entirely different."

"I agree."

"One more thing. The Paranormal Science Program at Hartford University was reinstated. Remember Ralph Booner? The guy with Duncan Doyle at the manor the night of the murder?"

"Yea, the one that Lauren said was so hot," Madison chuckled, tossing another French fry into her mouth.

"Well, his parents are mega-loaded and funded the program again, reinstated it completely. Now it is called the *Booner Paranormal Studies Department.*"

Madison's eyes widened as she allowed the news to simmer.

"But wasn't Ralph arrested for murdering his neighbor or something like that?"

"Yes, he was. Remember, he was never found guilty, the charges were actually dropped. Detective Chase said that he had accidentally hit his elderly neighbor while learning how to drive. She was like ninety years old. He backed into her with his car. He never saw her. She was walking her dog across his driveway."

"Holy crap. Oh my gosh, I've almost hit a guy in our neighborhood backing out of my driveway. That's why I park in the street! Remember that?"

"Yes, Maddie. That's why I don't jog in the neighborhood anymore!"

We both chuckled for a minute.

"But why would they call it murder if it was an accident?"

"It was the charge given to Ralph upon arrest because the elderly neighbor and Ralph didn't get along, something about him walking in her grass on occasion. The arresting police officer was coincidentally the elderly neighbor's nephew. It seemed the officer was more than upset at finding his aunt dead on the sidewalk and rushed to judge the situation," I explained.

"Got it. Must have been hard on everybody involved. Unfortunate situation."

I checked the time and noticed we only had a few minutes left before the bell would ring. Madison tapped on the lunch table.

"That's interesting. Well, all of that evidence rather takes some heat off the Hartford boys as far as being the last ones in an argument with the victim before the death. If they were arguing over the program being shut down, it doesn't seem like either would kill over money. Duncan had to know Ralph was that well-off, and judging by the cars and clothes that Duncan and Carden have, it doesn't appear as though they are hurting for cash either."

"It certainly minimizes them as suspects. In addition to the fact that this was obviously premeditated. It would have taken some time to make foxglove teabags. Lauren would have reported suspicious behavior if one of the boys had left the scene for a period of time prior to the murder."

"I concur. We should focus our efforts on the other suspects."

"But what about their opinions about the murder being paranormal or from a curse?"

"Ha! The Ohio Team already discounted the house as having paranormal activity. Second to that, you can't *prove* there is a curse on a house. We can look at the death records, though, and see if there is anything strange going on that might need to be addressed in court one day."

# 21 QUESTIONS

I shot a text to Lauren and Willow, who had both asked to tag along during the courthouse investigation of the Foster Manor. Both of the girls responded that they had made prior plans so Madison and I decided to go to the courthouse without them.

After school, Madison and I drove to the Godley Grove County Courthouse and marched straight to the records department on the basement level. We requested the archived records from the 1800's to the present, and the clerk escorted us into a darkened, musty room at the end of a long, barren hallway. The clerk piled up the microfiche records in a huge stack on the white, dusty Formica countertop next to the archaic microfiche machines. We took our places in the hard, orange plastic chairs in front of antiquated microfiche monitors.

"All right, Madison, let's search for birth, death and marriage records. Let's try to trace the Foster lineage as far back as we can. We know that Richard Foster is the one who built the Foster Manor so let's look for him first," I said warily, inspecting the machinery in front of me.

"Fiona, these things look ancient. Haven't these folks heard of the internet? It'd be so much easier if we could search on the web instead of using these weird contraptions," Madison scorned, fumbling with her microfiche.

"Agreed, but this courthouse hasn't made the updates yet. Just stick the negatives into the slot and use the knob to scan each one of these. It's going to take some time."

Madison finally located the switch on the back rim of the microfiche, and the light glowed, making an eerie cast upon her face. After about thirty minutes of sighs and groans, Madison made the first discovery.

"Fiona, Richard Foster died by gunshot and Eleanor Bendon Foster, his wife, died from unknown causes," Madison reported, scrawling the data in her notebook.

"What year was that? It's the same Richard Foster that built the manor, right?"

"Yea, it is him. Richard died in 1883 and Eleanor died in 1890."

"Well, that doesn't prove much. Are there any articles associated with Richard's gunshot?"

"Not around this time, but it is mentioned in a much later article that I found about the house's curse that Eleanor was the one rumored to have shot him. I actually found that article on the internet, but I printed it and saved a copy."

Another hour passed, and we pressed on through the years, building the pedigree of the Fosters as we viewed the glowing records on the microfiche screen. It was hard to keep track of time in this darkened room.

"Richard and Eleanor had two offspring. Albert and George Foster. Born in 1880 and 1882," Madison reported as she transcribed the dates into her notebook.

"All right, find their death records," I ordered, searching through my own pile of microfiche negatives.

"Hey, got something here. George Foster married Beatrice Hargrove Foster in 1902, and they had two offspring, George the second and Catherine. I'm after their death records now."

"Found the death records of Albert and George. Albert died of a suicide by hanging. George was poisoned. I found a news article, and it said that his wife, Beatrice, was the main suspect and jumped off the second story balcony onto the marbled foyer, killing herself. Her death certificate said blunt force trauma to the head from the fall. Now, what about their offspring, let's find their death records."

Madison bounced in her orange plastic chair as she wrote down the data from the microfiche.

"Got it. You won't believe this, Fiona. Catherine died via accidental death by George the second, by gunshot, and George the second died via homicide by gunshot."

I shook my head in disbelief. The evidence of homicides and suicides that occurred in the manor was insurmountable.

"Somebody needs to take their guns away!" I shrieked. "Found a marriage record for George the second and Victoria Radley Foster. Married in 1927, had one child. Gilroy Foster. There's our victim."

"All right, please don't say it…Victoria was murdered? You find her death certificate yet?"

"She killed herself via gunshot."

"And remember, Gilroy and Glenda's two sons died at only ten years old, unknown causes. Here is one more. Eleanor Foster had another child, seven years after her husband died. Her name is Francis Foster, and there is no father listed on her birth certificate. Francis was raised in an orphanage as her mother died during childbirth. Here is Francis's death record; she died of natural causes at an old age. Funny, she's the only one in the lineage that grew up away from the manor. In fact, she probably never even entered the manor if she was born in the hospital and went straight to the orphanage."

"That's wild. Most likely coincidence. Well, I can definitely agree it sounds like a very bad string of bad luck and a great case for the argument of gun control. However, I wouldn't go all paranormal just yet. Criminal activity runs in families, it's proven, it's carried in the genes."

"I suppose. Well, I think we have enough here."

Back at home, we arranged the pedigree on a poster board. It did appear as a strange trend for a family's lineage to all die such untimely, tragic deaths. I still wasn't going to give in to the curse or paranormal explanation of things. People learn by behavior, and criminal tendencies have been shown to be inheritable. That was a good enough explanation for me.

Madison and I hung out in my bedroom for a spell, sifting through the evidence. Using my corkboard, we arranged our data just like the one at the police station. We had evidence stuck on the board with pushpins that we moved around like puzzle pieces, trying to pull together the story.

"I get that this evidence is crazy, meaning it does support the *cursed house* theory. So we need to investigate some real suspects before the media gets wind of this and goes to town with it. We don't want the residents of Godley Grove buying into this madness, Madison. It will cause havoc in the jury room once they arrest a suspect and they go to trial."

"Pick a suspect. Who are you feeling right now?" Madison prodded, lying back on my fluffy pink comforter.

"Let me give the honor to you, Madison. Who do you want to investigate?" I said playfully.

"Let's go see Nic Dalton, Fiona."

"Madison, are you crazy? Why would we go see that man? Don't you remember how pompous he was?"

"Don't care. I'm firing up the Mini Cooper. I know exactly where his office is. If you don't come, I'll go alone."

I grudgingly climbed into the Mini Cooper. I thought this was a horrible idea. I remembered meeting this man the night of the paranormal investigation at the manor. I associated him with the rattlesnakes for some reason. He had arrived soon after the snake bit Lauren. He reminded me of a snake. I had hoped that Madison would choose someone easier to focus on.

We pulled up into a front spot in front of his office next to a car that I remembered as his, a relatively new model silver SAAB. Nausea settled into my throat as I looked at the stuck on lettering in the window. *Nic Dalton, Esquire. Real Estate Attorney.*

"Ugh, this guy makes me creep out, Madison!"

"Fiona, let's push through this. He has some questions to answer. You might be creeped out for a reason – because he's a murderer! I realize the police have him down as a suspect and are investigating him. However, he might accidentally tell us some things, not realizing that we actually work with the police and they listen to us."

We forged through to a cheaply decorated reception area. There were old, wooden chairs spread out like a classroom on top of a thin, crimson carpet. A small television was playing on top of a plywood decorative table. The receptionist was busy filing her fingernails, watching videos on YouTube, and tried her best to ignore that we had walked into the reception area. We asked her ever so politely if we could speak to Mr. Dalton. Obviously not wanting to be bothered, she waved us toward his door.

"Mr. Dalton," Madison faded in as she slid her hand on his office door, pushing it further ajar.

Nic Dalton had a dumpy stature at probably five foot six. He was losing his gray hair that trimmed around his face in a rounded mane. He removed his reading glasses from his globular cheeks, gazing at us callously with his cobalt eyes. His skin sagged carelessly around his sockets.

"Yes?" he inquired unpleasantly, placing the glasses on top of a pile of files.

"Mr. Dalton, we met at the Foster Manor. My name is Fiona Frost. This is Madison Christie," I said cautiously, standing by the wooden chair in front of his desk, waiting for him to gesture for us to take a seat.

He stared at us, studying our features, examining what we had in our hands. He gaped at the chairs in front of us and gave a snub of a nod toward them, "you have five minutes."

"Thank you, Mr. Dalton. I don't know if you are aware, but I have a federal grant that funds a forensic science training program. We echo the police department's efforts during criminal cases in Godley Grove as part of our program. If you don't mind, we have some questions for you," I outlined, hoping that he would be receptive.

"Shoot, now you have four minutes."

"Is it true that Ms. Glenda Foster is living with you now?"

"We are adults, you are a child. That is none of your business."

"All right, Mr. Dalton. Did you know Kosmo Wilder before the murder of Gilroy Foster?"

"I have no idea who that man is."

"But isn't it true that he was in the same fraternity as you in college?"

"I don't know. There were many members of my fraternity and it was long ago. Do you remember every toddler that went to daycare with you? I assume not."

"Where were you the night of the murder of Gilroy Foster?"

"Ha! There's the cliché question of the day. Knew that one was coming. I was in Las Vegas, little girl. It's already been verified by the police department. Your time is up."

"One more question, Mr. Dalton, if you don't mind. Why were your prints on Mr. Foster's medicine cabinet?"

"Mr. Foster asked me to retrieve his medication for him on occasion. That doesn't make me a murderer. It makes me a family friend. You should be talking to the real suspects, little one. Don't waste your time on me."

# 22 PLAN

Later that evening, after I got home, I noticed Haley's door was shut. I heard heavy metal music blaring. I knew that she was in there. I decided to leave her alone for now, but I did need to follow up with some questions about the locker bomb case and Josh Coleman.

I called Detective Chase and explained that Madison and I had gone to Nic Dalton's office, and our efforts were futile. Detective Chase explained that it was a rookie move for us to go there, and he could have warned us it wasn't going to be productive. I had a feeling that would be the case, but I allowed Madison to talk me into it so I was just as much at fault.

Detective Chase described that Nic Dalton did have an established alibi, and now that the digitalis medication wasn't the poison, but rather the foxglove plant in the teabag was the origin of the toxicity, he was nearly nixed from the suspect list.

I asked Detective Chase if it would be worth our time to visit Addie Coleman in jail. I explained that she would probably reveal information about her brother if she weren't, in fact, guilty of any real crimes. Exchanging cooperation for immunity in the case would be more than enticing to her, I guessed. Detective Chase thought it was a great idea, and we arranged the visit for the following afternoon.

I never saw Haley that evening or the next morning. I supposed she was humiliated, trying to stay low-key in the house. My mother said she had come straight home, grabbed some crackers and hadn't so much as peeped her head out of her room.

The next day at school, I was feeling exhilarated. I was in such a good mood, time flew by, and I was nearly able to get the case off my mind completely. Madison and I sat with Wolfe Nero at lunch, and he kept us so entertained, we didn't even discuss the case at all. Hanging around Wolfe always put me in an instant good mood.

Madison gave me a ride to the police station after school. She had to go shopping with her mother. Her mother still needed her to translate for her at times, as she moved from Japan after meeting Madison's father when she was twenty-two. She learned English on the fly when she moved to Godley Grove, and she still had trouble communicating. We found her to be more than charming when she didn't know what we were saying.

"Thanks, Maddie. See ya later!"

"Bye, Fiona! Good luck with Addie!"

I strolled into the police station, and the familiar strawberry cream-soaked dirty sock aroma bounded through my nostrils. Ms. Spinks waved hello and buzzed me in the green door. Detective Chase met me in the hallway and ushered me out into the parking lot to his beige Impala.

"Well, this should be fun," he chuckled, buckling his seatbelt and pulling out of the parking lot.

"Does Addie Coleman know we're coming?"

"No. It's never good to give the suspect a head's up. We want to catch her off guard, so she doesn't have time to think about what to say or contact anybody to discuss it."

"Makes sense. I guess when you're in prison, it's not like you are going to be too busy to talk or anything."

Once we arrived to the prison, I found that I had already become impervious to the lines of security we had to go through. I could see how one day, the nerves would subside, and the routine would become calculated if I had to interview a prisoner for something. Just like with dead bodies, as long as you ease into it, and don't dive in head first to freezing water, I found that you could get used to anything.

Detective Chase decided that it would be good if I sat in on the interview with Addie. He was mistaken that we were friends, however. I didn't know if I should mention that Addie was snarky to me and had mentioned that I needed to go to prom and stop my training in forensic science. Something in the back of my mind wanted me to taunt Addie by being on the other side of the table as she sat there shackled, in a bright orange jumpsuit. I always tried to live by karma, but it was tempting not to deliver my own dose of karma to her.

"All right, here we go. Fiona, just follow my lead, we need her right now," Detective Chase said, opening the door to the interrogation room.

Addie was already sitting there in the room, waiting. We said hello, and Addie seemed humbled. She wasn't the same snob that greeted me the day I saw her at the evidence desk. I found myself feeling guilty for wanting to take pleasure in this meeting.

"Addie, I hate to see you on that side of the table," Detective Chase said, bowing his head.

"You know I had nothing to do with it, Detective Chase. Can't you just talk to them and have me released?"

"Well, that is a possibility. You know that you are eligible for bail, have you contacted a bail bondsman?"

"Not yet. I really don't have the money to pay them," Addie lamented.

"I'll see what I can do, but first I need your help. You do know that the crowbar that was matched to the tool used in the locker bombing case at the high school was found underneath your bed in your bedroom at your home, right?"

"Yes, but—

"And it had your fingerprints on it."

"I know, but I found it in the hallway of my home and just put it there to get it out of the way. I think my brother might have set me up."

"Well, that's what you get for living with such a person," I added without a careful choice of my words.

Detective Chase shot a glance of disapproval to me.

"Sorry, Addie. I didn't mean it," I mumbled. "I actually live with a not-so-nice person as well."

"No offense taken, Fiona."

"Addie, the circumstances surrounding the red envelopes are also being looked at. The first note that Fiona brought in was lost after you received it, the second note only had your fingerprints, and the third had a prisoner's prints that you might have believed was being paroled. Because of a fluke that he couldn't shut his mouth about Fiona's dad at the last second, he remained in jail. However, you wouldn't have known that he wasn't being released because you were on administrative leave. All of the pieces of evidence surrounding your involvement in the kidnapping and the locker bomb are pretty strong," Detective Chase lectured.

"I know it seems weird, but it's all coincidence, I am innocent."

"I have a few questions, Addie. I need your help. Do you have any information about the Foster Manor murder?"

Addie sat up straight, her face melted into a state of anxiety.

"No, why would I?"

"We are starting to believe that all of these events are connected. Why would you," Detective Chase cleared his throat and continued, "why would Josh want Fiona off the Gilroy Foster case?"

"I didn't know he did?"

Detective Chase looked at me with a harsh expression. He stood up from his chair.

"All right, thank you Addie. I see this is a dead end."

Addie Coleman dropped her head in deep thought. The room was silent until Detective Chase turned the door handle.

"Wait!"

We twisted around to face Addie, a lonely tear streamed down her cheek.

"You've suddenly remembered something?"

"I didn't want to say it before because Fiona is here. But you should really look into Lauren Hope."

My blood boiled.

"Lauren Hope? Why do you say?"

"She was there the night of the murder. Her prints were on the tea canister. She made the tea for the victim; the tea contained the foxglove toxins."

Detective Chase quickly lunged toward Addie, raising a shaggy eyebrow.

"How did you know it had foxglove?"

Addie's face paled, she was openly nervous as she searched for her words.

"I heard that it did. It wasn't his medication, right?" she fumbled, hands trembling.

Detective Chase drew in a deep breath, staring at her mannerisms for a long minute.

"What else do you know, Addie?"

"Lauren was there with two boys from Hartford University. Josh heard her in the hallway talking to somebody about this guy, Ralph Booner. She said she would do absolutely anything to go out with him. If Ralph got into an argument with Mr. Foster the night of the murder. Well, I'm just saying that Lauren needs to be given a very hard look as a suspect."

I felt as though my heart was going to burst through my chest wall. Infuriation filled my veins as I clenched my teeth forcefully.

"Liar! Detective Chase, she is a liar!" I exploded, pointing at Addie's petrified face.

"Fiona, please calm down. You said yourself that Lauren is a tad boy crazy, and I don't think it is far-fetched to say that she wanted to date this boy. But Addie, that's a little crazy to say that a high school girl, one with no criminal history, would murder someone to date a boy."

"That is what I am saying Detective Chase."

I had to get out of the room before I physically attacked her. I had never had such raw emotion pushing me toward violence. I looked at Detective Chase in desperation, feeling the blood redden my face. He must have seen the rage brewing inside of me as he nodded and instantly turned to Addie.

"Thank you for your cooperation, Addie," Detective Chase motioned for me to follow him out of the room.

My vision was blurred, the heat seethed from my face.

"She is trying to throw you off. She obviously knows more details about the murder than she should. She's involved!"

Detective Chase patted me on the shoulder and nodded.

"I'm not going to rule out that someone in the crime lab didn't give her an update. Let's go check the visitation roster and see if any familiar names are there. It would have to be someone recent, however, because we just found out ourselves that it was the foxglove flower and not the pill bottle."

We sprinted to the reception desk of the visitor's area and found ourselves in a déjàvu situation, waiting for the guest register from the previous day. We carefully combed the visitors, and luckily, there was only a handful. Each one of the visitors had an established history of weekly visits on the register for other prisoners. We checked with the guard and asked if Addie had made any phone calls in the last twenty-four hours, and they checked the phone records. One call to her attorney was made. It was very unlikely that her attorney knew about the foxglove from the crime lab.

Detective Chase and I deliberated the situation in the lobby. We hatched a plan and then waited in the interrogation room once again for them to bring Addie back to speak to us.

# 23 FATHER

We explained to the guard that we needed to see Addie Coleman again. He escorted us into the interrogation room where we waited for over ten minutes.

Detective Chase received a phone call from the crime lab. I anxiously listened to his side of the conversation, barely following the revelations on the other end. When he hung up, he immediately explained what his lab had reported to him.

"Well, Fiona. It appears as though a witness has come forth with news about Glenda Foster and Nic Dalton. It seems as though they might have been involved in life insurance fraud and possibly forgery of Gilroy Foster's Last Will and Testament. But funny thing is, at the same time, it counts them out as suspects in a way."

"How could that be possible?"

"Well, Nic Dalton's paralegal is the witness. She reported that Nic switched out the Last Will and Testament of Gilroy Foster the day after the murder. If either Nic or Glenda were the murderer, don't you think they would have done this *prior* to the murder? It seems utterly careless, like a second thought, a reaction to the murder."

"Did the first will give anything to Glenda? Doesn't she automatically get half of everything because she was married to Gilroy?"

"No. The original will was filed by Gilroy six months ago and gave his entire estate to the city of Godley Grove."

"If Nic and Glenda were involved together, why wouldn't Nic say something six months ago?"

"The paralegal said their relationship only kindled recently. Glenda was going to file for divorce, but she had signed a prenuptial agreement with Gilroy Foster and was worried about losing the money from the Foster estate."

"What's that?"

"A prenuptial agreement states that she won't get any money if they divorce."

"She is obviously the murderer! She wanted his money so she did it!"

"Don't you think that if you planned to murder your husband with poison, you'd have all of your ducks in a row *before* the act? Nic and Glenda reacted. They didn't expect him to die that night. They might have been planning to kill him, but it wouldn't make sense that they would kill him and then have a kneejerk reaction like that by burning the copies of his original will in a barrel behind the manor the night of the murder. In addition, the life insurance policy that Glenda was about to purchase on Gilroy hadn't been filed yet. It was in Nic's office being reviewed. The day after the murder, Nic had his paralegal back date the policy before she filed it so it would appear as though it was filed previously to his death. The paralegal said that Nic knew many people over at the insurance company, and they would have done anything he asked them to do. They also altered the death certificate so Glenda could be paid. See, on a life insurance policy, if it's murder, you don't collect the money. The paralegal felt guilty about being asked to commit fraud and quit her job. She's moving to Silver Springs. She said she couldn't work for a man like Nic any longer, and that is why she was coming forth with the evidence."

"Yea, I guess that all makes sense."

"Something else, Fiona. The witness reported that Nic had planned to drive to your high school to threaten you to stop investigating him and Glenda. He figured you were sharp and might figure something out about them. He obviously decided against it, but he was going to issue you a legal letter to never step foot on his property."

"Wow. I did see his car drive through the parking lot at the high school."

"One more thing. Kosmo Wilder. Well, he was an old college friend of Nic's who fell on hard times lately. He wasn't homeless. His car was never broken down. He was hired by Nic to infiltrate his way into the manor. I'm sure we'll never know what they had planned for Kosmo to do, but Glenda was in on it and knew that Kosmo was going to show up at the manor that night."

"It didn't make sense that she'd allow a *presumed homeless man* to stay at the manor. What widow, grieving for her husband, would allow a homeless man that she had never met to stay in her home? It just wouldn't happen, and we were fools to believe it for a second. Grief or no grief, a stranger living in your home is creepy!"

"Especially after an unsolved murder!"

"No doubt! Maybe he was there to try to fool everybody into thinking the house was haunted? Maybe his job was to create ghost effects when nobody was looking?"

"That might be a great explanation, Fiona. If the house was certified as haunted, they'd be able to make a ton of money off the estate."

After a few more minutes, we sent a guard to see what the problem was with Addie being escorted back into the room. After another ten minutes, the guard came back with news that Addie had decided not to speak with Detective Chase and had elected to make a phone call instead.

"Can't you make her talk to you, Detective Chase?"

"It wouldn't do any good. She has the right to remain silent."

My phone rang. Forgetting to put it on silent, I grabbed the phone and noticed my father's picture on my screen.

"It's my father," I said, puzzled. I slid my finger across the screen to answer, "Hello Dad!"

*"Fiona. I was told that you are currently at the prison attempting to speak with Addie Coleman?"*

"Yes, uh, that is correct," I said cautiously as I gazed at Detective Chase with a guarded expression.

*"I just spoke with Addie Coleman's attorney. She's decided to make a plea bargain. I understand that you are with*

*Detective Chase. Will both of you meet me at the police station, she wants to talk to us all via Skype,"* Lewis Frost boomed from the other end of the line.

I looked over at Detective Chase who was in a panic, thumbing through his recent calls. He noticed a missed call from my father and showed me the screen, a despondent mask upon his face.

"Dad, we'll meet you at the station. We're leaving now."

Detective Chase looked into my eyes with confusion as I hung up the phone and stood up toward the door.

"Addie called her attorney. She told him to call my father and make a plea bargain. She wants to speak to all of us together so we're meeting at the police station. Are the FBI agents still there?"

"No, once the kidnapping case was solved, they headed out. They don't have jurisdiction over the local murder case," Detective Chase outlined.

"I'm relieved. I was cringing at the thought of having to see Agent Jonas again!"

"Not such a delightful chap, huh?" Detective Chase laughed.

Discussing the hypothetical reasons why Addie Coleman wanted to plea bargain, the car ride to the station was filled with chaotic energy.

We filed into the conference room of the police station; my father was in the seat in the middle of the room facing the large screen on the wall. His lanky assistant was situated by the media center and pulled up Skype on the screen. We took our seats and waited for Addie's call.

"Hello Mr. Frost," Detective Chase said, pouring himself a glass of water.

"Good afternoon, Detective Chase. Hello, Fiona. Addie will call in with her attorney at any moment."

"Do you know what her story is? She was just trying to pin it on Lauren Hope at the prison when we talked to her. That's not going to get her a plea agreement, right?" Detective Chase stammered.

"We will listen to what she has to say and then discuss. I'm no fool, Detective. I know when to make a deal."

"Yes sir. I know," Detective Chase responded sternly. "I was just taken off guard by what she said at the prison."

We sat in awkward silence, waiting for Skype to alert us to her call. Within a few minutes, her face appeared on the screen, and her attorney's face could be seen over her shoulder. My father sat up in his chair, surveying the screen.

"Ms. Coleman. Mr. Finstein," Lewis Frost said boldly.

"Hello Mr. Frost. My name is Addie Coleman. I've been arrested, falsely, in the locker bomb case. My brother Josh Coleman was also arrested for the crime as well as for the kidnapping of your niece, Haley."

"Yes, I am aware of the details of the cases, Ms. Coleman. I hear you have something to tell us about the Foster murder?" Lewis Frost said coldly.

Addie Coleman turned around to whisper something to her attorney; her black stringy locks were in full disarray. She swung her head back around to face the webcam, the camera lighting made her dark brown eyes appear as darkened hollow circles.

"First, I want to say that I did not have knowledge that my brother was with the kidnapping victim, Haley Frost, until the morning that we were arrested. That was the first time he brought her to the house. I have no knowledge of where they were before that time."

"Understood," Lewis Frost chanted.

"Second, I did not know that the crowbar was the tool used in the locker bomb at the high school. My brother left it in the hallway of my home, and I foolishly picked it up and put it under my bed to get it out of the way. I'm a lazy cleaner, I suppose."

"Noted," Lewis Frost sounded.

Addie turned around to her attorney once again for a long moment. She twisted back around to the webcam and cleared her throat.

"Third, I have no knowledge of what happened to the first kidnapping note that Fiona submitted to me at the evidence desk. It simply disappeared. I believe the courier misplaced it. She isn't supposed to submit evidence anyway, so I didn't think it was that important. I do admit that I mishandled the second envelope that was analyzed by the Silver Springs document analyst. My fingerprints were on it because I failed to put gloves on when I placed it in the evidence bag. I was reprimanded by Detective Chase for that mistake."

"Detective?" Lewis Frost inquired as he gazed at Detective Chase.

"Yes, that is correct, Mr. Frost. Fiona is not supposed to submit evidence on open cases but this envelope was evidence involving her personally that she discovered and it wasn't on an open case. At least, we had no idea that it could have been connected. I did officially reprimand Ms. Coleman for not using gloves on the second envelope submitted for evidence to the Godley Grove Crime Lab. She failed to follow the laboratory protocol of wearing gloves while processing evidence."

"Noted, Ms. Coleman. Please continue," Lewis Frost added sternly.

"I spoke to my brother on the phone, and I might have mentioned that a criminal, Gerald Smith, was to be released from prison. I was unaware that divulging this information to my brother was a criminal act as this is public information," Addie said before she was interrupted from her attorney sitting behind her. She turned around, whispered to her attorney for a moment, and then faced the webcam to continue, "I meant to say that it is not a crime to divulge common knowledge information. I did tell my brother Josh that Gerald Smith was being released from prison, but anybody that reads the paper could have known that. It wasn't against the law to tell him. I knew that Fiona went to the same school as my brother so he would be interested to know that Gerald Smith had threatened Fiona's family. I was just making conversation. If my brother went to visit Mr. Smith in prison, I had absolutely nothing to do with it nor did I have knowledge of it."

"Understood," Lewis Frost echoed.

Addie sat awkwardly in silence as she stared into the webcam. Turning around to her attorney once more, she drew in a huge breath. She was bouncing ever so slightly in her chair, obviously nervous.

"You should speak to Walter Hargrove about the murder."

Silence ensued in the conference room as my father stared at the screen on the wall. Detective Chase drew his eyebrows into a confused gaze as he bounced back and forth from the screen to my father's face.

"Walter Hargrove, the groundskeeper at the Foster Manor?" Detective Chase perked up in his chair, relaxing his eyebrows.

"Yes. He is my father," Addie's voice wavered. "You should also know that my grandparents' names are Victor Hargrove and Francis Foster Hargrove. You should be able to figure the rest out, you're smart."

"Francis *Foster* Hargrove?" Lewis Frost said softly. "Are you saying that you are an heir to the manor? Are you related to the Fosters?"

"That is exactly what I am telling you. Francis was a black sheep of the family. The Fosters didn't care for the Hargrove family very much, the history was buried. Richard and Eleanor, the ones who built the manor in the mid eighteen hundreds, refused to admit they had a daughter once she moved out and married Victor Hargrove. It was shameful to them."

"So what does this have to do with Walter? What is his motive for killing Gilroy?"

"Walter knew that Glenda Foster had recently fallen in love with Nic Dalton. Gilroy and Glenda despised each other for years. They were not in love. Not since their twins died in 1980. They always blamed each other and hadn't even spoken to each other in years. My father knew that he could blackmail Glenda out of the manor once he got rid of Gilroy Foster. Not only that, he was trying to scare Glenda out of the manor as well so she definitely wouldn't try to stay there. He's the one that unleashed the chandelier, trying to make you all think the house was haunted. He bragged about it to me. The manor is cursed, it does drives people to murder, but it isn't haunted. My father is the rightful heir to the estate, but he is definitely a man to be feared."

Detective Chase appeared baffled, "Why would you tell us this, Addie? If he is your father—

"He moved to Foster Manor as the groundskeeper way before we were born. I don't really know him. I strongly believe that he murdered our mother, Nancy Coleman, whom he never married. He made up a story that she moved away to Louisiana, abandoning us, but I don't believe it. I was close to my mother; she'd never just leave us. He only recently came into our lives, telling us that we could move into the manor once it was all his. We figured he was only using us. And he did tell me," Addie engaged into a stifled cry, gasping for air, she continued, "I think he murdered Gilroy's mother as well. Gilroy's mother hired him many, many years ago. When she found out he was an heir to the manor, I think that is when he killed her. My mother pretty much told me the story. My mother knew things about Walter Hargrove, and I think that is why he killed her as well. He knew I worked in the crime lab. He knew that if he were a suspect in the murder, I could turn him in. He has watched over Josh and me, trying to get us to commit to moving into the manor with him. Recently, he was trying to force us both to live there."

Addie burst into another fit of tears.

"It's all right, Addie. You are doing the right thing," Detective Chase assured.

"He's a very intelligent man. If you are going to catch him, you better hurry."

"Thanks, Ms. Coleman. You've been a big help. If your story checks out, we will work on the plea bargain," Lewis Frost said, scribbling notes into his leather bound notepad.

Addie's reddened expression was riddled with degradation as she shouted, "Fiona!"

I leaned into the webcam so she could get a clear picture of me before I responded, "Yes, Addie?"

"Josh and Haley didn't mean to hurt you. You were supposed to meet with your bio teacher that morning, all the way down the hall, away from the explosion. It was just a prank, a *mean* prank, but it wasn't supposed to be that big of an explosion, and they definitely didn't mean for you to get hurt. My brother had never built a bomb before. However, that's why Haley didn't want to go home. That's why they staged the kidnapping. Mr. Frost, my brother didn't kidnap your niece. I apologize for him being a rotten influence on her, but she was more than willing—"

"That is enough, Ms. Coleman," her attorney scolded as he walked over toward the Skype connection. "Mr. Frost, I'll be in touch," Mr. Finstein said, as he disconnected the Skype call.

# 24 ANSWERS

It felt surreal. I gave my father a quick kiss on the cheek before climbing into the car with Detective Chase. For a moment, I felt as though it might be my last kiss but quickly snapped out of the drama in my head.

"Fiona, do exactly what Detective Chase instructs you to do," Lewis boomed, giving a stern eye.

"Yes, Daddy."

The adrenaline coursed through my veins faster than my blood could travel as I buckled my seat belt. I had never observed an arrest before, especially not one of a murderer. What would it feel like to witness a murderer be arrested? I could only place myself in the countless crime dramas that I had watched on television, but no matter what I did in my head, the moment didn't feel real to me. It didn't feel as though I was in my own body, and it was though the world around me was a 360-degree television screen.

The police pulled away from the station, and we trailed the speeding caravan in the Impala. My heart picked up the pace as the Impala accelerated. The sirens emanating from the caravan in front of us failed to maintain the same rhythm, which made the noise overwhelming and chaotic.

"Do you think he will be there, Detective Chase? Didn't the movers say that everybody had moved out of the manor?" I shouted above the noise.

"No idea. He hasn't been a main suspect so we haven't been tracking him. We were duped, I guess you could say. It's making more sense as I think about it. You know, he has a greenhouse. I'll bet the foxglove plants are in there. We should have thought of looking there, I feel reckless. As far as the movers, they were only moving things from the manor. We didn't even think about the groundskeeper's quarters. However, since he was attempting to force his kids to move into the manor with him when he got rid of Gilroy and Glenda, we're pretty sure he's still there."

The sirens' energy, and the speed of the car seemed to build in the forefront of my consciousness, and my anxiety was replaced with exhilaration. This was definitely something I could get used to.

"Do you think he will put up a fight?"

"Well, even if he does, he's not that big of a guy. I mean, he's tall, but if you blew on him hard enough, he's likely to fall over," Detective Chase chuckled.

"But he could have a weapon, right? What if he shoots at us? We've already established he is a murderer."

"Fiona, don't worry. We know what we're doing. The front line will have bulletproof vests on and have been extensively trained. We stay back where it is safe until we are cleared to enter the scene. We will collect evidence once they arrest him. You can shadow, but as usual, do not touch *anything*. We will not be part of the arrest. We're meeting the rest of the crime lab there to investigate his quarters, the greenhouse, etc."

The flashing blue and red lights bounded through the iron gates, and each police car parked erratically in the circle drive, surrounding the estate. Detective Chase pulled the Impala behind the police car barricade. The heavily equipped officers piled out of their front row vehicles, rushing over to the quarters behind the manor, scattering into a formation around the residence. They moved in such a carefully planned effort, it was as if they were a rehearsed screenplay, and we were the audience. They waited for each member of the team to give a silent signal before knocking on the front door, shouting that they were the police. After a few minutes, a baffled Walter Hargrove opened the door and ambled out onto his porch with his lanky arms held high in the air.

They immediately handcuffed Walter and pulled him toward the nearest police car. Detective Chase gestured for me to exit the car. We stood next to the Impala with the rest of the crime lab personnel until the police officially cleared the scene.

"I don't understand what's going on here," Walter shouted, his bald head glowing brightly in the sunlight.

It still seemed like a dream to me. I was witnessing the arrest of a murder suspect, and it was hard to face the reality of it. I shook my head ever so quickly to snap out of my trance.

"You are being arrested for the murder of Gilroy Foster. You have the right to remain silent," the arresting officer chanted as he escorted Walter Hargrove to his car.

"But wait! I don't understand. I'm innocent! You've got the wrong guy! Glenda Foster is the one who did it! She was burning his last will and testament the night of the murder. It was the will that shut her out of everything!"

"Tell it to the judge, Walter," the officer said, shoving him into the back seat and shutting the door of the car.

"Well, Fiona. Let's follow the team into the greenhouse and see what they find. Stand back, and remember to not touch anything or we will lose the evidence. Keep your arms folded at all times in case you make it in a picture or video."

"Yes sir!"

We piled into the greenhouse on the side of Walter's house. It was well maintained, and within a few minutes, Pablo Sanchez from the crime lab identified the foxglove plant in the very back corner of the greenhouse. Pablo was the resident biologist in the lab. I thought he was a funny guy, and he had a strange fascination with seahorses.

The team took samples of the potting soil from nearly every pot in the greenhouse. They followed up with bagging the evidence of the foxglove plants before clearing the greenhouse and moving into Walter Hargrove's residence.

On Walter Hargrove's computer, they uncovered emails Walter had sent to his kids, Addie and Josh Coleman, over the past year. All of the emails outlined how horrible their mother was, and how Walter would, one day, be the heir of the Foster estate. The more recent emails demanded that the kids move into the manor with him when he inherited it from Gilroy and Glenda. He even outwardly threatened Addie and Josh in some of the correspondences. It was apparent that Addie Coleman had told the truth to my father. I felt ashamed because I actually found myself feeling sorry for Addie and even the school bully - Josh Coleman.

I now understood that Josh had a more than repulsive childhood that most people could never understand. It was most likely true that his own father killed his mother and probably more of his family members at the Foster Manor including Gilroy Foster. I could almost comprehend how that could make a child mean and emotionless as they grew up. I'd never pardon a bully or any of a bully's actions as far as what Josh Coleman had done to his victims at school, but I could at least recognize how he got the hideous way that he was as a person. I suddenly had a rush of appreciation for the cards that I was dealt with having such a good home and a strong upbringing. I always appreciated what I was given, but I realized that I was more than fortunate.

We ventured out into the garage of Walter's home. There was a car in the middle of the two-car garage with a white vinyl cover over it. The officer pulled the cover off and exposed the dark green Honda. The front end was smashed, black paint streaks and chips were scattered throughout the dents. No doubt, the black paint came from my VW. There was no license plate, no registration, nothing. Detective Chase called in the vehicle identification number and found that the car had been stolen a month prior from the Silver Springs Public Library.

"I wonder if those tires will match the second unknown treads found the day after the murder?"

"I'll bet they will, Fiona."

I looked over to the wall of the garage and noticed multiple aquariums on a steel shelf. I pointed to it, nudging Detective Chase.

"Well, I suppose we know where the snakes came from," Detective Chase sounded as he lifted a mesh cover from one of the aquariums.

There were at least five aquariums on this shelf containing various types of snakes, each with a handwritten piece of masking tape on the top rim of the container. The masking tape label had what appeared to be the species name. The tank with *Rattlesnake* was empty.

"I suppose that would be more than a coincidence that the snake that bit Lauren used to live in that tank."

"You are most likely correct, Fiona," Detective Chase snickered, dropping the mesh covering and gesturing for the crime scene photographer to get the pictures of the tanks.

The crime lab spent the next few hours processing the evidence at Walter Hargrove's house. They left the scene feeling more than confident that they had more than enough evidence for a solid conviction. Not that they needed it, but they even uncovered multiple shards of blue glass that were a probable match to the Grecian vase broken at the murder scene that were found in various locations of Walter's home. Detective Chase told me that it was the most concrete case he had ever investigated, and he thanked me and my lab from the bottom of his heart for our assistance in solving the crime. I couldn't have felt more honored.

The next morning, the club meeting was scheduled for 6 AM. The members were filled with a crazed eagerness as I described the events of the past twenty-four hours. Each member expressed regret that they hadn't been part of the experience, but everybody was glad that the case was resolved, and that Detective Chase acknowledged the club's involvement in the case. It was our first murder case, and we had each been a part of the resolution in our own way.

"Fiona, have you even spoken to Haley yet?"

"Ha! Madison, funny thing that you say that. She apologized to me this morning. Right before she left for the airport. She is going away to a boarding school in New Zealand."

"Your dad wasn't joking, was he?"

"It was only a matter of time, Madison. She needs to get her head on straight. This will be the best thing for her. She's just lucky that she wasn't there when Josh built the bomb and wasn't there when Josh put it in my locker, or she'd be doing jail time just like him!"

"What ever happened to Addie Coleman?"

"She was released. Got probation for hindering a police investigation. Her forensic career is over; she'll have to find a new line of work. I heard that she might inherit the estate of Gilroy Foster, though. It depends on how they interpret his original will if they can find it. He was hiding a bunch of cash from Glenda Foster, supposedly, and this cash isn't covered in his original will that he left to the city of Godley Grove. She'll probably be set for a while, so don't feel too bad for her."

"Won't Glenda get it all since she was Gilroy's wife?"

"There's something wicked going on with her and Nic Dalton since there's evidence that they were actually trying to hatch a plan to murder ole' Gilroy. They tried to hire someone about a month ago to kill him, and he went to the cops upon hearing of Gilroy's death. Glenda and Nic got into an argument over it a couple of days ago, started spilling the beans and pointing fingers at each other."

"Why didn't they tell us that? Aren't we supposed to be part of the investigation, Fiona? Why would they keep that from us?"

"We're on a *need to know* basis. We are studying the science of the investigation, not necessarily the investigation aspects. They need our analysis to be unbiased. If we thought that Nic and Glenda did it, we might look at the data differently. That's something we'll learn to do in time. Detective Chase knew we'd be unable to separate it, and our analysis would be skewed. As it was, nobody expected it to be Walter Hargrove."

"I did, I knew he did it!" Madison sang.

"Yea right," we both laughed. "Want to go to the mall or go watch a movie?"

"Let's go shop for prom dresses!" Madison shouted. "I got a date!"

"Really? With who?"

I was shocked. Madison would have told me news like this immediately.

"Carden Doyle," Madison smiled shyly. "He just asked me!"

"But prom isn't for months, Maddie!"

"I know, but he wanted to be certain he asked me first. So cute, right?"

"I guess so," I giggled.

"Speaking of prom, Fiona," a deep familiar voice sounded from behind me.

It was Wolfe. My heart started into a flutter, and I stumbled to respond.

"Yes?"

I thought for a second that I would lose consciousness as I spun around and locked eyes with none other than Wolfe Nero.

"K, it's settled then," he said with a spark of playfulness.

My heart started beating wildly, and I fought to remain calm.

"What? What are you settling?"

"You said *yes*," Wolfe said dryly, a glint of anticipation flashed in his eyes. He turned around and jetted out of the lab.

Madison's mouth dropped open, her eyes widened into elation as she stared at me and silently mouthed the words *oh my gosh.*

My mouth went completely dry as I gasped for air. My phone rang, and I pulled out the phone from my back pocket. It was Detective Chase. I was sure he was calling to congratulate us all on the case being solved. I swiped my finger across to answer and punched the phone on speaker so Madison could hear.

"Fiona. You'll never believe this. Can you meet me at the mouth of Arles Cave in five minutes?"

"Detective Chase! What happened?"

"Supposedly, a wannabe vampire cult from your school performed a ritualistic ceremony in Arles Cave and sacrificed some poor soul. A drifter stumbled upon the scene as it happened and then reported it at the nearest gas station. We're on our way to investigate. There's been another murder in Godley Grove, Fiona, and this one is said to be gruesome. This one's gonna hit the national news, and we have to act on it quickly. You in?"

# ABOUT THE AUTHOR

Dr. Bon Blossman (www.BonBlossman.com) is a published fiction author, C.E.O. and founder of the world's top international murder mystery company, (www.mymysteryparty.com), a recording artist, and a developmental physiologist. She is also an adjunct professor with over 17 years of college level teaching experience including a year of teaching forensic science to high school students.

Dr. Bon completed her Bachelor of Science in Pre-Medicine (Biology and Chemistry), her Master of Science in Biology (Microbiology) and her PhD in Biology (Developmental Physiology). She continued with a two-year postdoctoral fellowship in a developmental cardiovascular research program.

Dr. Bon is a member of Beta Beta Beta Biological Honor Society, Gamma Sigma Epsilon Chemical Honor Society, Phi Kappa Phi Honorary Society, National Scholars Society and is listed on the Cambridge Society's Who's Who List. She is also a member of the Society for Integrative and Comparative Biology, the American Association for the Advancement of Science and the American Institute for Biological Science.

Since 1998, she has published over five scientific journal articles in the fields of microbiology, mammalogy, and physiology, including a landmark paper in metabolic allometry, with her most recent research focused on the development of the embryonic cardiovascular system. She currently serves as an ad hoc reviewer for the National Science Foundation and the Royal Integrative Society.

# WANT MORE MYSTERY IN YOUR LIFE?

## BECOME A PART OF FIONA'S WORLD!

Head over to www.FionaFrost.com and read more about Fiona Frost and her friends, solve a quick whodunit challenge, purchase cool fan gear, a murder mystery party or work on the mystery of the month!

---

JOIN THE FAN CLUB AND GET IN THE MIX FOR FUN CONTESTS AND PRIZES! IN ADDITION, YOU'LL BE FIRST TO KNOW WHEN THE NEXT VOLUME OF THE SERIES IS RELEASED!

## CONNECT WITH FIONA FROST ON

**Facebook** and **Twitter** @ClubFiona